# HELL TO PAY

AN INFERNAL AFFAIRS NOVEL

# SHERRILYN KENYON

# PROLOGUE

"What do you mean I'm banished from Hell?" Lucian Teivel barely had time to conjure clothing before his best friend, the demon Sorath, ordered him away from his bed...and his four naked demonic bedmates who appeared as confused by all this as he was.

"I'm sorry, Luke. There's nothing I can do. Your father ordered us to escort you out."

"*Of Hell*," Luke repeated just to make sure he understood what was happening. He, his father's direct heir, was being banished from the only home he'd ever known...it made no sense whatsoever.

*Who the fuck gets banished from Hell?*

Aghast, he stared at Sorath in total disbelief. "I'm my father's favorite."

Everyone knew that. Lucifer bragged about it all the time, much to the dismay of every demon in this domain. In fact, his father loved to hold that over the heads of the rest of his children and demons.

"Favorite or not, Lucifer has ordered you gone. Now. *No* delay."

Luke stared at Sorath, a prince in his own right, and the leader of his father's greatest legion, and the ten demons Sorath had brought with him for this dubious task. Like Lucifer, Sorath was so beautiful he was hard to look at. He had dark skin and black wings that matched his soulless eyes and long, braided hair. Aside from Luke, he was the creature Lucifer trusted most with tasks such as throwing his beloved son out of his realm.

"Any idea why?"

Sorath arched a brow that basically questioned Luke's sanity for asking such a question. "Do you think for one heartbeat I dared to ask him?"

"Since your wings haven't been ripped from your back, I'd say no."

It still didn't make sense. No one had ever been banished *from* Hell. Not in all these centuries. How could this happen?

Granted, he lived to irritate his father. Mother, too, for that matter. And Lucifer had made the threat on more than occasion to toss him out on his ass.

Still, Luke had never once believed his father was serious with those booming threats.

Just pissed off.

Which, as Lucifer, was his father's normal state of being.

"Does my sister know?" Luke didn't give him time to answer. "Shaddix!"

She appeared instantly in his room, then drew up short

as she saw Sorath and the number of demons with him. Exceptionally tall for a she-demon, she was impractically beautiful. The kind of beauty that left people staring at her, wondering how her overlarge features came together so that she was attractive. And yet she was. Long black hair framed an unconventionally beautiful face.

And for once, she wasn't spewing hatred toward him. "I just heard. What happened?"

"I was hoping you'd know." While she wasn't Lucifer's favorite, she was his daughter, and her mother had been one of the original fallen angels who'd been cast out of Heaven along with his father. In Hell's pecking order, his sister technically ranked higher than he did, given that his mother was a hellhound.

But when it came to raw viciousness and brutality, Luke had no equal outside of their father.

Her brow furrowed by worry, Shaddix shook her head. "I've no idea. I know he's threatened it a lot in the past when you've angered him, but I never thought he'd actually do it. Not with the way he dotes on you."

For the first time in centuries, they agreed on something.

Luke growled low in his throat. The only reason he could imagine was that someone had seen him conversing with Remiel—the archangel of hope. Lucifer blamed Remiel for his fall from grace. Therefore, Lucifer hated that bastard with every ounce of venom he possessed...

And that was a lot.

Luke had been a forbidden friend of Remiel's for centuries. Why? He had no real idea. Other than the angel was funny and they'd often met in the human world while

Luke sought souls for his father and Remi had tried to protect the mortals from Luke's temptation.

Their friendship was the only thing he could imagine would cause his father to overreact. And it meant there was a tattletale in Hell.

He glared at his sister. "Someone betrayed me. Find out who."

Shaddix nodded while Sorath gave him a hard stare. "Does this mean you're leaving on your own?"

In other words, Sorath wanted to know if Luke intended to fight him. Normally, he'd do so without hesitation and just on principle. But right now, he didn't want to pummel his best friend.

He wanted to beat his father. Which would be nine kinds of stupid. A level of stupid he didn't need or want right now. While he knew he could defeat Sorath, he didn't stand a chance against Lucifer.

Grabbing his sword, he paused in front of Shaddix. "Find my betrayer."

"I will, and I'll keep asking Father to forgive you."

Forgiveness? From Lucifer?

Their tropical haven would ice over first. No, he would have to find his betrayer and cut off their head, but not before he beat them enough that they'd go before his father and tell Lucifer they'd lied.

The four demons in his bed began to weep. Without him here, they'd be relegated back to their pits.

Such a shame given their beauty and talents. He'd miss them.

But right now, there was nothing he could do to spare them their pain.

With all the dignity in his rotted soul, he walked past Sorath, then out of his room and toward the portal that led to the human world.

The portal shimmered in the dim light. In the past, it'd been something he'd stepped through without a passing thought.

Today might be his last glimpse of home.

And that infuriated him to a dangerous level. He met Sorath's gaze levelly. "Tell my father this isn't over."

Just as he was about to step through the shimmering portal, he heard a tiny voice.

"*Dominus*! Wait!"

He looked past Shaddix to see Helly rushing toward them. She wasn't a demon. She was an imp...his servant since the day his mother had whelped him. Short in stature, she was classically beautiful with perfect features, dark brown hair and an adorable pair of curved horns that rose out from just above her ears.

"I'm going with you, *dominus*. You don't need to be out there alone."

Leave it to Helly to be loyal. Either that or his mother had insisted. Senka would be absolutely livid over this. Not that Lucifer would care.

While his mother, alone, held a special spot in Lucifer's dark heart, theoretically Senka didn't control him. If she protested Luke's banishment, Lucifer would double down on it and refuse any leniency.

Luke's only hope was to find his accuser and make that bastard undo this.

"Thanks, imp."

Shaddix opened the portal.

Sorath met his gaze and held it. "I'll find out who did this to you and together we'll gut them."

Luke clapped him on the arm. "I will find out who did this and when I do, there will be hell to pay."

"So, who did you piss off to be sentenced to our little corner of Hell?"

Standing in front of a large, antique mahogany desk, Sorcha O'Malley blinked twice at the unexpected question. "Beg pardon?"

The woman who'd introduced herself as Bernadette Corwin lifted a stack of papers and straightened them. "I saw your service record. It's impressive and spotless. Means you must have pissed off someone significant to be sentenced to Infernal Affairs. So what did you do and who did you do it to? Details, please. I love gossip!"

Not something she was about to discuss, especially with someone she just met.

No one needed to know her dubious history that she was still trying to get over.

So Sorcha shrugged. "Don't know. Guess I'm just unlucky." And a little too accurate with her aim.

Uncomfortable with this line of questioning, Sorcha

cleared her throat and glanced about the old Victorian mansion that had been converted into an office building. The former living room was now a reception area and the woman before her was quite...

Something.

Tall, thin and with dark skin that was smooth and perfect, Bernadette was beauty incarnate. She had short sister locks that framed a face Sorcha could tell was used to smiling and laughing.

She liked her already.

Even if she was nosy.

"What did *you* do to be sentenced here?" she couldn't resist asking Bernadette.

"Girl...that is a long and lengthy list. Let's just say it involved a police captain, a night stick that went some place it shouldn't have, and a bite that may or may not have been infectious."

Sorcha felt her jaw go slack. That sounded almost as bad as what she'd done. "Wait... Seriously, what did you do?"

"Oh, you heard me." Propping her elbow on the top of the desk, Bernadette rested her chin on the back of her hand and smiled. "Not like he didn't deserve it. He did. Trust me, I wouldn't have risked rabies or parvo lightly. Anyway, I've been here five years and love it. You will too once you get used to your coworkers. We're all a little...unique."

"Bernadette! Would you stop trying to scare off the new hire."

Bernadette scoffed. "Not a new hire. She's a transfer, like me. I want to know the dirt on her, and I will find it." She leaned forward and whispered behind her hand to Sorcha, "That's my special skill."

Shaking her head, a short middle-aged brunette joined them. She held her hand out to Sorcha. "Captain Elana Reyes. Nice to meet you."

Sorcha shook her hand. "And you, Captain."

"Elana, please. We're not that formal around here." She slid an irritated glance toward Bernadette. "Will you get back to your real desk and let Ryan have hers?"

With an impressive dramatic gesture, Bernadette rolled herself back from the desk and stood up. "I wanted to meet the new one first. Shoot me."

"Keep it up and I might." Elana winked at Sorcha. "That's how *I* got sentenced here."

"That is true," Bernadette said. "Which is why I'm going upstairs right now before she gets an itchy trigger finger. See y'all later." She gave an impudent wave of her hand as she left the room.

Confused, Sorcha turned toward her new boss. "Is she another detective?"

Elana nodded. "My second-in-command, Lieutenant Bernadette Corwin. Her skill is intuition and clairvoyance, in addition to research. She's like a magpie on a shiny object."

"And yours?"

"I'm the boss at Infernal Affairs, which means my special power is not losing my shit when someone does something they're not supposed to. Let that not be any kind of encouragement for you to break rules. As my father used to say...shit rolls downhill. I will always have your back, but please remember that I really do have an itchy trigger finger. And everyone has a breaking point. Please don't be mine."

Given that she had a similar itchy trigger finger and father, Sorcha felt an immediate kinship with the captain.

She also suspected there was a lot more to the captain than she let on. In fact, she could feel something "special" about Elana Reyes besides patience.

"How many detectives are there here?"

"Eight altogether, including you." Elana stepped back and gestured to her right. "Shall I give you the grand tour?"

"Sure."

The captain indicated the room where they stood. "The front desk here is normally occupied by our office manager, Ryan Braddach. Not sure where she's run off to at the moment, but I know she'll be right back. She's extremely reliable." She led Sorcha past a small waiting area in front of a bay window to a set of double doors. "This is one of our interrogation rooms."

Nice. It held a small table and four chairs.

Along with a very thick chain that came out of the wall and made her wonder who or, more to the point, *what* they interrogated. That thing looked big enough to handle a rhino.

Down the hallway was a small kitchen with a gas stove and green cabinets. "Feel free to bring food for lunch or cook something as long as it's not too smelly. Christian Gutjar is sensitive to smell and will hunt you down to complain." Elana paused to give her a knowing stare. "Trust me, you don't want to get Chris started. There's no off switch."

"Good to know."

Elana led her toward stairs that had a black runner down the center. "Four of the offices are on the second floor and there are two more on the third."

Sorcha could just imagine the endless trudging of stairs that lay before her. "Is there an elevator?"

"Sadly, no. But if anyone has mobility issues, we meet them on the main floor or the garden level."

"Garden level?" Sorcha liked the sound of that. Something about being in nature always soothed her.

"It's the walkout basement, but it lets out into a garden. There are two offices down there—yours and your partner's—and another interrogation room."

"Son of a donkey eating turd ball! Screw you and your afterlife. Sheez! Give it a rest, you giant asshole! I hate you so much! Can't you haunt the cemetery across the street? What is wrong with you?"

Sorcha drew up short at the deep masculine shout that echoed through the second-floor hallway.

Elana shook her head. "That'll be the Chris I was warning you about. He's very creative with his language." She motioned her toward the office in the far-left corner. Knocking once, she pushed open the door. "There a problem, detective?"

He gestured toward the window. "Winslow...making me crazy as usual. Tell him to go bug someone else or I'm banishing him into the light." He picked up a roll of paper towels and began dabbing at his desk and crotch where water had been spilled. "It's sad that I can't have a single sip because someone—" he glared at the corner "—won't stop knocking my drinks over." He growled low in his throat. "Two seconds! Two effing seconds. I swear to all that's holy that I left the cap off my water to reach for my phone and boom... I'm going to kill him! Except I can't. But oh! It's so unfair."

Elana slid her gaze to Sorcha to explain. "Winslow was poisoned by his wife and died in this bedroom. As a result, he knocks over any drink brought in here. Apparently, he's trying to save the occupants from his bad ending. Make sure you have a lid on any container you bring in here. Chris, meet Sorcha."

She waved awkwardly at the tall blond man who reminded her of a modern-day Viking. "Hi."

"Hi. Sorry for the rough language and hostility. I'm normally very calm. This has just become a major pet peeve for me...and I'm having a crappy day."

Sorcha definitely understood those. She'd been having way too many of them lately. So much so that she was beginning to wonder if the devil had put a target on her back.

Elana closed the door and pointed to the room across the hall that had the captain's name on it. "My office is there and Bernadette's is next to it."

"Cap?" Bernadette stuck her head out of her office as if on cue. "Need you. Sorry. Can't wait."

Elana nodded. "Feel free to explore." She handed Sorcha a key. "As I said, your office is on the garden level, just off the stairs. It's the one without a name on the door. I'll catch up to you."

Then she was gone so fast that Sorcha barely had time to blink.

Okay, then.

More curious about her own space than anything else, she headed for the stairs they'd just walked up only to learn that they didn't go down past the main floor.

Scowling, Sorcha turned around, looking for another set of stairs that would lead down to the garden level. "This is odd..."

She glanced out the window to see that there was a wrought-iron balcony on the backside of the house.

Hmm...

She started looking through rooms to find out how to access the balcony. Maybe it had stairs to go down.

As she passed through the foyer again, she saw an attractive young woman in the corner.

Sorcha didn't speak to her. Not out of rudeness. Rather because she knew it was a residual haunting—a ghost that didn't even know Sorcha was here.

Since this was her first day on the job, she didn't want to expose her "unusual" abilities too soon. Even if it was Infernal Affairs and she knew they'd understand because she'd been hired for them, she just didn't want to be exposed yet.

Which also made her wonder where Winslow had gone.

Chris might have looked to the corner, but it'd been vacant. So she knew he didn't share the abilities she'd learned a long time ago to hide from others. Even those familiar with the paranormal had a hard time accepting her "gifts" at times.

They were frightening for everyone.

Especially her.

At the end of the hall, she finally saw the outside spiral staircase at the back of the house that went to the garden level, along with a door that opened onto the balcony.

Relieved, Sorcha went outside and paused as she was assaulted with the roar of raucous heavy metal music.

What in the world? Given the volume, she was amazed that it hadn't been rattling the windows inside the house.

By the time she reached the grass, she realized it was

actually Christian metal music. Not what she'd first thought.

Completely unexpected.

It was also hot as Hell out here. *Gotta love Savannah, Georgia in September...* She pulled her jacket off as she paused to get her bearings.

The two lower offices and interrogation room were on her right. But what caught her attention was the pool to her left. Or more to the point, the attached hot tub that held a man leaning back in casual repose against the brown stone ledge.

No, not a man.

*A god...*

Even from her distance, she was mesmerized by what she saw. Long wavy dark brown hair laced with blond streaks and a body made for sin. Water sparkled invitingly against deeply tanned skin stretched tight over rippling muscles that said he spent way too much time working out. Best of all, he held just enough shadow on his cheeks and chin to be sexy and not gross.

Damn, he was savage. Raw and just absolutely compelling.

There were no other words for him.

*A man this hot...*

Yeah. He had to know he turned women, and probably a fair number of men, into molten pools of stupidity.

And while she liked to pretend she was above her baser hormonal urges, she knew it for a lie. This man penetrated every single level of protection she'd carefully erected around her broken soul.

*What the utter f—*

Someone clapped her on the back, startling her...

It was Captain Reyes. "His name is Luke. And he's your new partner."

*Are you kidding me?*

Of course, he was her partner. Why would she think otherwise?

*My luck never changes. From bad to worse.* Sorcha silently went off in frustration over that news. "What?"

*Why?*

Elana stepped around her. "I need someone on the straight and narrow to keep him on the righteous path. He's a handful."

*No shit! Look at him.* She could only imagine how arrogant and annoying he'd be. She was not looking forward to this. At all.

*I'm going to shoot another partner. Great. God only knows where they'll send me next time.*

Probably jail. Which she'd barely avoided in New Orleans. Her head was already pounding at the thought of another trial where she'd be grilled and lied about.

Another mug shot she'd have to live down.

*Effing awesome.*

The captain led her toward her new partner and that powerful aura that made her heart pound even harder. He didn't bother to move or twitch at their approach. Not until they stopped in front of the hot tub filled with water that appeared to be boiling.

The music turned down on its own.

With his arms stretched out along the stone-carved lip of the tub, Luke still had his head leaned back against the edge as he casually sunned himself while he should be working. He wore a number of chains with charms she couldn't quite make out and each of his fingers held a ring. His expensive sunglasses gave no clue as to his mood or where he was looking. "I just found my happy place, Elana. Don't put me on task. Not right now." His voice was deep and smooth, like whiskey and thick velvet. He should be on radio…

"Sorry, champ. Duty calls. Need you to get dressed and take Sorcha to Peachtree City to check out a Dire Wolf sighting."

He scoffed nonchalantly. "The Dire Wolf lives on Witcher Road in Newnan. There's not one in Peachtree City."

"The call's from the city police department that has had multiple reports. It's legit. Need you to check it out. Maybe your friend has a relative?"

Growling like said Dire Wolf, he lifted his head to look at them. With a slow, seductive smile, he pushed his sunglasses up on top of his head.

As he did so, Sorcha had to look away.

*Holy shit.* She hated to be redundant, but it was all she could say. He was hotter than Hell's half acre without those sunglasses.

*How could you be even better looking without them?*

It wasn't fair or right.

Forget radio, this man should have gone into acting.

The last thing she'd expected was for his eyes to be an amber-gold so intense that they appeared to glow in the sunlight.

He was everything she hated in a man and yet he was

the sexiest thing she'd ever seen. This was the alpha male to rule them all.

*Damn. Just damn.*

With a deep, intimidating sigh, he rose up out of the water like the god Poseidon coming out of the ocean. All he needed was a trident in his hand.

Heat rushed through every part of her.

That made him grin even more salaciously. "Don't worry, love. I know how irresistible I am and I try to keep it in check."

Okay, that offended her. "Pardon?"

"Those are *my* superpowers...among others." And with that, he left them and headed toward the four-car garage that was across the yard from their offices.

But as her gaze went over his sculpted back, she saw dozens of horrible scars. Some appeared to be from a whip of some kind, and others looked like knife and claw marks.

*What the hell?*

Had he been a lion tamer? What could have caused all those?

Scowling, she turned toward Elana for an explanation.

Elana shrugged. "I don't even know where to begin and I'm not sure you'll believe me if I tell you."

Great.

"Can I request Christian as my partner?" she asked her captain.

"No, he already has one. But Luke isn't what you think nor is he the egotistical monster you're assuming." Elana paused. "Actually, he's worse, but again, not for what you think."

"Meaning?"

And still Elana hedged. "Are you religious at all?"

"I didn't think you could legally ask me that question."

"This isn't HR related. It's more a way to determine how receptive you'll be to the truth."

Now Sorcha had to know. "I'm open to things. Why?"

"Luke Teivel is the son of Lucifer...and he's been banned from Hell."

# TWO

*Luke Teivel is the son of Lucifer...and he's been banned from Hell.* The captain's words repeated themselves in Sorcha's head.

Sorcha had absolutely no idea how to react to that. Her first instinct was to laugh and leave. Any normal person receiving that information would definitely run for the door.

But she wasn't normal and neither was Infernal Affairs. This was an organization set up to deal with preternatural things regular law enforcement couldn't handle. She'd known about them most of her life. Her father, who'd been a police captain in Jackson, Mississippi, had told her stories of working with them during the late eighties when they'd been founded.

Because of her "abilities" that had kicked in during her teenage years, her father had recommended her to Elana.

But the son of Lucifer...

How was that even possible?

"You're kidding."

Elana shook her head slowly. "Believe me, I know how it sounds. When we first encountered him...it was quite spectacular. Yet here we are."

Yeah, okay... "And how are we here?"

"I was banished from Hell. Let's leave it at that."

Sorcha gasped as Luke's deep, resonant voice intruded on their conversation.

How on Earth did a man that size move so silently? At least six-five, maybe six-six, he towered over them.

And he was dressed black on black, including a long leather coat in the simmering heat. How he could stomach that in this humid weather, she had no idea. She was only wearing a white V-neck T-shirt and black slacks and she was roasting.

But there was one question she had to have an answer to. "What does someone do to get banished from Hell?"

Again, that infectious grin spread across his face. "That's the question, isn't it?"

Yes, it was. "Did you deserve it?"

His grin turned charming. "Of course, I did. Pissing off Old Scratch is what I do best." He winked at her. "Now saddle up, detective. We're heading out."

Sorcha's jaw fell open. Uh, yeah. Heading off alone with the son of the devil who'd been banished from Hell just didn't seem like the smartest or sanest thing to do.

She looked at her boss.

"You heard the demon. Saddle up." Chuckling, Elana headed back toward their offices.

"Do I get a gun?" she called after Elana.

"Won't need one with Luke as your partner. And if you shoot *him*, you'll only piss him off."

What did that mean? Sorcha was afraid to ask. Had someone tried to shoot?

She glanced over to see that Luke was quickly making strides back toward the building where he'd vanished to change from his black board shorts into a black shirt, jeans and coat.

Rushing to catch up, she was quickly rethinking her decision to take this job. Not that she had any choice after what she'd done.

*Why...why did I shoot my partner?*

For the first time, she regretted it. Was this her punishment? To be paired with a partner she couldn't hurt?

"It'll be fine," she said under her breath, mocking her father's words. "You'll fit right in. It'll be the best job you've ever had. You'll love it there! Savannah's awesome! Just wait. You'll see."

Luke paused at the first garage door to turn and frown at her. "Psychotic episode or Tourette's?"

"Pardon?"

He waved his hand at her. "Your...whatever mumbling. Is it a psychotic episode or some other thing I need to know about? Is it a one-off or something recurring I'll have to explain to others?"

"Call it frustration. Shock. Denial. Disbelief...incredulity. I like that one."

He snorted. "Yeah well, working with you isn't my perfect tea party, either. I'm not exactly thrilled by those who have ties to my enemies."

"What?"

He reached down to open the garage door manually.

"Oh, don't play all innocent like you don't know your blood-line. I can smell it on you."

What was he talking about? "Apparently, I don't. What do you know that my family failed to tell me?"

After lifting the door, he froze. "Nothing. If you don't know, there's probably a reason for it and I shouldn't have said anything." He wagged his eyebrows at her. "Shall we?" He gestured toward...

Sorcha looked at the old vintage car and felt her heart sink with vicious dread. "Is that...*Christine*?" Which would make total sense given that he was the son of the devil. Why not have Christine as his car?

He gave her a droll stare. "No. Not even. Don't you dare insult this lady like that. Christine was a boring average automobile. This...this is a Gauguin Red 1957 Chrysler 300C. The first muscle car ever made. Built for speed and luxury, she was innovation incarnate. The first of her kind. The perfect marriage of aggression and beauty. And she is always forward looking. A perfect example of modernity and putting the past behind you while remaking the future into what you want it to be. She's just like me. A perfect being."

Wow...

Where did she even begin unpacking that statement?

"You don't suffer from any lack of self-esteem, do you?"

"I do not." He pulled the keys from his pocket as he opened the car door and got in.

Sorcha went to her side and had to admit the car was exceptionally pretty for an antique.

And damned if he didn't look incredible sitting in it. The huge convertible fit him to a T.

As she sat down beside him, he leaned across her lap.

"Uh, what are you doing?"

"Relax," he said, opening the glove box. He pulled out a red University of Georgia ball cap and handed it to her. "Long hair and convertibles make for a mess."

"What about you?"

Of all the things in the universe, he pulled a pink hair tie off his gearshift and tied his hair up in what had to be the manliest man bun she'd ever seen and given the fact she absolutely hated man buns and thought them completely stupid, that said something.

"You look like you should be a biker."

"Hell's Angel?" he shot back with that infectious grin.

She rolled her eyes. "Are they demons too?"

"No...but some of them will have a nice long conversation with my dad when they cross over."

Awesome.

"Turn on the radio, please. I need music."

Sorcha gasped as a tiny woman came out of nowhere and leaned forward between them from the backseat. Around the age of twenty, she had straight, dark brown hair with high arched brows and dark red lips. There was a mischievous air to her that said she was always plotting something.

Sorcha's heart pounding from startled alarm, she scowled. "Where did you come from?"

"Hell," she said with a shrug. "It's not as bad as you think...it's worse."

Sorcha turned toward Luke. "Explain?"

"Imp, meet Sorcha. Sorcha, Imp." He turned the car on and it roared to life like a rumbling beast.

"Imp?" Sorcha asked.

She nodded. "You can call me that or Helly. I answer to both with an equal dose of restraint and resentment."

Interesting. The name Helly somehow seemed to fit with her lip piercing and dark clothing. She looked like someone who would hang out with Luke, except she was as tiny as Luke was huge.

But Helly's presence definitely confused her. "I thought you didn't have a partner."

Helly snorted. "Not his partner... I'm his damn-it-dog."

"Excuse me?" Had she heard what she thought she had? "Damn-it-dog?"

Helly shrugged nonchalantly as Luke pulled out of the garage, parked and went to close the door manually. "You know, the thing you curse because it's always getting in the way. I was assigned to him at birth by his mother. She's a real bitch." She snickered at that.

Sorcha was surprised that Luke took the fact Helly called his mother a bitch in stride.

*Okay, then. I guess he's not close with his mom.*

She had no idea what to make of them as Luke returned to the car and got in.

But damn, he made an incredible sight with that sexy, masculine swagger. She hated how alluring a beast he was even wearing a long coat on a hot summer day.

*Put it out of your mind.*

So much easier said than done. Especially when someone was that innately delectable. "So where's this Peachtree City?"

He pulled out of the driveway and headed down the street. "About four hours away. Depending on how many police cars I have to blow past."

She winced at his words. There were few things she hated more than traveling...and in a car it was double grueling. Even with a sexy driver. "Can you teleport us there?"

He passed a droll stare toward her. "You're with Infernal Affairs. Don't you know anything about demons?"

"A great deal, but with you being the son of the devil, I'd expect you to have more abilities than most."

Luke cleared his throat as he caught Helly's amused gaze in his rearview mirror.

His new partner wasn't wrong.

But giving strangers insight into his abilities was as likely as Helly giving someone her real name. Such things allowed others to have power and control over them. The less people knew, the better.

So he grinned at Sorcha and turned up the radio.

She listened for a few minutes, then turned it down. "Skillet? Why do you keep listening to Christian music? Isn't that a little off brand for your ilk?"

"Ilk?" Luke repeated. "There's a word you don't hear every day." He glanced over at her and shook his head. "As for my music, I love Christian rock. The faith? The message? There's no sweeter reward than handing the faithful over to my dad. At least that used to be my goal. Now, I'm trying to think of a way to start reclaiming those souls I helped damn and really pissing off Old Scratch. Bastard deserves it. And I love revenge."

Then he did the most shocking thing of all. He actually quoted the Bible. "Vengeance is Mine saith the Lord. I shall repay."

But she supposed it made sense. He'd probably read the

Bible more than she had, and given her Baptist grandfather and upbringing…

Impressive.

"How many souls have you damned?"

He flinched as if he honestly felt guilty about it. "We don't talk about that. Ever. The past is the past and we don't revisit bad territory." There was a deep undercurrent to those words. One that sent a shiver down her spine.

Given his parentage, she would have thought he reveled in harming others.

That tone said she couldn't be more wrong.

"Noted. I'll never bring it up again."

Helly leaned over the seat to give Sorcha a huge smile. "He's being really standoffish because he doesn't know you yet. I promise he's a lot of fun once he gets used to you."

"I'll take your word for it."

Clearing his throat and glaring at the demon imp, he changed the subject. "So where are you from, Detective O'Malley?"

Sorcha almost didn't answer, but what difference would it make? Not like he couldn't look it up in her files, and given that he was a detective who knew her name, she would assume he'd already investigated her. "Moved around a lot. I was born in Jackson, Mississippi. Spent most of my youth between there and Richmond whenever I stayed with my grandparents. Norfolk, Birmingham, New Orleans. Now Savannah."

"Nice list of cities. Personally, I've spent a lot of the past century in Sin City."

That surprised her. "Vegas?"

He nodded.

"Never been there, but I'd love to see it."

"I'm sure you'll get your chance. We get sent there quite a bit. My father owns several casinos and hotels. Makes for a lot of chaos, and our kind of crime."

Sorcha widened her eyes. "Really?"

"Yeah. I'm sure you can imagine the deals certain people are willing to cut in order to have their dreams come true. It's why my father's agents own prime real estate there and in Hollywood."

That was a terrifying thought. "So there really are deals with the devil?"

"Oh yeah. Sometimes for great wealth. Some trade for things as simple as a bag of rice. Funny the value people place on their immortal souls."

Yes, it was. Worst part of her job was seeing how little some people thought of themselves and others. How little they valued anyone's life. It only made sense they'd value their immortal soul even less. "Is there anything you'd trade your soul for?"

"Peace."

By the look on his face, she could tell that had popped out of his mouth before he could stop it.

And the answer surprised her greatly. "As in world peace?"

Clearing his throat, he turned the radio up again, letting her know he'd had enough conversation.

Fine. She pulled her phone out and started reading. Helly leaned back in the seat and sang along with the Skillet songs. For a tiny imp, she had an incredibly powerful voice.

It wasn't until they pulled into Peachtree City that she realized it hadn't taken them four hours... It'd barely taken two.

"How did we get here so fast?" she asked as he stopped at the police station.

Getting out of the car, he winked, refused to answer, and headed for the entrance.

Helly climbed out of the car without using the door. It was only then that Sorcha realized exactly how tiny the imp was. Probably four-nine or so. She definitely didn't come close to five feet. "Those are the powers he doesn't talk about. He has a lot of them." She opened the door for Sorcha. "C'mon. This is always fun."

Was it?

More like scary, given the company she was with.

Sorcha got out of the car and followed Helly into the gray building to find Luke waiting in the tiny lobby for them. It might not really have been small. Just the overwhelming size of him filled it.

"The detective's coming," Luke said.

Helly grinned. "Which one?"

"David."

Jumping with glee, she clapped her hands together. "He's my favorite!"

Sorcha wasn't sure what to make of the imp's enthusiasm. Helly was oddly fun and extremely exuberant over very little. How Sorcha wished she could be that way, too. And it seemed strange behavior for a Hell imp.

Then again, what would she know about how such creatures behaved? Unlike Luke, she hadn't been assigned an imp at birth. Which really seemed unusual given that Helly appeared younger than he did.

Or maybe that was the size difference between them. Because Helly was so small, it was easy to think of her as a kid. Except the imp had exceptionally large breasts. Something Sorcha didn't want to focus on, as she'd always been self-conscious about how small hers were in comparison to others.

That thought was still in her mind a few seconds later when a well-muscled bald man came through the door on her left. He cracked a huge smile as soon as he saw Luke and Helly. "Good to see you two. What have you been up to?"

Luke didn't hesitate with his answer. "Trouble. Always."

"Of course, you have." David glanced to Sorcha before he spoke again to Luke. "Another new partner?"

Luke nodded. "Yeah. I ate the last one. He got on my nerves so much that it became a moral imperative. This one seems a little more tolerable. And if not, I hope she's tastier."

Sorcha felt her eyes go wide as David laughed. *I really hope that's a joke.* With Luke, she couldn't quite tell.

Without another comment, David handed a folder over to Luke. "As you can see, Redwine Road is where the sightings first started, then they moved to Peachtree City proper, and it has decided this is where it likes to play. It's a giant white wolf that usually comes out around midnight and terrorizes the villagers. It seems like every night someone calls, and we've had two officers catch sight of it over by the Avenue around ten. I'm hoping it just wants Starbucks and not one of the workers leaving to go home."

With a noncommittal humph, Luke opened the folder

and thumbed through reports. When he came across a photo, he paused. "Ring camera?"

"Yeah. That was over on Sweetwater Oaks. One of the houses on the lake. Came right up to their porch. I think it even smiled at the camera."

Snorting, Luke handed the printout to Sorcha.

Her jaw went slack as she saw the neolithic-sized wolf that was maybe four or five feet from the front door of a white brick house. The beast's shoulders were far more developed than other wolves she'd seen pictures of. But that made her curious. "Are there wolves in Peachtree City?"

David shook his head. "There aren't many in Georgia. Period. At least not in any significant number. The handful we have are gray and red wolves, and they're either hiding up in the mountains or down in the Okefenokee. Not that I knew that a week ago. I checked with park services and they said that even in those known areas, they rarely if ever have someone report a wolf sighting. We've had twelve of them in the last month." He pointed to the picture she held. "All of them describe *that*."

Luke nodded. "All right. We'll get started and I'll let you know what we find. Hopefully, this will be a regular wolf and not something we have to move on."

He inclined his head to Luke. "Thanks."

They headed out of the building, back to Luke's vintage car.

Sorcha waited until they were all in before she turned toward her new partner. "Does David know who you are?"

He shook his head. "Only Infernal Affairs needs to know. Others aren't so receptive and I don't need the peasants revolting."

"Excuse me?"

"Humans are terrified by the truth. Easier to deny it than believe it. If they know I'm Lucifer's son, it means Hell is real and they have accountability for their actions. Which in turn means religion isn't some myth they can sneer at and dismiss. Once they realize that, they panic. Panicky people are extremely dangerous, especially in large numbers, and they do very stupid things. Not to me, because they can't do anything to harm me. I'm currently Teflon. But to the rest of you...it just gets unnecessarily messy."

"Meaning?"

"Heaven won't have me and I'm banished from Hell. Purgatory is Earth. So here I am, trapped, until my dad calms down and welcomes me home. It's shitty to be me and I don't want others to try and put me in a lab or cell somewhere. I'm not here to hurt anyone. I just want to find my way home and avoid killing the natives." He put on his sunglasses.

Those words made her curious. "How do you know Heaven won't have you?"

He pulled his sunglasses down to the tip of his nose to give her an *are-you-serious* stare over the top of them.

"Okay. Okay. Stupid question, maybe. But are you sure?"

"Yes. To get in, I'd have to repent and I regret nothing... other than this conversation and the one time I tried a knock-off brand of Coke." He pushed the glasses back into place, then picked up his phone, dialed a number and put it on speaker.

After several seconds, a woman answered in what had to be the thickest Southern drawl in history.

"Hey, Laura. How you doing, hon?" Luke asked.

"Everything's just peachy, peachy, tall, dark and mysterious. But I know you didn't call to check in on little ole me, Mr. Luke. What is it you need?"

"Oh," he feigned being hurt. "You wound me with your suspicion."

"Not suspicion, sug, when it's true. You never call unless someone's seen a wolf, and no, it wasn't me. I wasn't there."

"How do you know it wasn't you? I haven't even told you where."

"Don't matter where 'cause I know I haven't been flaunting myself lately. Ain't no one seen my birthday suit unless they've been peeking in my windows—and if they have, then that's a whole other crime. So I know I wasn't there and didn't do it. Whoever they seen was probably just having a bad day or someone saw a neighbor's dog and panicked."

Sorcha bit back a laugh. The picture David gave them was definitely *not* a dog.

"You have any friends or family in Peachtree City?" Luke asked.

"None that I know of and I'm sure they'd tell me if they came that close to my town. Be rude if they didn't."

Luke stroked his chin. "Anyone turn anyone?"

"No. Definitely not. This is my territory. I'd have the throat of anyone who trespassed and did such a thing. Not to mention, it'd be just plain rude."

Luke passed a grimace to Sorcha. "Then we might have a problem."

"How so?" Laura asked.

"I'm in Peachtree City and there is definitely a Dire on the prowl. If it's not you, it's a close relative."

She went silent for several seconds before she spoke again. "Text me the address and I'll be there as quick as I can." Laura hung up.

Luke shifted through the papers and then texted Laura the location of the last sighting.

"Where are we going?" Sorcha asked.

"Whitlock Family Cemetery on Northlake Drive. It's less than five minutes from here." He turned the car on and headed out of the parking lot.

Interesting. Sorcha looked over the files they'd been given.

David was right. All of them were within a narrow geographic area. "Why do you think the wolf's staying in one place and not moving on?"

"Not a clue. That's not normal Dire behavior. They're usually very careful and avoid populated areas when roaming. When they do settle, they do like Laura and rarely shift. It brings too much heat, and they'd rather not be seen. One going up to a stranger's door and smiling for the camera… not what they're about."

"Know a lot of them, do you?"

He shrugged. "My mother's a hellhound. Being canines, they tend to run in the same circles. Have a lot of shared behaviors and…friends."

Interesting to know. Sorcha looked over her shoulder at Helly who was using her hand to swim in the air flow as they drove. "For real? His mother's a hellhound?"

Helly put her hand down and grinned. "What he's not telling you is that his mom's the Alpha of all the Hell packs, including the Dires who live in Hell. Makes her exceptionally dangerous and powerful."

Sorcha scowled as she realized what Helly had meant when she'd called Luke's mother a bitch...and why the imp had laughed so hard about it.

Oh.

But that left her with another question. "So a dog gave birth to a baby boy? How does that happen?"

He laughed. "Hellhounds are shifters the same as a Dire. The primary difference is that the Hounds are enslaved to my father...and they tend to be black in their canine forms, even though they could be any color they want. It's like a uniform to them."

*Who knew?*

He turned left and then pulled into a parking lot behind a Bank of America.

Frowning, she didn't see anything that resembled a cemetery. Just a pizza place, bowling alley and such. "Why are we stopping in a strip mall?"

Luke turned off the car and got out. He jerked his chin toward the woods across the street. "Cemetery's over there. We'll have to walk."

Helly jumped out over the back while Sorcha left the car by more conventional means.

They followed Luke across the street to a small asphalt trail that headed off toward more stores. It was a curious path that made no sense to her. "What is this?"

"Golf cart path. Peachtree City is famous for them." He lifted the sunglasses to perch on top of his head so he could glance about with those gorgeous amber eyes.

"I thought that was *The Villages* in Florida."

He shook his head. "Peachtree City predates them by decades, and you don't have to be over fifty-five to live here.

They have over a hundred miles of golf cart paths. Makes it one of my favorite places."

"Really?"

Tucking his hands in his pockets, he shrugged. "I like quaint things."

That seemed very out of character for him. Then again, she didn't really know him that well.

Still...

Sorcha followed Luke to the cemetery that had a tall chain-link fence around it. It looked innocuous enough, except for the three wandering spirits she saw. One a few feet from her and two who appeared to be speaking off to the side. "So, Lassie. You picking up anything?"

Luke gave her a shit-eating grin. "I see dead people."

His words caught her off guard. She wasn't used to being around others who could see what she did. "Do you?"

"And so do you."

Her body went cold. "Pardon?"

"I'm not the humans at IA. I know you see Willie standing almost on top of you. John and Cecilia are the two who are arguing over their graves."

That wasn't comforting at all. How did he know their names and more importantly... "You can read my mind?"

"No. I heard the change in your heartbeat when you looked toward them." Then he screwed his face up. "And yes, I can read minds, but I wasn't reading yours." He made a cross over his heart.

As she began to panic, Luke moved to stand in front of her. He put one hand on each of her shoulders. "Breathe, Sorcha. Deep and even. The rate you're going, you'll have a heart attack before Laura arrives."

Because she was trying to decide what was most disturbing. Him touching her and the way she really wanted to take a bite out of that luscious body. Him reading her mind. His ability to hear her heartrate.

Or the fact that he could see what she did.

No one had ever been able to see the entities who haunted her. It was comforting and...

Highly disturbing.

All of a sudden, something rustled in the woods near them.

It wasn't a golf cart.

Luke moved in front of her to protect her at the same time a giant white wolf came rushing at them. It launched toward them, then transformed into a tall, incredibly beautiful woman with white-blonde hair.

"You're scaring my new partner, Laura."

She looked past him to where Sorcha stood. "Sorry, hon."

Luke tsked. "No, you're not."

"Of course not. Like you, I don't believe in apologizing. Except for when I first meet someone and scare them." Laura wiped her hands together as she surveyed the area. "I know this'll be a giant surprise to you, but there's nothing here."

Sorcha was confused as Laura turned in a small circle near Luke. "What do you mean?"

"No Dire has come near this place...ever." Laura turned back toward Sorcha. "I'd know if they had. We leave a very distinct scent. And it usually lingers like a dead polecat."

That made her stomach sink. "If there's no Dire Wolf..."

"What is everyone seeing and reporting?" Luke held his

hand out and the police folder appeared in his palm. He pulled out the photo and showed it to Laura. "What is this?"

She scowled as she took it and saw the image. "A Dire."

"So what's a Dire not a Dire?" Sorcha asked.

Luke sobered with an intensity she found as disturbing as when he'd rested his hands on her shoulders. "Trouble."

# THREE

Sorcha sighed as they investigated the last sighting location in the woods that led to a Kroger parking lot where the wolf had been spotted two days ago.

Just as with the other sites, Luke and Laura felt and smelled nothing.

"Is it demonic?" she asked. "Maybe it's just a really big animal?"

Laura pulled her blonde hair back with a ponytail band. "Has to be a demon or other critter. It's definitely not my breed and a demon would be the only thing I can think of that could mask its scent from me. Even if it was another kind of shapeshifter, it would leave a scent I could detect."

That was all Laura kept saying.

"Why would a demon be roaming the woods of a small town?" Sorcha looked at Helly.

The imp shrugged. "Not a demon. I'm an imp, but it could be all kinds of reasons. Maybe they're hunting the set of *The Walking Dead*? A lot of demons have crushes on Norman Reedus."

Laura snorted. "That's set in Senoia...one town over."

Luke laughed as his phone rang out with ACDC's *Hell's Bells*.

"Really?" Sorcha asked.

Ignoring her, he held the phone to his ear. "Hey, Captain. What's up?"

While he took the call, she watched a golf cart of teenagers ride past them with their radio blasting.

Laura shook her head. "Good to be young, eh?"

"I wouldn't know. My mother says I was born ninety." Sorcha frowned as she saw a shadow among the trees. "You live here?" she asked Laura.

"Close by. Why?"

Hands on hips, Sorcha saw another golf cart speed by. The occupants all waved at her. "This is an unusual place. I've never seen anything like it."

"Yeah, I know. I grew up in North Carolina and moved here a few years back when I came down for a conference at the movie studio. I fell in love with it. Are you from Georgia?"

"Not at all."

Laura tsked. "Watch out in Savannah, then. With your sensitivities, it's going to test you."

She wasn't kidding about that. Sorcha had only been there for less than a week and it'd been hard on her already. "I've noticed."

Luke hung up and walked back to them. "Sorry, Laura. We gotta go." He glanced at Helly and Sorcha. "We have a more pressing case in Savannah."

Sorcha arched a brow. "How so?"

"Dead college student. The captain wants us back as soon as we can get there. This is high profile with the news crawling all over it."

"What about the Dire?" Sorcha asked.

He met Laura's gaze. "Can you keep an eye out and let me know if you find anything?"

"You know I will, cutie pie. Last thing I need is someone bringing attention to my species. We only need one Dire per region, and I've claimed this one as mine."

Luke inclined his head. "Understood. I'll be in touch once I find out what's going on in Savannah." He gestured in the direction of the Kroger parking lot where they'd left his car. "Shall we, Lady Detective?"

Sorcha had no idea why that gave her a bit of a chill, yet it did. "You know, you're awfully polite for a demon."

He led the way along the path. "We're not all bad. And as Imp noted, I'm technically another species. Demons are their own thing. But they can be quite charming when they want."

Helly grinned. "He's right. Charm and perfection are what they're known for."

"Really? I always thought it was soul sucking."

Luke sighed heavily. "Hard to suck someone's soul when you're an asshole. And for the record, you can't take a soul. It has to be given over freely. So demons come in slick and insidious so that they can charm you out of it. As I'm sure you know, people are attracted to shiny." He cracked a grin at her and threw his head back playfully so that his hair rippled around his shoulders. "It's why I shine so bright. I like being the candle to the moths."

Sorcha laughed at his exaggerated teasing. "Now, that's the kind of arrogance I expect from the son of the devil."

"Not arrogance. Just truth. We're not at all like the ghosts you see."

He was right about that. "True. Ghosts don't try to possess anyone."

Luke paused to pin her with a frightening glare. "You don't know much about demons, do you?"

"Not really. I've tried to avoid them as much as possible. But I have definitely dated a few...on accident."

Passing a look to Helly, he started walking through the woods. "Just like people, they're not all alike. There are many different races of demons. And a complicated hierarchy."

That was something she definitely didn't know. "Really?"

"Yeah. The ones who want to take up residence in others...they're bottom feeders and are as hated by us as they are by you."

Huh... She'd have thought they were revered. "Why?"

"Because humans lump us together. Just like there are slimy humans, there are slimy demons. Those bastards make us all look bad."

And Luke definitely wasn't slimy. Proven by the fact that he opened the car door and held it for her.

Sorcha slid in as Luke walked to the other side and joined her. Pulling his hair back with the pink tie, he waited for Helly to get in and be situated before he turned on the car and headed back.

"So what do the higher-level demons do?" Sorcha was curious about the aforementioned hierarchy.

He gave her that wicked lopsided grin before he answered in a gravelly tone. "Seduce."

That one word hovered between them. It wasn't helped by the sudden image in her mind of him making love to her. Worse? She could practically feel him in her arms. His hard, muscled body moving under her hands.

*What's wrong with me?*

This wasn't like her. At all.

And yet she was attracted to him in a way she'd never been attracted to anyone. She'd heard the term "sex on a stick" most of her life. He was the only one she'd ever met who gave that term meaning.

Luke glanced over at her as he headed toward Senoia. "I've rendered you speechless."

"I've noticed that you like to shock me."

"Don't take it personally. I like to shock everyone."

"Is that what has you banned from Hell?" she asked in a teasing tone.

But it sucked all the humor out of him.

Helly leaned forward to whisper in her ear. "Don't joke about that. He's very sensitive about not being able to go home."

"Oh, sorry. I didn't know."

Luke let out a long-drawn breath. "Not your fault. I'm just not happy being here. Believe it or not, I prefer Hell to this world."

She had a very hard time believing *that*. "How? Why?"

"Better the hell you know than the heaven you don't."

"That's not a saying."

"But it's how I feel. All my family is there and most of my

friends." He glanced over at her and smirked. "And no. Your uncle Ted isn't burning in any of our pits."

While it bothered her that he'd heard her thought, she was relieved to know that. "Thank you."

"Don't thank me. I had nothing to do with it. I mean, it was close. He definitely had one foot in Hell the whole time he lived. But he managed to pull it out at the last minute when it counted."

Given the criminal tendencies of her uncle, that made her very curious. All her life, she'd heard her father say that if anyone was going to Hell, Ted would be driving the bus. "How so?"

"Regret. Contrition. He admitted what he'd done and sought to make it right. It's not enough to ask forgiveness. You must feel the weight of your conscience and truly wish you'd never given pain to others. That's a lot harder than you think. Most want to blame others and never take responsibility for the evil they do. Nothing in life is worse than someone who feels justified in their hatred or bad acts. That's when the real evil takes over and does the worst damage to this world. And it's how people end up damned."

Sorcha hated how true that was. "Yeah. Too few want to face the truth of what they've done and who they've hurt." Like her ex. He'd been a rotten piece of shit. One who'd gone out of his way to cause her and others pain.

She despised the word *narcissist*. It was used way too flippantly by those who wanted to label others and who didn't really comprehend its meaning. But having been in a five-year relationship with one who still wouldn't let her go, she knew exactly the mental anguish such people caused. Bert had never once been able to face anything he did.

Everything was her fault and she was the one who caused him to hurt her.

*Why do you make me do these things, Sorcha...*

Luke reached over and took her hand. "Don't worry. Bert will pay for what he's done. You're not his only victim, and he has no remorse that will redeem him."

"You sure?"

"Beyond. He's not your uncle. He's been earmarked as ours for a long time now."

She appreciated his support, but... "I'm not sure I wish him to Hell for what he did to me."

"Oh, it's not your wishes that damn him. Trust me. It's his actions. And he will *never* change."

"How do you know that?"

Again, that terribly salacious smile. "My superpowers."

She should be offended by the way he said that. But he was charming her with those hellish ways.

He let go of her hand and gripped the wheel.

Wanting to change the subject to something less personal, she went back to the original matter. "What details do you have about our murder in Savannah?"

"SCAD student."

"SCAD?" Was that some new slang she didn't know?

"Savannah College of Art and Design. It's one of the local universities."

She winced as an involuntary image of her sister went through her mind. "Did the murder happen on campus?"

He shook his head. "In a cemetery. Reyes thinks it looks like a sacrifice of some kind."

That surprised her. "What?"

"Yeah. We get those sometimes. College kids are tricky.

They play with things they shouldn't. Sometimes those things turn deadly. The police believe this is either gang related, human stupidity, an occult slaying, or that it might be paranormal. They're not sure and Reyes doesn't want to make the call without my looking the scene over."

"Why?"

"Because I won't be guessing. I'll know instantly if my side had a hand in it."

That made sense. "Do you think it's demonic?"

"No idea. The devil and demons don't do as much as y'all think. Most of the world's evil comes from humans and their own inclinations."

That was an interesting thought. "How so?"

Luke shrugged. "People are so quick to damn themselves with their deeds and thoughts that there's not a whole lot we have to do. But the worst are the kids who find some book in the library or online with instructions on how to summon the devil or a demon. They do it for fun, thinking it's a lark or that they can control the demon, or offer to trade their souls for their deepest, darkest desires, which is normally something stupid like love, fame or wealth. For the most part, we ignore humanity because they're so petty and ripe for the plucking without any effort on our part. There are only a handful of souls we go after."

"Such as?"

"Those who are devout or really altruistic. They're the diamonds we seek. The souls we'd normally never be able to claim. But if you wear them down...there is a breaking point where everyone gets desperate enough to make a deal to stop the pain. If you can get *them*, you've accomplished something."

"How do you wear down someone like that?"

With one hand on the wheel, he shrugged. "First, we try the usual. Greed. Gluttony. Fornication. Wrath. Apathy. Pride and of course, envy—the true original sin. It's in people's natures to destroy themselves."

That didn't make sense. "The original sin was done by the devil who tempted Adam and Eve in the garden of Eden."

"That's what they say, but they're wrong. The gift of knowledge isn't a sin. Innate curiosity might get you punished, but it won't condemn you. Besides, the devil didn't make Eve bite the apple. Her jealousy did. She wanted what she wasn't supposed to have, and she was jealous God kept it from her. Mark, chapter eight. *Get thee behind me, Satan: for thou savourest not the things that be of God, but the things that be of men. For what shall it profit a man, if he shall gain the whole world, and lose his own soul?*"

Luke winked at her. "Those are the souls we seek. The ones who aren't hypocrites and the ones who are destined for glory. A demon's job is to derail their righteous path by any means necessary. We don't bother with the ones who seek us out. We get those by default."

What he described horrified her. "Why would you ruin people who are trying to do right and live without harming others?"

He shrugged with a nonchalance that irritated her. "My father turned against God, and he hates those who refuse to do the same. His goal is to get as many loyal followers pried loose as he can. No reason, other than jealousy and revenge against the father he once loved. He was punished and hurt and so he seeks to do the same to others. Like so many out there, the devil wants to share his pain."

She took a minute to think about what he said. "So God and Lucifer aren't locked in an eternal battle between good and evil?"

Luke gave her a droll stare. "Do you really think Lucifer is on equal footing with God? If he was, he wouldn't have been thrown out of Heaven. Nor would he have stayed in Hell. He'd have gone back and reclaimed what he lost."

"Then why doesn't God stop him from all the evil he does?"

"*He will deliver his soul from going into the pit, and his life shall see the light. Lo, all these things worketh God oftentimes with man, to bring back his soul from the pit, to be enlightened with the light of the living.*"

"Another Bible quote?"

Luke nodded. "Job."

"Awesome. Care to speak it in English?"

"God doesn't mind the test. Without doubt, there can be no faith. Those who are worthy can't be swayed or knocked off course for very long. They'll find a way to ignore temptation and keep to the straight and narrow. Or repent for a momentary lapse in judgement. Like you and me, Lucifer is merely doing his job. God seeks and favors those who might falter, but who will stay the course, in spite of every miserable thing thrown at them."

Suddenly, Sorcha realized how very little she actually knew about the devil. "I never thought of it that way."

"Most people never think about it at all." Luke stopped at a light. "Want to know something else?"

"Sure. Why not?"

He used the rearview mirror to glance at Helly in the backseat. "His name isn't really Lucifer."

Her jaw went slack. "What?"

"Lucifer means 'light-bringer.' That was never his name. Like Satan, it's merely an epithet others use for him."

Huh...that *was* fascinating. "Then what's his name?"

Helly leaned forward to whisper in her ear. "We never tell anyone our real names. It gives them power over us."

"Really?" she asked.

Luke nodded.

"Then your name isn't Luke?"

"Hell no, it's not. Nor is it Lucian."

"Then what is it?"

"That's a secret I'll only give to the woman who holds something more than my body."

# FOUR

"Well, that was unfortunate."

Luke passed an annoyed stare at Remiel as the archangel appeared by his side in the Catholic cemetery he'd been called to about the student murder. In his human form, Remi was almost as tall as Luke. Shoulder-length, wavy blond hair that he'd pulled back into a ponytail, and eyes so blue that they appeared electric. His white, golden-tipped wings were currently hidden. Though it would be amusing to see them contrast with the angel's jeans and black button-down shirt. "Not as unfortunate as my being seen with you in public," Luke quipped.

"I still say our relationship had nothing to do with your banishment."

Right... Luke completely disagreed. "My father hates you with every beat of his callous, black heart."

"Samael doesn't hate me. He's merely angry that I didn't

join him in his rebellion and no one holds a grudge better than he. That being said, I'm sure he's over it by now."

Luke laughed. "That eternal hope in you is annoying, my friend."

"We're all creatures of habit and birth. Should I toss a bone for you?"

"Ha, ha." Luke rolled his eyes at the reference to his being part hellhound. "Low blow."

Remiel smiled. "Sorry. I'm feeling a bit...puckish over the waste of that young life. She had such promise. I weep at the cruelty."

"Yeah." Luke wasn't happy about it himself. It'd been a brutal murder that he was sure the poor kid hadn't deserved.

But at least one thing was clear... "This wasn't one of us." There was nothing demonic about it. Well, other than the gore. But even that was over the top for his kind.

Unless they were really pissed off.

Sometimes if they wanted to make a point.

"It wasn't human, either."

"You sure?" he asked Remiel. "Humans can be far more vicious than any of our ilk. I can see a human doing it for some sick and twisted reason...like she didn't compliment someone's shoes. Their senseless cruelty is legendary." Luke knelt by the girl's side. Someone had shredded her horribly and then ripped out her throat. Her face was so badly battered that he couldn't even tell what she'd looked like before her attack.

This had been ruthless. Savage.

Human.

"Where's her soul?"

He looked up at Remi's question. "What?"

"It's not here, lingering as it should be. No psychopomp was dispatched to escort her to her final place, and I don't detect her soul in any dimension. What happened to it?"

That made a good point. If no psychopomp had come here to gather it, then her soul should be wandering about the grounds with the ghosts.

And it wasn't, which left him with an interesting list of possible culprits. "It was done during daylight." That meant no vampires were involved. Sadly, though, the list of soul-eaters who could walk in daylight was a long one.

Rising to his feet, he sighed. "Any ideas?"

Remi smirked. "You're the detective."

"And you're the asshole."

Remi laughed.

But at least Remi had pointed him in the right direction. They were hunting someone who'd stolen the girl's soul.

No, Luke realized as he glanced about and considered what Remi had said about it not existing in any dimension. They were looking for something that had eaten it.

Sorcha dried her face that she'd just washed. Six years on the New Orleans police force and she'd never once vomited.

Today, she made up for it.

Never in her life had she seen anything more gruesome than the crime scene in the graveyard. She doubted if Jack the Ripper had been worse.

"You okay?"

She caught sight of the captain in the mirror and

blushed at having been seen like this. Like she was a rookie on her first crime scene. "Yeah."

"It's always hard when it's a young person."

True. The girl had been no more than eighteen or nineteen. Sorcha was just grateful she wasn't the one who'd have the awful job of notifying the girl's parents. The very thought made her want to vomit again. Those poor people.

"Do you see anything?" the captain asked.

Sorcha wiped at her face one last time and shook her head. "There's nothing I'm picking up on. What about Luke?" She'd left him as soon as she'd seen the mangled body someone had placed near a marble statue of a dog named Prince.

Two seconds later, she'd emptied her stomach in the nearest bush and had made a trail to a local construction business and into the bathroom where she currently stood.

"He's not picking up anything either. Was hoping you might be able to see the girl's ghost."

Shocked, Sorcha froze. "What?"

"Your father told me what you can do. It's one of the reasons I hired you. We could use a medium on staff. The last one we had...didn't work out."

Sorcha could imagine the trouble a medium would have, given everything she'd seen in the office, alone. Never mind everything else that haunted Savannah.

What more was there that she didn't know about this job?

"Was she Luke's partner, too?"

The captain shook her head. "No. Chris's. He had a hard time dealing with her. She really didn't like Winslow."

How could anyone not like Chris and his ghost?

Right now, she'd give anything to have them as her biggest problem, because all she wanted was something to calm her nerves from a sight she was sure she'd never unsee.

This one would haunt her as much as her sister's.

Reyes handed her a can of ginger ale. "Believe it or not, that'll help."

"Thanks." Sorcha took the offering and popped the lid. She wasn't a big ginger ale fan. But right now, she'd welcome anything to settle her stomach and get the awful, bitter taste out of her mouth.

"Take your time. I'll be at the crime scene when you're ready."

Even though it was the last thing she wanted to do, Sorcha took a deep drink, then followed after her captain. She really didn't want to see what was left of that poor kid again.

Think about the student's family and the pain it'd cause them. No one ever got over the death of someone so young.

She knew that better than anyone. *I miss you, Siobhan.* Sorcha felt the loss of her twin sister every single day. It was why she'd entered law enforcement. Losing someone you loved was hard. Having no answers about their death or watching their killer go free was worse.

It left a devouring fury deep inside the soul that never abated. One that hungered for justice.

Explanation.

No one knew anything about Siobhan's death. No witnesses. Just a crime scene with gory photos she'd memorized in hopes of finding out something. Someday.

All she'd ever found was pain.

No answers.

*Don't think about it.*

She couldn't change the past. All she could do was get answers for others. Make sure they didn't live with the guilt and mystery that she did.

Trying not to make the poor girl Siobhan's substitute, she returned to the cemetery and headed for Luke who was talking to a tall, gorgeous blond man. There was something about him that seemed ethereal and raw. Dangerous and yet comforting.

Strange combination.

"Sorcha." Luke inclined his head to her as she joined them. "This is Remi."

"Hi." She smiled at the stranger.

A frown darted across his face before he returned her smile. "Nice meeting you...wish it was under better circumstances."

"Yeah." She pulled the blue latex gloves from her purse and the shoe covers. Last thing they wanted was to taint evidence or track anything home. "Are you with Infernal Affairs?"

That widened his smile and showed her just how exquisitely handsome he was. "More like *Eternal* Affairs."

That confused her. "What?"

Luke laughed. "Remi's the archangel Remiel."

Her jaw went slack. "No way... You're kidding."

They both shook their heads.

"A demon and an angel...friends?"

"Luke's not really a demon. He claims that status, but his father is an angel and his mother a hound. Demons don't enter into his genetic code."

Her partner snorted. "Remi is overly literal, as in he's ASD on steroids. It's one of his more annoying traits. And I assure you, my father would be highly offended hearing you classify him as an angel. He considers himself the first demon."

Remi sighed heavily. "His pride...ever his downfall."

"Stubbornness is ever yours."

Remi gave Luke a gimlet stare. "Let ye who be without sin..."

"Oh, I'm casting that stone, brother. Just be happy that this time it's not at your head."

Tsking, Remi stepped back. "I shall leave you two to your business. Just be careful. We don't know what we're dealing with." And with that, he looked about to make sure no one was watching them and vanished.

She shivered at his actions. "Does he do that often?"

"Yes, but generally not in public."

"What about the *we* comment?" she asked. "You work with him a lot?"

"Not at all. He's the archangel of hope who sometimes guides the souls of the faithful into Heaven."

"Is that why he was here?"

Luke scowled at her. "You ask a lot of questions."

She tapped the badge clipped to her waist. "Investigators usually do. Kind of goes with the whole detective territory."

Snorting, he jerked his chin toward the body beside the family plot where the dog sat in eternal repose. Too bad she couldn't ask it any questions. It would have seen everything that happened here.

"Remi said that no one had been dispatched to claim the

girl and he didn't detect her soul in any of the known realms."

Now she was really confused. "What does that mean?"

"No soul. No psychopomp. No happy-ever-after or not-so-happy-ever-after...means something else took her soul, or worse, devoured it. And whatever it was is probably the one who killed her."

"That's disturbing."

"More than you know. No one likes a soul-eater. On any side. It's...unnatural."

Sorcha made a face. "I would have thought they were among your father's favorites."

"Soul-stealer, yes. Soul-eater, hell no. Pun intended. My father makes it a source of pride to take every soul he can from the Creator. But to destroy one...that pisses off everyone. It's absolutely senseless to waste a perfectly good soul, even an evil one. They all have their uses. And that use isn't for food or destruction."

In a weird way, that made sense.

Helly joined them. She was eating a large ice cream cone. "Are we done?"

"No," they said in unison.

She let out a long, exasperated breath. "Fine. I'm going to sit in the AC while you sweat in the heat. Unlike Luke, I hate being hot." She flounced off toward the car.

Which made Sorcha realize something. She *was* sweating. Horribly. Luke on the other hand...

"Aren't you hot in that coat? It's nine thousand degrees out here."

He smirked at her. "From Hell? Remember? This is the arctic tundra to me. Why do you think I was in a boiling hot tub in the sun? Since they kicked me out of my home, I freeze all the time. It's miserable. You're lucky I'm not in a parka on the equator."

"Is it really that hot in Hell?"

"I'm not sweating, am I? Because I'm used to a *lot* hotter than this. I cannot say this enough. Hell is *hot* and I like it like that."

Terrified by what he described so casually, Sorcha drifted toward the bagged body that was being lifted onto a Gurney by the coroner. The regular LEOs—law enforcement officers—were finally clearing the scene.

Even though she could no longer see the girl, she kept her gaze averted. It was the kind of death that lingered.

In an effort to divert her thoughts, she started on the obvious. "There's not enough blood here, given the severity of her injuries. She was obviously killed elsewhere."

"Agreed."

Sorcha glanced around the cemetery that was similar to the one across the street from their offices. There was a school nearby, and a *lot* of homes.

Granted there were trees to block some line of sight, still... "This is a very public place to dump a body."

"Again, agreed. And while it's nowhere near as popular a tourist attraction as Bonaventure or Colonial Cemetery, it still gets its share of looky-loos."

Frowning, Sorcha glanced at the road not that far away. "So how did they do it without being seen?" It made no sense to her. A passing car could easily see suspicious activity and report it.

Luke shrugged. "For one of my kind, easy. Teleportation. Portaling. Hell, we could drop a body and just mind fuck anyone who saw it. Burn out the cameras. The real question is, could a human do it and not be seen?"

She turned around, looking at everything. "I don't see how. Unless they were really lucky. But there are so many cameras nowadays, it's getting harder and harder to commit a crime and not be seen. I can't tell you how many crimes we solved in New Orleans with a simple Ring camera on someone's door. What other creatures are you thinking?"

"Demons don't usually kill their victims. Defeats the purpose of what they're after. But if they did, they could open a portal. Jump in and out. Never be seen."

That was a good start. "Aside from demons, who else uses portals?"

He gave her an arch stare.

"Okay. Apparently, it's a long list. I'm just trying to understand it." Because portals weren't that common in her world, even as bizarre as it was.

Sighing, Sorcha went toward the grave where the body had been placed. "Hagan lot... Patrick and Mary. Died 1912 and 1921 respectively. Along with Prince the dog—he loved his master." Extremely weird, as was the fact that the entire lot was one giant marble slab and fenced in with some impressive coping and decorations that included a very large, ornate cross, towering over the graves. "You think the dog or Hagans have anything to do with it?"

"No."

"That your evil powers speaking?"

Luke scratched at his ear, looking less than pleased. "Don't need my powers here. Can't imagine anyone trying to bring back someone from that long ago. Unless it was a writer for a term paper of some kind. Anyone else would know it was pointless...and gross to try and raise a body that old. Zombie bokors go for the recent dead."

"You're not funny."

"You say that, but I know the kids who go to school here. You'd be amazed what some of them have done or will do to get what they want...especially when it's an A for a test or paper they don't want to write or study for. There's only so much AI can do."

She would deny it, but there had been a time or two when she'd been willing to sacrifice the proverbial goat while in college.

And when it came to her roommate...

Maureen was very lucky Sorcha hadn't sacrificed that boyfriend-stealing-bitch to the goddess of sanity. Had Maureen not stolen her boyfriend, Sorcha wouldn't have ended up with Bert.

Still...

Reyes walked over to them. "Any insights?"

Raking both hands through his thick dark hair, Luke shrugged. "I didn't do it. I'm innocent. Don't believe what the dog tells you. Everyone knows Prince is a liar."

The captain rolled her eyes. "What about you?" she asked Sorcha.

"I didn't do it, either," she couldn't resist saying before she shook her head. "I got nothing except a possible headache." She glanced toward Luke. "Maybe fleas."

Reyes laughed.

There was a glint in his eyes that said Luke might be amused, but if that was true, then he needed to tell it to the rest of his face. Even so, the smirk on his lips was adorable.

"Anyway, we are in accord in that we have no idea what happened."

Reyes nodded slowly. "Can you find out? That is, after all, why I'm paying you the little bucks."

Putting his hands in his pockets, Luke shrugged. "I'll ask my deems and see what they say."

"All right. They're wrapping up the evidence." Reyes clapped Sorcha gently on the shoulder. "It's been a long day. I'll get the reports from the police as soon as they're filed. Why don't you head home, and we'll see you in the morning."

Sorcha stifled a yawn. She was rather beat. Reyes was right, it'd been a long day. "Thanks."

Luke dug his keys from his pocket. "I'll take you back to the office."

As they headed for his car, she realized that Helly wasn't waiting for them. "Don't you need your imp?"

Making a face, he shook his head. "She'll get back when she's ready."

Should Helly be out on her own? Sorcha wasn't sure it was a good idea to leave a Hell imp on the streets unattended. "You leave her often?"

"She's a grown imp. Much older than I am. And she doesn't need a car to travel."

Sorcha opened the door and glanced back toward the area where the student had been placed so unceremoniously. "Don't you worry about her?"

"Not at all. And you shouldn't either. It's the humans who should be afraid."

Great. That was even worse. "Will she hurt them?"

"Only if they try to hurt her first and then...payback's a

pissed off imp and if we're lucky, we can film it and make big bucks on TikTok."

And with that she was definitely afraid as he turned on the car and its huge engine roared to life.

Helly was out on the loose and so was an unknown killer who could be some preternatural predator, or a psycho hunting students.

Her head really hurting now, Sorcha pulled out her pad to jot down a few notes as Luke drove.

Neither of them spoke as he returned her to her car that was parked across the street from their office.

Sorcha got out and hesitated. "Guess I'll see you in the morning."

"I'll be here. Even though I hate mornings with the burning passion of a thousand suns...or the heat of my father's deepest pit." After winking at her, he drove off toward the garage.

She stood there for a moment, looking back at the building where her day had started. Infernal Affairs. Had she made a mistake by coming here?

In one day, she'd investigated a Dire Wolf sighting, met a shapeshifter, an angel, several ghosts and had ended up with a slaughtered college student whose image would haunt her for eternity.

And met the son of the devil and his Hell imp.

Heck of a first day.

"Terrified of tomorrow." But a weird part of her couldn't wait to see what would happen next. It'd been a long time since she felt this stirring of excitement. Since she'd actually looked forward to something.

*I am definitely not right in the head.*

Yet as she opened her car door and glanced up at the window in the front room of their offices, she caught sight of the ghost she'd seen earlier that day.

The ghost waved at her and smiled.

Before she could stop herself, Sorcha waved back. Then she quickly got in, hoping no one had seen her do that, and went home.

Luke parked the car in the IA garage and turned off the engine. He should probably complain about the fact that he lived where he worked, but it made it highly convenient to live over the garage of their offices.

It made his morning commute tolerable.

"You like your new partner." It was a flat statement, not a question.

He pulled the keys out and glared at the dash of his car. "Did I ask for your commentary, Delilah?"

A shadow rose away from the radio to manifest in the seat beside him. Slowly, she became the sultry vixen who'd damned Samson. Her dark, wavy hair fell to the middle of her back. In spite of the fact she was thousands of years old, she appeared in the form of a stunningly beautiful woman in her mid-twenties. One whose beauty was such that Samson hadn't stood a chance.

Thankfully, Luke wasn't Samson. Even though Delilah had been after him since he'd hit puberty, she wasn't his type, and he found her constant stalking annoying. "Why are you pulling out of the car, D? Spying for my father?"

"Never. He doesn't need me to do such. He has spies aplenty. I'm bringing you a message from Sorath."

That sounded off. "And that is?"

"He has a theory on who did this to you."

Then why would he send her to tell him and not come himself? Something wasn't adding up. "Theory or fact?"

She shrugged. "Does it matter?"

More than anything. He wasn't about to react over a theory. But if Sorath knew who'd betrayed him...

That, he would definitely act on.

"Why are you in human form?" Normally, she remained as part of his car, leaving it only to carry messages to and from Hell.

She climbed onto his lap. "Care to catch up?"

Luke caught her wrists to keep her from embracing him. "I don't need a haircut. Thanks."

"I'd never do that to you."

Yeah, right. And he'd never trust anyone so treacherous. Her record with men...

While Luke could be stupid for a pretty face...

He wasn't an absolute moron.

"Tell Sorath I'll be in touch, and stay in the car when you're in this realm."

She pouted. "Surely, you're tired of humans by now. Don't you want better company?"

"Tired of the human world, not humans. Now go. You're wearing out my patience." Not to mention, he had something much more pressing to see to.

With one last huff, she vanished back into his dash.

Luke took a moment to savor the quiet, knowing it wouldn't last.

By the time he entered his apartment upstairs, the voices were back in his head. All the whispering and begging. Those who were trying to make deals and those who wanted out of bargains they'd made.

He heard them all.

There had been a time when he would have sought out the more desperate souls for his father. Damn shame they weren't on speaking terms. He was really good about bargaining and delivering souls that made his father proud.

But those days were over.

He would never damn another human. Never make another bargain. Even if he regained his status, he wouldn't be his father's pride anymore.

*Fuck him.*

If only he could purge the voices, Luke would be thrilled.

"What did that bitch want with you?" A pair of bright red eyes glowed in the shadows between his couch and the far wall.

He'd know that sultry, growling feminine voice anywhere.

Luke closed the door and locked it. "What are you doing here, Mum?"

"I smelled Delilah in human form. Given her history with you, I had a feeling she was harassing my favorite child."

"I'm your only child." Luke used his powers to turn on the lights. As he did so, the black Xolos hound turned into his tall, elegant mother. Her amber gold eyes stood out against her dark skin, making them appear to glow. She wore a bright silver crescent moon amulet suspended between her intense eyes.

With a tender smile, she approached him and reached up to gently cup his cheek. "I've missed you."

"Miss you, too." He pulled her in for a hug.

She yanked playfully at his hair before she took a step back. Her long black gauzy robe rustled with her graceful movements as she entered the small kitchen. "This place is beneath you."

"You say that every time you visit."

"It's true every time I visit. I weep to find you in such a state. How do you stand it?" With a wave of her hand, she tidied up the counters he'd left a bit crowded. The one truth about Senka...she couldn't stand clutter of any kind.

Turning back toward him, she pinned him with that glare that usually caused demons to wet themselves. "What did that bitch want?"

"She said Sorath knows something about my banishment."

Scoffing, she waved those words away dismissively. "Not true. Sorath has nothing. If he knew, he'd have told me so."

"How about you?"

"Your father won't discuss it. Sammy is still quite angry at you. He won't even allow me to mention your name in his presence. Worthless bastard."

Only his mother could use that nickname for Samael Lucifer. She got away with things no one else would even dare because she was the only creature alive his father fully trusted.

"I will find the one responsible for this and when I do—"

"You will let me deal with them," Luke reminded her.

Senka screwed up her beautiful face. "If you insist."

"I do."

Helly appeared at the door, then pulled up short as she saw his mother. She bowed respectfully. "My lady."

Senka inclined her head to the imp. "At least this one is loyal and knows her place. Something I won't forget when you've returned to your standing. I will make sure your imp is well rewarded."

If only she knew what Helly said about her in her absence, she might think differently. Thankfully, none of it had ever gotten back to his mom.

And he definitely would never tell. He liked his imp in one piece.

Senka moved to stand before him. "I'd best be off to torture Delilah. Need something to improve my mood." She tugged at the stud earring in his left ear. "I hate this thing. Make it go away."

He wrinkled his nose at her. "Bye, *Mata*."

She stepped back to go, then hesitated. "You know your new partner?"

"Yeah. I met her today."

She gave him an irritated stare. "Be careful. She has things after her as bad or worse than you do. They've already taken her sister. And they are coming for her next. I don't want you hurt because you're near her when they strike."

He wasn't worried. The list of things that could hurt him was very short. "I'll be careful. But what is after her?"

"Ancient powers. They're all around her. Can't you feel them?"

No, he couldn't. That wasn't like him. All he knew was

that she wasn't fully human. His assumption had been that she was a half breed like him.

But if his mother was correct...

There was a lot more to her. "Can you give me more than that?"

"I don't know more than that at present. Just be watchful, child."

"You, too."

With a nod, she vanished in a cloud of smoke.

"What was she talking about?" Helly asked as she flopped on his black leather couch. "Who's after Sorcha?"

"No idea. Sorcha said nothing about a sister." And the voices in his head gave him no clue about Sorcha's past. Other than her uncle Ted and one other dead relative from a long time ago, he knew nothing about her really. That was highly unusual for him. "I thought she was a halfling human."

"People think you're human."

True. There were a number of creatures who could hide their real natures. Generally not from him, but on occasion...

There was a lot more to Sorcha than he'd originally thought. And for some reason, that thrilled him to no uncertain end.

But right now, he couldn't afford to be distracted. He had to find his betrayer.

And figure out what had mangled an innocent college student. Most of all, he needed to know what game Delilah was up to. She didn't just randomly extricate herself from his car. Never in history had there been a greater shit-stirring bitch than she.

If she had any part in his banishment, hers would be the first throat he'd take.

*Things always get worse before they get better.*

And he felt trapped in a midnight hour from which he couldn't escape. More than that, he felt as if his enemies were getting the better of him. The saddest part was that he didn't know who those enemies were or why they'd targeted him.

*They're Hell demons. Does it matter?*

Not really. They'd succeeded in upending his life. But he wasn't done with them.

*They're probably not done with you, either.*

That was a sobering thought. Along with the fact that they were out there. Living their lives, thinking they wouldn't pay. Thinking they could just keep fucking with him without any consequences.

They couldn't be more wrong.

He would find them. And they'd curse whatever bitch had shat them into their worlds. Because at the end of the day, no one knew better how to punish someone than the son of the devil who was bent on vengeance.

CHAPTER

# FIVE

S orcha stood in her new office with her hands on her hips. It was so...

Plain. Icky?

Hard to tolerate?

Definitely.

Four boring beige walls. A white erase board with the word "asshole" written in permanent red ink. An awful green metal desk the likes of which she had never seen outside of old movies. A cheap rolling chair and two tan, metal filing cabinets that held enough rust on them that she was sure she'd get tetanus just from opening a drawer.

"What am I supposed to do with this?"

Someone knocked on her door.

Depressed over the nightmare that would be this office, she went to open her door only to find a sexy Luke on the other side, holding some kind of green potted plant and a cup of coffee. He flashed that gorgeous grin at her. "Morning, new partner."

"Thought you weren't a morning person."

"Oh, I am not. Don't let this act fool you. I'm pretending to be human for your sensibilities 'cause I don't want to scare you off on your second day." He looked past her to the whiteboard. "Oh, I forgot about that."

Luke walked into her office so that he could put the plant and coffee on her desk. He snapped his fingers and the word "asshole" vanished.

"Should I ask?"

Again, that adorable grin. "About the word or the snapping?"

"Both."

He shrugged nonchalantly. "Rob was a douche. Couldn't stand the bastard. *Asshole* was a step up from what I normally called him—and is a body part that wouldn't offend Reyes's more delicate sensibilities and force her to get an HR department. I had no idea that when the word scribbled itself across the board one night while he was working late that it would mentally break him. Had I known that, I'd have done it a lot sooner." He laughed. "You should have seen him running through the yard, screaming he was being stalked and haunted."

"By you?"

"Who knows? Like I said, he was a paranoid douche who made me sick to my stomach. I can't stand a..." He grinned as he caught whatever profane insult he'd almost said.

She watched as the words "good morning, beautiful" drew themselves on the board. "That's better."

Yes, it was.

The plant floated over to the filing cabinets, then set itself down.

Luke screwed up his face. "It is shit in here, isn't it?"

"I've worked in worse."

"Really?" Running his thumb along his bottom lip, he shook his head. "Want to peek into my office? Get some decorating ideas?"

"Sure." She'd see it sooner or later. Might as well stick her head into the devil's den and get it over with.

He led her to the office next door to hers. The first thing she noticed was that he didn't need a key. He simply waved his hand over the doorknob, and it opened. How she wished she had those evil mind powers, especially given how many times she locked herself out of her house.

One time, she'd even managed to do it while holding her keys in her hand. She still hadn't figured out why the lock had broken, but it'd taken her hours to get back inside.

Locks hated her.

As Luke walked in and turned the light on, she laughed.

"Isn't this just a little on the nose?" His office was a haunting thing to behold, and she just couldn't believe it looked like this. "And seriously, how did you get all this stuff in here?"

The room was like Dr. Who's TARDIS. Much bigger on the inside than outside. He had matte, jet black bookcases that held images of adorable young angels carved along the top and bottom. The shelves were covered with all kinds of occult and new age titles, along with history books. Some in languages she couldn't even identify.

On the wall behind his desk, there appeared to be an arched gothic church window that looked out onto a beautiful forest, complete with deer. Actual black velvet curtains hung down the wall as if the painted arched windows were real.

Flanking the mural were two...

Lamp posts? Only they were statues of knights set on black marble columns with something that appeared to be a flickering torch held in the raised hand of each one.

There was even a jet-black crystal chandelier hanging from the ceiling.

Like the shelving, his huge black desk had angels carved into it, along with two black skull candelabra set on the edges. She assumed his PC must be inside the desk as the top held only a monitor and black, skull-skinned keyboard and mouse. The matching leather chair on wheels looked more like a throne than the average office seat.

Even his evidence board was black and covered with interesting black sticky notes with silver writing about the student they'd found last night. But what intrigued her most was the fact that it was a Smart Board.

Latest tech.

Wow...

This was a far cry from her awful, outdated space.

Luke put his hands in his coat pockets. "Sometimes, I like being on brand. It sets a tone."

"And Captain Reyes was good with the purchase order for all this?"

He laughed, then stopped abruptly. "Oh, hell no. She'd have had an apoplexy if I'd tried to requisition all this on the feeble IA budget."

"Then how...never mind." He was the son of the devil. It was obvious that he wasn't used to going without.

Or being denied anything.

Even without his infernal father, a man that good looking seldom heard the word no.

From anyone.

"Want me to fix your office?" Luke offered.

Why did that make her so nervous?

Probably because making a deal with the devil's son was never a good idea.

"Fix it how?" she asked, cringing inwardly at the thought of working inside something reminiscent of Wednesday Addams' bedroom. While his office was interesting, it would give her nightmares to work in something this gothic.

"To your tastes, not mine. I don't want to give you nightmares. I'm aware of the fact that I'm an acquired taste."

Had he heard her thoughts? If he had, he gave no clue about it.

And to be honest, she was a lot more tempted than she should be. "How much will it cost?"

He sucked his breath in sharply. "It's a dear price, I'm afraid."

She could imagine. "My soul?"

"God, no." He closed the distance between them until she had to look up into those mesmerizing eyes. The air between them was rife with an energy she couldn't explain or identify. Whatever it was, it made her breathless. Her heart raced.

"I don't do that anymore," he said in a low tone that caused her to hold her breath. "It involves the hardest thing on the planet. Much more valuable than most souls..."

Why was she enjoying this game? It should piss her off and yet she couldn't resist his unholy charm. She actually wanted to step closer to him. "And that is?"

He leaned down as if he were about to impart a major secret. When he whispered in her ear, it sent a shiver over her entire body. "A please and a thank you."

She scowled. Luke was such a strange beast. "Those aren't hard."

He gestured over his shoulder toward the street. "You been out there lately? Politeness waved bye-bye to humanity a while back. I'm sad to say. It was one of the things I used to like about coming here."

Clearing her throat, she stepped back before she gave in to the need to kiss those sexy lips. "Yeah. I feel that. And yes, if you could please help me redecorate, I would be eternally grateful." As soon as those words were out of her head, she remembered the "asshole" on her whiteboard. "Out of curiosity, you're not the one who made it look like it currently does, were you?"

He flashed a devilish grin. "Aren't you glad I like you?"

Definitely, but she would never say that out loud. No need to feed his abundant ego.

"I think so." She wandered over to his smart board. "By the way, I love this. I've always wanted one."

"Okay. Done."

Was he serious? "Really?"

He nodded. "Yeah. Why not? They are handy for what we do. Makes it a lot easier to share info. I highly recommend them."

Was he that rich or could he just make things like this

appear with his powers? Both were terrifying to think about, but one was a lot scarier than the other.

Just what all could he do with nothing more than a thought?

She narrowed her gaze on him. "Are you ever going to tell me what your powers are?"

"Rather not say, but I'm glad they work in the human world. Bad enough to be kicked out of home. I'd hate to have been stripped of my powers, too."

"Wonder why your father left them intact?"

Luke shrugged. "I'm not about to defend my father and say he's a nice guy who was misunderstood. He's really not. But he's not always a bad dad. For all his faults, he was once an angel and sometimes...rare times...those instincts return when he lets his guard down."

In a weird way, that made sense. "I never really understood his rebellion. My preacher grandad always said Satan became angry because people had freewill and angels didn't. Is that true?"

"If angels didn't have freewill, how could they disobey and rebel?"

Another thing she'd never thought about. He was right. The angels would have needed some degree of freewill to do that. "Then what happened?"

"Simply put...jealousy. Root of all evil."

"I thought that was money."

Luke shook his head. "Money only comes into play because people are jealous someone has more of it than they do. I can't say this enough. Jealousy is the real root of everything bad. All throughout history. It was even the cause of the first murder."

Cain and Abel. He had a valid point.

But one thing didn't make sense to her. "Why would an angel be jealous of humanity?"

"Grass is greener over a septic tank. No matter how good someone has it, that person always thinks someone else has it better or easier. And instead of being grateful for what they do have, they want what they perceive someone else has that they lack or that it's something that person they hate doesn't deserve. My father was a fool for envying mankind, and the worst part is that he knows it, but will never admit it. If he did, he could return to the fold. But *that* will never happen."

"If that's true, I almost feel sorry for him."

Luke snorted hard. "Don't. *Sympathy for the Devil* is a Rolling Stones' song. At the end of the day, my father will *never* repent or admit he was wrong. You know the old saying, better to reign in Hell than serve in Heaven."

"Is that how you feel about it?"

"I reign nowhere and never have. Don't want to. I'm just a spoiled kid who isn't happy he got tossed out on his ass without warning. Ambition wasn't in my vocabulary until a year ago when I found myself naked and freezing on a Savannah sidewalk."

She sucked her breath in sharply between her teeth. "Is that really what happened?"

He nodded slowly.

Sorcha winced in empathetic pain. "That must have been awful."

"Yeah. I had clothes on when I was tossed. I don't know if it was my dad or Sorath who thought it'd be funny to remove them when they dumped me in the human world. Either way, I'm still not amused by it."

"Sorath?"

"One of the fallen angels who chose the wrong side." He sighed. "Had Imp not been with me when I was banished, I don't know what I'd have done."

Leave it to Helly. "She got you clothes?"

He shook his head. "I can conjure those and I was quickly in a parka before the old lady in front of me could scream and call the police...then again, given the lecherous smile on her face, I don't really think that was her intention with her phone. Pretty sure there are photos of me naked online somewhere."

She laughed even though there was a part of her that wondered if she'd be able to find those photos.

"I heard that." Luke winked at her.

Heat filled her cheeks at his teasing tone.

Clearing her throat, she gestured at his work. "Anyway, what is all this on your board?" It looked like he'd been busy on their case after she'd left him last night.

There was a preliminary police report. Police pictures from the crime scene and a list of possible perps off to the side.

"Yeah," he said, dropping his deep voice a full octave. "I bet you want to see my full board, baby."

She growled at his suggestive tone, even though he was good looking enough to get away with what would be offen-sive from anyone else. Reyes was right. He was definitely a handful. "Would you stop! I'm here to work."

"A'ight." He picked up a remote and turned the board on.

Which made her curious about one thing. "Why do you

have physical pictures taped to it? Doesn't that defeat the purpose of having a smart board?"

"Lazy. I haven't put the files into the system yet, and there are things I'm not sure about. Don't want to go to the trouble of adding photos and info until I know I need to. It tends to clutter my thinking."

That made sense. "Gotcha." She walked closer and saw a list that was written on what appeared to be old parchment. "What's this?"

"Quick list I made of soul-eaters."

It was quite long. She pulled it down so that she could read it.

*Revenants, Wendigo, Vampires, Draugr, Lamia, Ammit the Devourer, Wanyudo, Soucouyant, Bakeneko, Nekomata, Daimons, Valravn, Bubak, Ankou, Cat-sith, Kasha, Raven Mocker, Shinigami, Slaugh, Boo hag and witches.*

The last one made her curious. "Bit prejudiced to put witches on here. They don't kill and eat children, you know? One of my best friends is a witch."

"Trish isn't the only kind of witch out there. Like Trish, there are those who use it as a religion, and I mean them no disrespect. Then there are the Witchbreeds who are born with powers. Those are where the old legends and stories come from. They are completely different from religious witches or Wiccans. Honestly, we should come up with another term for the Breeds because they do blacken the names of those who are honest and decent."

A knock sounded on his door.

"Come in, Yuichi."

The door opened to show a young man around thirty.

Sorcha was five seven and he was maybe an inch taller with jet black hair and sweet brown eyes.

Luke inclined his head to him. "Sorcha meet Detective Nagata Yuichi."

"You go by your last name?"

Yuichi smiled. "I'm Japanese and Luke is honoring me by saying my name as we do. Family name first."

Oh. "Sorry. I knew that. I just wasn't thinking. Not enough caffeine yet." She took a sip of her coffee that was perfect.

"All good." He gave Luke an arch stare. "Got your text that you wanted to see me. What did you need, big guy?"

"Talk to me about Wanyudo, Bakeneko, Nekomata, Kasha and Shinigami."

He gave him a stern frown. "I'm sure you know they're yokai."

"Yeah. And?"

Yuichi shrugged. "They're different kinds of yokai? Not sure what you're asking me."

Luke jerked his chin toward the paper in her hands. "We're looking at soul-eaters. Since those yokai are more your wheelhouse than mine, I wanted to ask you about them. Would any of them be interested in murdering a college student and taking her soul?"

Yuichi screwed up his face as he considered that. "The Wanyudo are nasty bastards. Not only do they steal souls, they eat children and torture their parents with it. When they appear, it's always a male face in the center of a burning wheel. Legends say that if you see them you'll die and they take your soul. Or if you have a child, they'll kill the child instead and take the kid's soul."

Sorcha felt sick to her stomach. "Seriously?"

He nodded. "Yeah. Not my favorite yokai. They're so bad, my mom didn't even use them to threaten me with when I was a kid. She was too afraid of them to mention their name."

"What about the others?" Luke asked.

"Bakeneko, Nekomata, and Kasha are roughly the same. They're all kaibyō…cat yokai. Bakeneko and Nekomata are often confused with each other and they overlap. They have a lot of shared abilities. Biggest difference is a Bakeneko has one tail and a Nekomata has two. There are some tales that they have taken souls, but they usually prey on those who deserve a bad end. It's said that they take the souls to make sure evil doesn't return to this life through reincarnation or any other means. Kasha are also Bakeneko, but they usually eat a corpse, not a soul. There might be something written about souls with them, but I'd have to research it. Like I said, they normally eat corpses."

Luke nodded. "Thanks. That helps. I can mark them off the list." He took the paper from Sorcha's hand and used his finger to strike through the names as he'd already done with the vampires. Another impressive power. "Any other soul-eaters in Japan?"

Yuichi considered it for a few seconds. "You mentioned the Shinigami, but they don't take souls. While they're attracted to places of violent death, they go there to possess someone…usually someone evil so that they can cause more evil." He smirked at Sorcha. "They are definitely something my mom used to scare me with as a kid and it's why she hates my job. She's terrified I might come in contact with one and cause it to stalk and kill me because I'm evil for not calling my mother more often."

She could relate. "My mom loved the boogeyman. That and the invisible venomous snakes under my bed she swore would bite me if I left it after bedtime. 'Course that ended after I peed in my bed because I was too afraid to go to the bathroom. Wish I'd done that sooner."

They laughed.

She looked at Luke. "What did your mom scare you with?"

He shrugged. "That she'd tear my throat out and eat my heart if I disobeyed her."

Not what she was expecting to hear. "No, she didn't!"

"Hellhound. They do that to misbehaving pups. If you can't listen, you don't deserve to live. Why would I doubt her? Not to mention, she could always say she'd let the devil have me...and in my childhood that really meant something."

"Well..." Yuichi cleared his throat. "I'll never complain about my mom threatening me with yokai again. I'd much rather have those fears than yours." He looked back at Luke. "Anything else I can help with?"

"That's it. Thanks for narrowing the list."

"Anytime. If I think of something else, I'll let you know." Yuichi left them alone.

Sorcha took the list back from Luke and looked at what was left. *Revenants, Wendigo, Draugr, Daimons, Lamia, Ammit the Devourer, Souruita, Valravn, Bubak, Ankou, Cat-sith, Raven Mocker, Slaugh, Boo Hag* and *witches.*

She took another drink of her coffee. "Why did you need

to consult Yuichi? Didn't you know the difference between the yokai?"

"I'm not omniscient. And while I have a general knowledge of many paranormal creatures, I don't know intricate details about the ones I never interact with. Like you know Germans live in Germany. You might even know some of the language, but chances are you don't know what their favorite communal brand of beer is or what time they usually sit down for dinner. What kind of Easter traditions they celebrate, etcetera."

"Point taken. But being who you are, I would have thought you'd have interacted with most of the paranormal creatures."

"First, not my thing. Again, I was a lazy, useless layabout. In Hell, ambition will get you horribly tortured. So the only ambition I had was to stay in my room as much as possible and remain on my father's lesser bad side."

"You mean good side?"

"He doesn't have a good side. Or even a blind side. You step into his presence and you're risking a lot."

Okay, then...

She returned her attention to his list. "Are vampires really a thing?"

He arched a brow at her question. "You lived in New Orleans and you don't know?"

"Never saw one...other than cosplayers and those who identified as vampires."

"Then be grateful. Daimons and vampires *love* to steal souls. Though it's more a Daimon thing than a vampire one, and the body was dumped in daylight. Back in the day, that would have precluded Daimons, too...now, maybe not. A lot of them have converted so that they can walk in daylight again. But it definitely takes vampires off the list. They hate daytime almost as much as I do." He pulled his cell phone from his pocket and texted someone.

"Law enforcement?" she asked.

He shook his head, then rocked his head side to side as if reconsidering the no. "I guess he could be considered law enforcement, just not for humans."

"Like us, then?"

"No. Dark-Hunter."

# SIX

Sorcha was still confused by who he was texting. What was a Dark-Hunter? "Are they similar to ghost hunters?"

He gave her an irritated glower. "Not even. They're immortal warriors who sell their souls to a Greek goddess for a single act of vengeance...rather a cheap sale if you ask me. Personally, I'd demand more, but that's what happens when you don't realize your worth... Anyway, after they give up their souls, they serve the goddess Artemis so that they can keep Daimons from stealing human souls. It's definitely a thing in their world."

Wow. She wasn't sure how to even begin processing that. "You know, there are so many things I wish I wasn't learning on this job. And these Daimons are in New Orleans, you said?"

"They're all over."

"So, there's a Dark-Hunter here?" she asked.

"Three actually. But Kieran MacAllister is the one I talk to most."

His phone rang.

"Speak of the devil." Luke answered it and put it on speaker. "MacAllister...how you doing?"

"Sitting here with me *baffies, tassie* and box. Couldn't be better. You, mate?"

That was one impressive Scottish accent on that man. She could barely understand what he was talking about.

Luke didn't seem to have any problems translating. "Sounds like fun."

"I know that's not why you're calling. So what's it, then?" Kieran asked.

"We have a dead college student. Something took her soul. Was wondering if it could be Daimon related."

"*Ah dinnae ken.* What did the body look like?"

"Bloody. Torn to pieces."

MacAllister sucked his breath in through his teeth. "Not one of ours, then, mate. Daimons don't waste time on that sort of *laldy*. Too feared of getting caught."

"How many Daimons are in the city?" she asked.

"Hello, there...didn't tell me we had company. Is she tidy?"

Luke laughed. "For a *toonser*, aye."

Sorcha shoved playfully at Luke. "Would you two stop speaking in code? I'd like to follow this conversation."

Luke wrinkled his nose at her. "With the name Sorcha O'Malley, I'd think you could follow it."

"Irish is different from Scottish Gaelic. *Is fearr Gaeilge briste, ná Béarla clíste.*"

Kieran laughed. "Nicely done, lass. Only understood a wee bit of that."

Luke winked at her before he spoke to Kieran. "Aye. She's a *stoater* for someone who thinks broken Irish is better than clever English."

When Kieran spoke, she could hear the smile in his voice. "Well then, lass, to answer your question, we have a fair nest of them here in Savannah. Not too bothersome much of the time. But every now and again, they come to town to pick off some tourists...maybe a college student or two if they're in the right mindset for it. But they mimic a vampire in attack. Two marks on the neck, and not a soul to be found. It's what feeds them. They don't normally desecrate the flesh. No need in it, really. They like to be quick, lest me or me boyos come across them and decide to free the souls they took."

That actually made sense. Thick accent and all. "Thank you so much."

Luke snorted at her. "Appreciate your time, Kieran. Thanks for marking another creature off my list."

"*Haste ye back*, Chief." He hung up.

Luke slid his phone into his pocket. "So we're left with Revenants, Wendigo, Draugr, Lamia, Ammit the Devourer, Souruita, Valravn, Bubak, Ankou, Cat-sith, Raven Mocker, Slaugh, Boo Hag, and my personal fave, witches."

Ouch. "That is still a really long list. Something tells me they won't be as easy to wade through as these last few."

Luke nodded as he reviewed the list again. "We can probably take Ammit off. Normally those souls are taken in the Underworld. Not this one."

"Then why did you add it?"

"I was being thorough and listing every beast I could think of who might have skin in the game."

"I can't believe with your powers that you can't narrow it down more."

He gave an adorable shrug. "That's why we have Infernal Affairs. As many powers as I have, preternatural beings are really good at covering their tracks. Some of them have had centuries to perfect their skills."

"Fair point." Sorcha sighed as she considered what they needed to narrow it down. Honestly, she had no idea.

So, she decided not to make that decision. "Which one do we tackle next?"

He screwed up his face at the list. "Let's try the Raven Mockers."

"Why them?"

"Why not?"

Why not, indeed. Shaking her head, she bit back a snort. Why did she enjoy playing this game with him? Normally, it would infuriate her and yet she enjoyed Luke's silliness. "Okay...but how do we do that?" She assumed it'd be hard to find a Raven Mocker.

"We take a ride over to Tybee Island."

"Why?" She was beginning to feel a little repetitive with her questions.

He leaned forward as if imparting a big secret to her. "It's where my Raven Mocker contact lives."

She rolled her eyes. "Why aren't you texting or calling him?"

"He's not a tech-friendly raven. I've always wondered if it comes from an aversion to power lines or some other Luddite tendency. All I know is if he has a number, he hasn't shared it with the likes of me. Might be because I'm an asshole. Or he doesn't like me...no, can't be that. I'm adorable." He held his hands out to indicate his body. "Who could resist this, right?"

Groaning at his play, she finished off her coffee and put the cup in his black dragon trash can. "So, who's this Raven Mocker you know?"

"Sequoyah Tanamara...whose first name means sparrow. Weird name for a raven, if you ask me. But who am I to question his mother's choice? I'm so unhappy with the godawful thing my mother stuck me with that I refuse to use it."

Yeah, he was an odd duck, since they were being fowl about this. But she strangely liked him.

"And what exactly are Raven Mockers?" She'd heard the term and seen it used in fiction, but her information was sketchy at best.

"They're Cherokee in origin. And like a Daimon, they take souls to elongate their lives. Normally, they only prey on the dying. If they're not driven off when a person dies, they will consume the soul as it leaves the body."

"That doesn't sound like our perp."

"Unless the girl was dying from her attack, and a Raven Mocker saw her and decided to consume something handy. We really need the coroner's report, but Conspiracy's still working on the body."

What? Was he talking in code again? "Conspiracy?"

"Kyle Craley. He's the ME."

Sadly, Sorcha knew if she kept this job, she'd meet that ME and become well acquainted with him soon enough. "Why do you call him Conspiracy?"

There was that evil grin again. "You'll find out soon enough. Bernadette prefers to call him Creepy Craley."

"Again, why?"

"You'll find out."

And the way he said that made her stomach shrivel. There was something up with the coroner.

Lovely...

Deciding it could wait, she moved on with her questioning. "What about cameras? Any on the street or on houses?"

"Oh yeah, and they showed nothing. No one following her from her dorm. No one fleeing the cemetery afterward... another reason why I know it's an IA case and not one for the regular LEOs."

"I'm impressed. You really are an investigator." And he'd done a lot of work on this after they parted last night. "Where in Hell did you learn your skills?"

Luke seemed to approve of her punnage even though he didn't comment on it. "Reyes is a great teacher. Bernadette, too. And they have these amazing things called books...you won't believe all the kinds of information in them. Procedural manuals, too. Online government sites. Learn tons of stuff when you use them."

She scoffed at the sarcasm. "I would say we need to have you do school appearances, but that very thought terrifies me."

"Why? I like kids."

"As a rule, or for dinner?"

Luke laughed. "As a rule. Imp says I function on the same mental level. So we tend to get along."

She completely disagreed. There was nothing childish about him. Not even child-like really. He was all man.

Or demon.

Luke pulled his keys out of his pocket. "Time to fire up Delilah and piss her off."

"Pardon?"

"My car. She hates when I wake her before noon." He checked his watch. "Nine is guaranteed to cause a galactic hissy fit and make me happy about it."

"Your car has feelings?"

"You've no idea." Chuckling, he headed outside, then waited for Sorcha as she went to the door of her office to lock it. He stopped. "Check it before you go."

Curious as to why he said that, Sorcha opened the door and gasped. Then she gaped. Her walls were now a beautiful dark gray accented by white and peach. There was a gorgeous shabby chic chandelier made of metal peach tulips that hung over a contemporary white desk with brass accents. Her desk chair was a chic white leather that looked unbelievably comfortable. There were fresh cut flowers on her filing cabinets that were now made of white wood. And on the far left wall hung the smart board she'd always wanted.

"It's the best! Thank you!"

"Anything you want changed?" he asked.

She shook her head and before she could think about what she was doing, she hugged him.

Luke was stunned by her actions. Only the damned he'd spared from their torment had ever shown him any kind of gratitude. And that had always been sexual in nature.

He'd never experienced an innocent hug. Neither of his parents believed in such.

And it did the strangest things to his breathing. Something that wasn't helped by the scent of lilac and woman that hit his senses. She smelled like warm sunshine.

Smiling up at him, she pulled back. "Nothing at all. You must have really hated your former partner."

He had no comment. Not when his body wasn't currently under his control.

When he could finally speak again, his words came out a lot gruffer than he meant for them to. "Yeah...glad you like it."

Giggling the way he imagined she must have done when she was a girl, she locked the door, then gave him a becoming pout. "I hate to leave now. I want to sit in there and sip coffee while playing with my new board."

Those words sent an extremely vivid image through his mind. Inappropriate and very hot. "There's something else I'd love for you to play with."

Rolling her eyes, she headed for his garage. "Keep it in your pants, big guy. We have work to do." She paused to scowl at him. "Do we have an HR agent?"

"Why? You planning to report me?"

"Probably should, but I doubt it'd help. Knowing what little I do about you, you'd probably hire someone to take the class for you."

Spinning his keys on his finger, he wagged his brows at her. "You're learning me. Beware. Next thing you know, you'll be offering me your soul and nowadays I'd have to turn you down."

"Did you really barter souls?"

"My primary function...aside from lazing about." He bent down to open the garage. "I would say I regretted it, but I never took the soul of anyone who would miss it.

Besides, you'd be amazed at how many people can't be tempted."

That *was* surprising. Most of the people she'd known wouldn't hesitate to trade their soul for a winning lottery ticket. "Really?"

"Yeah. Those who usually barter with us have dark secrets. Never ceases to shock me the cruelty that lies in the hearts of those who look so harmless. Others look vicious and wouldn't harm anyone. But the ones we take... You'd never know the depravity in such an innocuous vessel. Sadly, people make the wrong judgment calls all the time. I really feel sorry for your kind. In many ways, this is the real Hell. My home is more of a sauna."

"Because you weren't being tortured there."

"True. But remember the ones who are, deserve it for the people they hurt and the deeds they chose to do of their own free will. Hell's a maximum-security prison, not a halfway house."

She paused as he opened the garage door. "You really never feel sorry for them?"

"Hell no. Just desserts. Those on the fence are given chances for redemption. We only get the ones who are vicious and unrepentant. The ones who more than earned punishment."

He saw the darkness that shadowed her eyes and it actually made him feel bad for her, as he felt that pain inside himself. She was thinking about her sister.

Strange how that finally popped into his mind, and he knew instantly that the two of them were twins.

And how much her sister's death tormented her.

Luke winced as he felt her grief like it was his own. Like

most sets of twins, they'd been unbelievably close. An image of them lying in bed and laughing together went through his head.

One of a thousand memories that tortured Sorcha.

Damn. Empathy wasn't something he normally struggled with. It'd mostly been a foreign emotion for him. But right now...

"I'm sorry your sister's not here with you."

She actually burst into tears.

"Oh wow...what the hell?"

Covering her face with her hands, she drew a ragged breath. "I'm sorry. I'm sorry. I'm really not an emotional person. You just have no idea how much I worry about her. Worried that..."

Before he could stop himself, he pulled her in for a hug to comfort her. Something he'd never done before, but he didn't like seeing his partner in pain. It made his own body ache in response and that stunned him.

*Why do you care?*

He shouldn't. He never had before. Yet Luke couldn't deny these new feelings that broke loose inside him. Emotions he couldn't afford to feel. In Hell, pity and empathy were a weakness that could get someone buried in a pit he didn't want to think about.

Luke winced at memories he wished he didn't have. Mistakes he never should have made.

Now, he was making another one by comforting someone he should shove away.

If only it was that easy.

"It's okay, Sorcha. Just breathe. Everything's okay, even if it's not right."

For several minutes, she stood in the circle of his arms, shaking.

Finally, she pulled back to stare up at him and offer a smile that almost warmed his freezing body. "Do you know who killed her?"

"I wish I could give you that answer. It's amazing and humbling what I don't know. Such as what happened to our college student or why I was banished from home." Who had betrayed him. And what happened to her twin.

He'd love to be able to answer that for her.

"We will find out. I promise."

Sorcha nodded as she pulled her emotions into check. He wasn't omniscient. She'd figured that much out. And it surprised her that he didn't know why he'd been banished. "No one told you what you did?"

He shook his head. "My father doesn't explain himself to anyone. Least of all me."

That made sense.

She supposed the devil didn't need to. He was too used to ruling. Why would he explain himself to anyone? Even his own son.

Putting it out of her mind, she went to his car to find Helly sleeping on the backseat underneath a bright pink Hello Kitty blanket.

"Should I ask?"

Luke laughed as he gently nudged Helly. "Why are you out here, Imp?"

"Your mom told me to watch Delilah. I'm watching Delilah."

He scoffed. "You're sleeping."

"Was and intend to return to it." She rolled over,

clutched her stuffed dragon pillow under her head and sighed as she closed her eyes.

"Does she always do what your mother tells her?"

"We all do what my mother tells us. Including the devil. No one wants to cross my mother. She holds on to a grudge like a lover."

That was an interesting thought. "She that scary or that powerful?"

"That vindictive." He opened the car door and got in.

Sorcha pondered the new information as she joined him.

With an evil laugh, Luke tried to start the car.

It sputtered with what honestly sounded like anger.

Luke tsked. "I know, D. Wakey, wakey, eggs and bakey."

The car engine didn't even attempt to turn over this time.

Luke let out an elongated breath. "Don't piss me off, Delilah. I'm not anymore of a morning demon than you are. Now, wake up...time for work."

"I hate you!"

Sorcha arched a brow at the angry growl from the car speakers before the engine sputtered to life.

"Know you do." He pulled out of the garage, then left the car to close the door.

As he did so, Sorcha scowled. "Why don't you have a garage door opener?"

"Delilah's a petty creature. If I use one, she sabotages it just for spite. It's easier to open and close it manually than give her a way to piss me off."

Okay, there was definitely something up with the car. "So, the car *is* possessed?"

"What?" he asked as he returned.

"The car. She is like Christine."

He laughed. "Nothing like Christine. Delilah wasn't born on an assembly line. And she's not really the car. She likes hanging out in it to get under my skin because she knows I love the car and she's determined to suck all my joy out of it."

"Yes, I do."

Bug-eyed, Sorcha cut a glance to the car radio that spoke to them. "Hello?"

"Whatever. Tell the human to leave me alone. It's too early in the morning to conversate."

He passed a droll stare toward Sorcha as he pulled out on the street. "It's too early in the morning to conversate with the car," he repeated.

"You do everything she says?" Sorcha couldn't help asking.

"Rarely do I do anything anyone says. I'm vicious that way."

He was definitely something, but she wouldn't say vicious, per se. At least not to her. He'd actually been exceptionally nice and even kind.

The last thing she expected, which was why she was beginning to look forward to being with him. In spite of his hellish origins, he was a lot of fun.

Trying to distract herself from his...*je ne sais quois*, she pulled her electronic tablet from her crossbody bag.

Luke glanced over to it as they stopped at a light. "What's that thing you keep using?"

"It's where I keep my notes and case files."

"Yeah, but it's not a laptop."

Turning it on, she smiled at him. "Remarkable tablet."

She pulled the magnetic stylus from the side of it. "I can handwrite my notes, and it'll convert them to text files when I'm done so that I can import them into my reports. And now I can import them onto to my amazing smart board in my beautiful office, thank you very much."

"And they say I'm the one who does magic. That sounds like all kinds of evil to me."

"Only when a gremlin strikes. Maybe lightning."

He laughed. "I'll try and keep the gremlins from your equipment."

For some reason, that sounded almost like a come-on line. Then again, most of what he said sounded that way. With that deep, gravelly voice, he could turn the most innocuous comment into something sexual. She would say it should be a sin, but with his parentage, it most likely was.

She'd heard the word *incorrigible* her entire life. It wasn't until meeting this man that she understood the real meaning of that word.

He was the epitome of incorrigible. And he reveled in it.

Putting his sexiness out of her mind, she opened her tablet and started taking notes. "So...how long have you known this Raven Mocker?"

"Not sure. Probably a hundred years or so."

Shocked by his words, she paused her stylus. "One hundred *human* years or dog years?"

He growled at her. "Hellhounds have the same years as a human and I'm a lot older than I look."

Apparently. He looked around the age of thirty. "Does that make you immortal?"

"Makes me something." He clicked his tongue. "True

fact, only God is immortal. The rest of us have a guaranteed off switch of some kind.”

“Including your father?”

“Including my father.”

That *was* fascinating to know. “For real?”

He nodded. “No matter how omnipotent they seem, there’s always a way to kill something. Even things that don’t bleed.”

That was *very* interesting. “Good to know.” And it was.

*Everything has a kill switch.*

That meant that whatever took her sister could pay. She made a mental note of that.

And remained silent as they drove over to Tybee Island where a quaint little white house was set off by itself near a waterway.

“Catalina Drive?” she asked, surprised that something paranormal would be so normal in appearance.

“You expecting Mockingbird Lane, Elm Street or something more obvious?”

She laughed. “Not really. But this is quite a perch.” It was a small home with a little porch and a nice view of the sawgrass and water.

Luke didn’t say anything else as he parked in front of the garage and turned off the car.

Helly came awake with a loud yawn. “Oh, hey. Sparrow’s. What are we doing here?”

“Visiting,” Luke said dryly.

Stretching real big and then yawning again, Helly turned her back to them. “Tell him I said hi.”

“You’re not coming with us?” Sorcha asked.

"Naw. I see him a lot." And with that, she went back to sleep, clutching her dragon.

Sorcha passed a bemused stare to Luke as he headed for the door. "Did you know?"

"What? That Helly hangs out with questionable beings? Yes. You should have seen her in Hell. She was always finding someone to torture."

Sorcha didn't want to think any deeper on that subject, so she stared at the house. She wasn't quite sure what she'd expected as a Raven Mocker's home. It actually looked like any well-kept, unassuming place.

And when Luke knocked, a short, skinny man in a black tee and jeans answered.

Not what she was expecting.

At all.

While the man appeared a bit gaunt, he was cute enough with dark eyes and short black hair.

He took one look at Luke and slammed the door in his face.

Had he screamed first, it would have been hysterical. As it was, Sorcha had to press her lips together to keep from laughing.

Luke tsked at her, then spoke to the door. "Really, Sequoyah? Open the door before you make me angry."

The door opened slowly. Sequoyah let out a long, tired sigh as he braced an arm against the door and leaned on it while glaring at Luke. "Why are you here, evil spawn?"

"Why don't you have a phone?"

"Don't like to be disturbed. You should understand."

And while they stood on his porch, a group of ravens landed on the white railing to watch them.

Bemused, Sorcha stared at the group suspiciously. "Look. A murder of ravens."

Sequoyah passed her an irritated glare. "Conspiracy, treachery or unkindness. Murder is for crows. We're *not* crows."

"Sorry. I didn't know that." But personally, she'd rather be in a murder than a treachery, unkindness or conspiracy. They sounded awful.

What did the world have against ravens to call them that? Other than the fact that they looked rather scary in a group. Even the half a dozen that currently eyed them.

She had a sudden urge to cross herself.

Sequoyah inclined his head to the group of his friends. "We're fine. No need to pluck out eyes, right now." He stepped back to let her and Luke into his house.

Even so, the ravens remained on the railing like silent paladins, ready to attack over any insult they perceived.

Sorcha glanced at them through the window as she moved to the center of a sparsely decorated living room. Her mind kept replaying scenes from Alfred Hitchcock's *The Birds*.

She forced her thoughts away from the movie that had given her nightmares for a month after her sister had made her watch it when they were kids.

Clearing her throat, she looked at Sequoyah. "I didn't know Georgia had ravens."

"We're a very small conspiracy. Most of our brethren hide north. In the mountains." He passed a hateful glare toward her as he moved to stand beside his white sofa and crossed his arms over his chest. "We were run off a long time ago."

She didn't miss the bitterness in his tone. "You sound like you hold a grudge."

"I'm a raven. Of course, I do. It's what we're known for."

Yeah, there was something very sinister about Sequoyah. It made the hair on the back of her arms stand up.

"I always heard ravens were playful," she tried again.

"We can be. Unless you do us wrong. We hold on to that shit."

Luke cleared his throat to get her attention. In the small room, Luke physically dominated it. "They also mate for life. Sequoyah's wife was killed by an enemy. It's made him a bit crabby in his old age."

Her stomach sank at the thought. "Oh, I'm so sorry. I didn't know. That's awful. My deepest condolences."

Sequoyah shrugged with a nonchalance she could tell he didn't feel. "Why are you here, Luke?"

"We have a dead college student who's missing a soul. Any of you been hungry lately?"

"We're trying not to make any additional enemies so we only go where we're invited these days. You're looking for a different circus." He walked over to the side table to a bottle of water. "Why would you think it was us?"

Luke pulled out his phone and handed it to Sequoyah. "She was severely torn up. Didn't so much think it was one of you who killed her as much as one of you might have sensed her dying and decided to take an easy meal. Was hoping one of you might have seen who did this to her."

Sequoyah appeared less offended by those words. He held his hand up to signal one of the birds outside.

It moved from the railing and transformed into a tall,

Goth woman. Beautiful, with long black hair and dark eyes ringed in thick black eyeliner. She came in through the front door and passed a bored look to her and then Luke.

"What's going on?" she asked Sequoyah.

Sequoyah handed her the phone. "Anyone venture near the college lately?"

She took the phone and shook her head. "We don't normally go there. The students have a nasty tendency to follow us around and throw food at us. Stupid entitled shits. They act like we're pigeons." She handed the phone back to Sequoyah, then looked up at Luke. "Hard to take their souls when so few of them have one these days."

Luke snorted. "Hard to disagree given the number of them who try to sell their desiccated souls to my kin."

With a heavy sigh, Sequoyah passed the phone back to Luke. "Have you talked to any Daimons?"

"Just a Dark-Hunter."

Sequoyah scratched at his chin. "Try the vampires, then. Granted they've fallen out of public favor lately. But some of them do still haunt the campus, looking for *Vampire Diary* fans to prey on."

Sorcha cleared her throat. "It's *Vampire Diaries*. Plural."

Sequoyah responded with an arched brow and a peeved glare. "Like I care."

"Sorry we bothered you." Luke turned toward the door.

As Sorcha started after him, the woman stopped her and cocked her head in a very bird-like manner. "There's a darkness inside you. Don't let it grow any larger."

Those words chilled her. "Pardon?"

Instead of answering, she returned to being a raven and flew from the room.

Confused, she glanced to Sequoyah who shrugged.

"Starla's complicated. But she sees things others don't."

"Meaning what?"

He shrugged again.

Okay then. Those words were haunting and terrifying. She definitely didn't care for the bird people. They were very unnerving.

Her heart pounding, she followed Luke from the house. "Long way to drive for nothing except an ulcer I could have done without. Now I'm paranoid."

He snorted. "I'm always paranoid."

"Well, with your genetics, I get it, but I don't like this feeling. What darkness? Am I damned?"

"Not yet."

"Not *yet*?" she repeated. Those flat, dry words didn't help her mood at all. "What do you mean by that?"

"Nothing," he said with a grin as he opened the door and got into his car.

"I'm really not liking this job at the moment." Or Luke, either. Couldn't anyone answer one damn question?

"There are worse jobs to have."

"I shudder to ask."

His grin widened. "Helly? You want to take up the challenge?"

She didn't move from her sleeping position on the backseat. "Working the shit pit in Hell...not sure what is worse. The ones being shit on or the ones who have to clean it. Either way, that pit is awful as they're being doused in the scat of those with serious intestinal woe. Then there's scraping road-kill off the highway that leads to Hell...in the desert...at four in the afternoon. Those who are chosen to be the guinea pigs for Hell's new torture devices... I can tell by the sounds of their screams that is a really horrific job... Finally, there's the poor souls in test audiences for bad movies and hokey TV shows."

"Copy editors for technical manuals," the car said through the radio.

"Delilah for the win." Luke chuckled.

"They really have those jobs in Hell?"

Luke nodded. "Made worse because no one gets paid there. They do that shit for free. Pun fully intended."

She groaned out loud at his bad joke. "So, my takeaway is that I need to be in church more often."

"Couldn't hurt." He pulled his hair back into that strangely sexy man bun.

Awesome. "This job is going to make me crazy."

Luke backed up, out of the drive. "Life makes me crazy. Nothing is more of a mind fuck than humanity. Give me the damned any day. They're usually much more dependable. Evil things do evil things. When it's human, it looks all warm and fluffy like the Monty Python bunny. Turn your back...it goes for throat."

He had a valid point.

"Bert," she said under her breath.

Luke arched his brow. "Tourette's Syndrome again?"

"Ex-boyfriend who randomly sends me into it. He was just what you describe. A genuinely *nice* guy. Mr. Harmless. Opens the door for you. Pretends to be unable to hurt anyone or lie. Goes to church on Sunday, pretending to be kind and decent. Biggest fucking liar and vindictive bastard ever born. Wouldn't know the truth if it tackled him to the ground and choked him out...which I'd like to see it do, just once."

"I know the generic losers you're talking about. Would it make you feel better to know there really is a special place in Hell for them?"

"Actually, yes."

"Then take heart. We love to torment them for eternity, and Hell is the one place no one believes their bullshit. We do actually make them choke on it and other, sometimes literal, shit, too."

Wow. It was incredible how that little bit of knowledge lightened her day.

"Then I'll never mention him again."

Luke shrugged. "Doesn't bother me. Get it off your chest so it doesn't fester. Nothing good ever comes from keeping things bottled." The sincerity of his comment shocked her. He meant that.

"Thank you."

He pulled out of the gravel drive and headed back toward town.

"Where are we going now?"

"Talk to a wicked witch. Maybe get some food."

CHAPTER
# SEVEN

Sorcha held up her phone. "I have a witch on speed dial." While Trish might not be wicked, she could be evil, depending on the topic.

And her mood.

But in all honesty, Trish was the only reason Sorcha was still here. How many times had she called Trish, crying after she'd lost her sister? She couldn't begin to count them all. Not once in all these years had Trish rolled Sorcha's calls to voicemail. And Sorcha wouldn't have blamed her for doing it.

It'd been such an awful time.

Even at the funeral, it'd been Trish who'd held her hand and promised her that one day she'd learn to smile again.

That they would find the one responsible.

*Justice will be met.*

Sorcha clung to that hope, just as she held her friend in a special place in her heart.

Luke passed a knowing look at her as if he heard her

thoughts. And with him, he just might be listening. "Patricia Owen. The Grand Witch of Nashville...how is Trish doing?"

The question surprised her. "You know her?"

"The devil knows all witches. Haven't you heard?"

She snorted. "That's not true. For one thing, Trish doesn't believe in the devil. He's not part of her religion."

"You don't have to believe in something for it to be real. I don't believe in love, but millions of beings would tell me I'm an idiot and that it exists."

She was surprised by his confession. "You really don't believe in Cupid?"

He gave her an irritated smirk. "Only fools and children believe in something that made up. I rank him right up there with the Tooth Fairy."

"And the Taj Mahal is what?"

"A building in India."

She tsked at him. "An eternal, enduring testament to love."

"A building," Luke repeated.

"You *are* jaded."

"I'm a realist with eyes. Only thing love is good for is sending deluded souls to Hell because they bought into that snake oil and drank it whole."

She couldn't argue that with him given the fact that those being sent to Hell fell within his wheelhouse, and he was the resident expert. "I feel bad for you."

That actually caused him to slow down. "*You* feel sorry for *me*?"

"Yeah, I do. Love might be corrupted and abused by some, but it's real. For better or worse."

He inclined his head to her. "The last thing I want is to

force my opinion on anyone. If you want to believe in love… more power to you."

"Now you're patronizing me."

"I'm really not, Sorcha. I envy you the ability to stand by your belief given the nightmares we've seen. You look at someone and you think they have someone else's best interest at heart. I look at someone and I see them looking at the other person as an extension of themselves or a tool to be used. An enemy they're conspiring to take down. Looking for a way to leverage the relationship to benefit them and not the object of their affection."

"Are you saying your fiercely protective mother sees you as an extension of herself?"

"Hell, yes." Wide-eyed, Helly sat up in the backseat and leaned over to stare at Sorcha. "He's her sacred embryo. He has no life outside of her and if he tries, she might eat his ankles just to hobble him so he can't stray far from her."

Her jaw fell open. "You're serious?"

Helly nodded fiercely. "Mama is very possessive of her property and Luke is definitely hers. She doesn't share him with anyone. Not even his father."

That was a scary thought. No wonder Luke felt like he did. His father threw him out for no reason and his mother thought of him as…

A chew toy? Weird and gross analogy considering it was his mother they were talking about, but given what Helly said, it might not be far off the mark.

She shivered, then decided to change the subject. "So who's this witch you're talking about?"

"An old friend of Bernadette's. They went to high school together."

That was interesting, indeed. "Did Bernadette introduce you?"

He nodded as Helly returned to her spot in the backseat. "You'll like her."

"I like most people."

He gave Sorcha a disbelieving scowl. "Since when?"

"Always."

Luke snorted. "Oh, okay. If you want to believe that. Far be it from me to destroy your delusions."

Though his tone was teasing, it still irritated her. "I'm not delusional. I'm a people person."

He scoffed at Sorcha's words. "Have you seen yourself around others? You're always fidgeting. You have a moat wider than the Grand Canyon. For someone who likes them, you sure go out of your way to keep them as far away from you as possible. Dodging questions. Deflecting. Trust me, you are *not* a people person."

Damn. He wasn't being a jerk. The bastard was really observant.

*He's a detective, idiot.*

Of course he'd pay attention to something like that. It was actually unnerving how that intense amber gaze of his took in everything. Stripped down everyone he passed.

Even fully clothed, she felt naked.

"Do you always know what someone's thinking?" she asked.

"Most of the time, I choose not to pull any individual thoughts out of the chaos I hear. It's exhausting enough to be in *my* head. Last thing I want is to hear the petty concerns of others." He paused, then deepened his voice into a mocking tone. "*My feet hurt. I hate my boss. Why do they always screw up my order. My ex is a lying jackass who should be run over by a bus…*" He sighed heavily. "Ninety-nine percent of all thoughts are wasted, and I have better things to do, so I block it out."

"You can do that?"

That evil grin flashed. "I can do a lot of things. Some much more interesting and pleasurable than others."

That intended innuendo gave her goosebumps, even in this wretched heat. "What exactly are your powers again?" Yes, she kept asking that one question. At this point, she was hoping to wear him down until he gave her the information she wanted.

Or at least annoy him enough that he would eventually answer.

"Mine to bear and use…sparingly. Believe it or not, I don't like taking unfair advantage of others."

That was new and unexpected. "Doesn't that fly in the face of your demon persona?"

"Remember, he's not really a demon." Helly flounced back to her seat.

They kept saying that. Maybe it was time she started believing them because he didn't act like a demon.

He was an enigma that was unlike anyone she'd ever met.

Which made her wonder something. "How many cases have you worked since you've been at Infernal Affairs?"

Luke shrugged. "Don't know."

She found that hard to believe. She always kept a running tally of how many cases she worked on a small board. Her goal was to close every one. So far, she'd been lucky. She'd closed the majority of hers…

But there was always the handful that refused to be solved. Those that kept her up at night, wondering what fact she'd missed. What piece of evidence had eluded her.

How the poor families were coping with their undeserved heartbreak.

So, she found it difficult to believe that Luke didn't keep records about his. Was it possible that he didn't care?

Luke shrugged nonchalantly. "I never look at what I've done. Only what I need to be doing. The past holds nothing for me. It's just a bad nightmare and who needs those?"

And it was an anchor that forever held her tethered to that one cold January night that had changed everything in her life. That one second when the police had shown up on her parents' doorstep to tell them that Siobhan would never find her way home.

It was as eternal as the anger she still felt over the fact that her sister's ghost hadn't come to her.

Why could she see other ghosts and not Shy? Why had her sister avoided her? It hurt on a level that defied explanation.

And it was one she'd never understand. Any more than she'd fathom why her sister had to die so young and so tragically.

Life wasn't fair and that unfairness made her want to scream until her throat bled. Time hadn't made any part of this easier to bear. In some ways, it was worse now. When her sister had first died, there had been a strange numbness that clung to her.

For three months, she hadn't shed a single tear.

Not until she'd accidentally spilled Siobhan's favorite perfume in the room they'd grown up in. That one stupid act had sliced through the cocoon that had shielded her from agony.

Sorcha had screamed and then wept for the next six months. Nothing and no one, not even Trish, had been able to stop those tears that had flowed even while she slept.

To this day, she choked up every time she thought of her sister.

Every happy memory was tainted because Siobhan wasn't here to share it with her.

Sorcha still had her sister's number programmed into her phone. From time to time, she'd even call it just to hear Shy's voice again when her voicemail picked up.

*Hey caller! This is Siobhan, not Sorcha. If you're actually calling me and not my twin, I'm busy chasing dreams. Please leave a message and I'll call you back as soon as I can. Unless you're a creditor or SPAM. Then you can kiss my ass. If this is Sorcha...text me, bitch! And if you're my parents, sorry for the language. Yes, you taught me better. Love you. Toodles.*

God, how she missed her sister and her off-beat humor and optimism. The world was a much darker place without Shy in it.

No doubt that was why their parents had kept Shy's phone active all this time.

It was hard to let go. Even harder because they had no explanation. No real closure.

Clearing her throat, she sighed. "I like knowing how many cases I've worked and solved." How many families had a closure that forever eluded her and her parents.

He glanced over to her. "Oh, I can answer how many unsolved I have. None. I always solve them."

She arched a brow at that. "You have *no* unsolved cases? At all?"

"Not with Infernal Affairs. The only thing I can't solve is who knifed me in the back. But I will find them and when I do—"

"There will be hell to pay," she finished for him.

"Exactly." Luke picked up his phone.

"Who are you calling?"

"Lorelei O'Shaughnessy. The Grand Witch of Savannah."

The title startled her. "Is she a member of Black Onyx?"

He nodded.

That explained so much. "She's in the same coven as Trish. That's how you know about *my* friend."

"Exactly. Sometimes my powers aren't so mysterious."

She felt like an idiot. "And you've been to the Black Hat Ball, haven't you?"

"Last year. I'm hoping to be invited back. It was a lot of fun."

Made sense. Trish's coven threw a huge invitational ball every Samhain to celebrate the season and their religion. "I knew I should have gone. I could have met you a year ago."

"Glad you didn't."

"Why?"

Luke's grip tightened slightly on the white wheel. "Fresh out of Hell. I was in a bad place, bad mood, and nothing like I am now. You wouldn't have liked me."

"I don't believe that."

"It's true," Helly said. "I can vouch for it. He was very unhappy about being here. If they don't invite him back to the ball, I know why."

Hmm.

Luke dialed his phone.

"You know, holding a phone while driving in Georgia is illegal."

He laughed at her words. "D! Take the wheel."

Sorcha gasped as he let go of the steering wheel and the car kept driving. It even turned. "There's no way a car this old is self-driving. What is up with this thing?"

"Delilah's driving for me." He turned the phone speaker on and then returned his grip to the wheel. "Oh ye of little faith."

Far be it from her to question him.

"Hello?"

Sorcha arched her brow at the soft, Southern drawl. That had to be one of the most feminine voices she'd ever heard.

"Hey Lady L. It's Luke. How you doing?"

"Just fine, sweet pea. Sipping my coffee and plotting destruction. What are you up to this fine early morning?"

"Here to pick your brain."

"Well, that sounds all kinds of painful. Can't imagine there's anything I know that you don't, but by all means, amuse yourself."

Sorcha smiled at the woman's humor.

"What do you know about Witchbreeds?" Luke asked.

"Don't much like them as a rule. Put them in with the Sims and Malums for making the rest of us look bad. Why?"

"I'm looking for a witch who might have the ability to take a soul and keep it or possibly destroy it."

"You personally want to take a soul and need a witch to do it, or someone took one already and you're trying to find who was dumb enough to be such an inconsiderate ass?"

She definitely liked Lorelei. The woman was quick.

"They took a soul and we'd like to get it back."

Lorelei went silent for a second. "Well...only a handful of witches would even consider doing something awful like that. Bad, bad form, you know? You're talking the darkest of dark. I can only imagine a Malum being mean...and dumb enough to try. Or a really lucky Sim who downloaded something that went wrong."

"What about a Cunning?"

"Nope," she said definitively. "Healers would never tamper with a soul. Defies everything they believe in. You're talking someone into necromancy or worse. That's not a Cunning's gig."

"You know any Malum?"

Lorelei sighed. "Unfortunately, and I'm embarrassed to say that I regularly interact with a few."

"Can you hook me up?"

"You're determined to ruin my morning, aren't you, sweetie?"

"Sorry, darling," Luke drawled. "I hate to take you from your Zen. But I don't want to tell anyone else that their kid isn't coming home. I'd like to stop this bastard before they kill someone else."

Lorelei sucked her breath in sharply between her teeth. "That's below the belt."

"I know."

"Fine." She let out a sweet sigh. "You could at least say you're sorry."

"Yeah, but you'd know I didn't mean it and I hate being insincere. Especially with you."

"Hmph." Lorelei clicked her tongue. "Well, the one I'd try is Senechal Villan."

"Sounds like an STD."

"You're awful, Luke. And he kind of is. You know how the Malum are. They're terrible people and even worse witches."

"No comment. Where can I find our STD?"

"He works nights, so he should be home this morning."

Sorcha snorted at her words. Of course, he would work nights. Was he also a vampire? She was dying to ask but didn't want to interrupt.

"Text me his address. That way he won't know you outed him."

"How you figure that?" Lorelei asked.

"I'll tell him a demon sent it to me. Put the fear of Hecate in him."

Lorelei laughed. "You do that, handsome. Good luck."

Luke ended the call. "I hear you over there."

Sorcha blinked innocently. "Hear what?"

"All those questions in your head. Lorelei is just like your Trish. She's Wiccan and not scary at all. Hell, she's so tiny, I could put both her and Helly in my pocket." In spite of the law that said he wasn't supposed to be touching his phone, Luke scrolled through his photos.

"I really wish you'd keep your hands on the wheel."

He snorted in response. "Delilah isn't going to let us wreck. She wouldn't risk damaging her girlish curves." He handed her his phone.

Sorcha looked down to see a beautiful woman with reddish-blonde hair. He was right, she came up to about Luke's waist. Tiny and gorgeous with a pair of mismatched eyes. She should probably hate her, but the smile and gleam in her eyes said she was kind and spirited. "Lorelei?"

He nodded.

Wow... She looked more like a secretary or nurse.

"Wicca is just a religion to most. Those who practice it look and act like everyone else."

"You say that, but I've seen them do some rather awful—"

"Sims and Malum," Luke said, cutting her off.

"And those are?"

"Sims are the ones who practice without any real power. What they do, they do to shock others. They want the attention of being different and counter to the mainstream. Most of them barely understand what they're doing so they do occasionally conjure something they shouldn't. For the most part, they're posers. Children acting without a clue. Then you have the Malum who practice so-called *dark* arts. The Malum can come from any group, including the Breeds who do it out of sheer malice toward the world and everyone in it. That is when they are truly dangerous."

Her head was beginning to ache from trying to keep everything straight. "I'm still fuzzy on all this."

"Witchbreeds are what you probably know as Cambions, Nephilim or Changelings. They're the children of humans and some supernatural creature...which is what can make them terrifying. They're what Hollywood pretends all witches are. Beings who are born with real supernatural powers they can't always control or understand."

"The ones who cast spells."

He winced at that. "All of the groups cast spells and even make potions. Witchbreeds have psychic abilities to boost whatever it is they do."

"Oh."

"Yeah. Big *oh*."

"What about Warlocks?" she asked.

"Mundane term for practitioners. Wizard, warlock, sorcerer, etcetera. They all fall under the five categories... Witchbreed, Witch, Cunning, Sim and Malum."

That was good to know, but it left her wondering something. "So, who created this list?"

"A descendent of Margaret Aitken." He said that so matter-of-factly that she felt like an idiot she had no clue who that was.

"And Margaret Aitken is who?"

"One of the Witchfinder General's flunkeys back in the Seventeenth Century. A vindictive bitch who saved her own ass by accusing innocent people of being witches and watching them literally burn."

"That's awful."

"Yeah, but in the end, she burned, too. Sadly, not before she killed a lot of innocents."

"And so this Margaret came up with the first list—"

"No," he said, cutting her off. "Even though the Witchfinder General and his group were discredited and disbanded in the seventeenth century, some of them continued on with his mission to rid the earth of witches. That group is still around today, causing problems and looking for those they deem witches to punish and expose. About five percent of IA cases every year deal with their current pain-in-the-ass membership preying on someone. Either an innocent or an actual witch."

"Really?"

He nodded. "Their current members assume the names of the original cast of clowns. Matthew Hopkins, Christian

Caldwell, Margaret Aitken, John Godbold, John Cotta, John Stearne, Roger Nowell and Henry Chauncy. So we have no way of knowing how many of them there actually are. What their real names are or were, etcetera. All we know is that someone claiming to be Aitken's descendent wrote their training manual called *The Hexenhammer*."

"You mean the *Malleus Maleficarum*?" *The Hammer of the Witches*. "I thought Heinrich Kramer wrote that."

"The original one, yes. Kramer was a nut job who was disavowed by the Catholic church and most anyone with a brain. But two hundred years later, the next group of idiots came along and decided to expound on his work. So, they wrote their own operating manual, *Hexenhammer*, or what should have been rightly termed *Hexenhammer II, The Age of Anti-Enlightenment*." He glanced at her as he stopped at a light. "I can send you the PDF, if you want."

"Sure. Sounds like a good, fluffy bedtime story."

"Just make sure you have your Chucky doll nearby for cuddling when you get scared."

She laughed. "Where are we going?"

"Washington Av."

Since she wasn't that familiar with Savannah yet, she had no idea what kind of neighborhood they'd see.

But given the fact that the man's name was Senechal Villan, she was expecting something less than stately. Something definitely spooky.

She couldn't have been more wrong as they pulled into a ritzy neighborhood and stopped in front of an impressive mansion. One that was reminiscent of an old German or Tudor-style home. Mostly brown brick, it had gingerbread trim and a very Alpine feel. Nothing spooky about it.

Other than the possible price tag.

"Nice house."

Luke didn't comment as he turned the car off. "Were you expecting a trailer?"

"Not sure. Trish lives in an adorable 1920s bungalow. I guess I assumed he'd be in something similar. Definitely wasn't expecting a multimillion-dollar mansion...with brass bird feeders." Which was an elegant touch on a well-mani-cured lawn. The upkeep on the lawn alone was probably more money than her rent. "What were *you* expecting?"

He shrugged. "Wasn't expecting anything. I keep an open mind. One thing my past has taught me...never judge. The man who looks fine and upstanding is probably a wife-beating pedophile who cheats the IRS or worse, and the biker who makes people tremble at his approach is just as likely to be the one who donates his spare time to homeless shelters or other humanitarian causes. The Malum come in all shapes and sizes."

Still...

"His name is Senechal Villan."

"To be fair, Villan was once a popular English name and had nothing to do with actual villains. All it meant back then was that someone came from a nondescript village and they weren't a farmer."

Bemused, she snapped her head toward Luke. "Seri-ously? Where did that come from?"

"My travels in medieval England. You'd be amazed how many Villans were willing to give up their souls to stay healthy during plagues."

Not really. She might have been willing to give up the ole soul depending on the plague. It definitely wasn't the way she wanted to go into eternity. "I have to wonder. Are you just making shit up or is that for real?"

"It happened." Helly grinned at her from the backseat. "Luke doesn't lie. He might withhold information, but he never lies about anything unless he's screwing with a bad guy."

Sorcha turned and looked at Luke for confirmation.

He nodded. "I have no fear of consequences. Liars lie to avoid something they're afraid of, or to pump up their egos." Clicking his tongue, he winked at her. "My ego is super pumped...in case you haven't noticed."

"Oh, I did. You let that flag fly freely."

"Yes, I do." He got out, then turned toward Helly. "You staying in the car or coming with us?"

"Too tired to get out and walk, and you won't let me fly in public. Y'all have fun." She laid back down on the seat.

Pulling his hair tie out, Luke pushed his sunglasses up on top of his head as he waited for Sorcha to join him on the sidewalk.

Damn... He was something else. There was something unnatural about his charisma and beauty. No man had a right to look that edible.

*You have got to get a grip. He's your partner.*

Yes, he was. But this close to him, she really wanted to take a bite out of that luscious hide. It was hard to stay focused with someone who was just so...

*Je ne sais quoi.* That was the only way to describe him.

Doing her best to ignore his massive sex appeal, Sorcha followed him up the expensive brick walkway to the front door.

Luke rang the bell and they waited.

Given the quality of the home, Sorcha half expected a butler to answer it.

Maybe Lurch.

Instead, it was a humongously tall man around forty, wearing a pair of khaki pants and a striped button down—how he'd found clothes to fit a mountain was really the question of the day she wanted answered. And the word *huge*...massive understatement. This man towered over Luke and probably weighed twice as much.

Or more.

Damn. Just damn. She hoped she wouldn't have to chase him down and try to cuff him. It'd probably take half a dozen cops.

In fact, she had the cartoon image in her mind of him slinging officers off and sending them flying. Too bad he had short, curly brown hair because bald would have helped him look even more like a cyclops than he already did.

"Can I help you?" he asked Luke in a rather high-pitched voice that didn't match his appearance at all.

"You Senechal Villan?"

Suspicion darkened his brown eyes as he swept his gaze over the two of them. "He's not here. Can I take a message for you?"

Luke let out an evil laugh, then pulled his badge from his pocket and held it up for the man to read. "Don't lie to me, Sen. I tend to react badly when people do that."

Rage darkened Senechal's eyes, but so far, he wasn't trying to kill them or run so she counted that as a victory. He jerked his chin at her. "You Five-O, too?"

The unexpected slang caught her off guard. "I am." She pulled out her own badge and held it up for his inspection.

There was now a tension in the air that was so thick it almost choked her.

His gaze returned to Luke and stayed there. "You're not human."

How did he know that?

Luke quirked a bemused grin. "Never said I was. If you want to run... I don't mind chasing. Bigger the better, I always say. But you should know that it never goes well for those I catch up to. And I *always* catch them. The chase just pumps enough adrenaline in me that I like making it hurt." The gravelly way he said that sent a chill down her spine.

As did the hopeful grin on his face as if Luke were savoring the thought of chasing Senechal.

Senechal considered those words before he stepped back and let them inside his immaculate home. The marble foyer was just jaw-dropping. Straight ahead was an alcove with a real suit of armor in it.

"Love what you've done with your mansion," Sorcha said.

His answer was a flippant "humph." Closing the door, he turned to face them. "I hate inviting evil into my home."

"Not a vampire. I don't have to be invited." Luke inclined his head toward Sorcha. "Neither does the human."

Those words didn't amuse Mr. Villan at all. "Why are you here, officer?"

"Detectives," Luke corrected. "We're looking for creatures who like to mutilate college students and steal their souls."

"So you thought, what? Rattle the local Wiccan? I'm not the only one, and last time I checked, my religion is protected under the First Amendment."

Luke scoffed. "Definitely not impinging on your right to practice whatever religion you choose. But not even the First Amendment allows human sacrifice. The state gets a little miffed when covens eat people."

"Are you trying to piss me off?" He stepped forward to physically intimidate Luke.

Luke laughed at his efforts. "You might want to take a step back, little man. I'm not afraid of you and given who my parents are, you don't want to glare at me. If they take offense—and they might—you're going to have a really, really bad day. But I'll be amused. Nothing like the smell of blood in the morning to make me deliriously happy."

Out of nowhere, Helly appeared immediately beside Luke. Her eyes were solid black, and she sported a pair of fangs along with a set of curled horns that were above her ears. "You need me, *dominus*? Who do you want me to kill?"

# EIGHT

Sorcha stared at the "imp" that currently appeared more demonic than she'd ever imagined. *Just what have I gotten myself into?*

While Helly was still tiny, she was terrifying in this form. Enough so that Sorcha stepped back and made room in case she needed to run screaming from the mansion.

Luke gently put his hand on Helly's shoulder to keep her in place. "We're good, Imp. No need for bloodletting...quite yet."

Senechal went pale instantly at the sight of Helly. "You have your own imp?"

"I do."

He went down on his knees. "Forgive me, *dominus*. I didn't realize who you were."

Sorcha arched a brow at that.

Luke passed an amused smirk toward her. "He still doesn't really know who I am. But he's getting there." With a heavy sigh, he turned back to Senechal. "Get up. I'm not my father. And you're not Luciferian or a Satanist. Groveling doesn't appeal to me, and while Dad likes it, it doesn't cause him to suddenly discover mercy. It just amuses him before he rips out your spine and beats you with it."

Senechal rose to tower over them again. "I don't know anyone who would take a soul. It's not particularly helpful to any Malum I know. We can't use it for a spell, and my coven's charter forbids such acts. I don't know any Malum who would dare such a sacrilege."

"Could you use it to barter with?"

Both of them turned to stare at Sorcha for her question. "Well, could you?" she asked again.

Luke considered it. "Actually, you could in theory, but I've never known anyone to do that."

"Me, neither." Senechal scratched at his cheek. "A soul holds no intrinsic value to any Malum. Maybe a Witchbreed? They might have use of one for who knows what."

"Well, this just sucks." Luke growled low in his throat. "We're back to square one." He turned to Helly. "Guess we're out of here, Imp."

Helly wasn't so quick to leave. Instead, she continued to glare at Senechal as if she was every bit as tall and not some tiny, little gnome who barely came to his knees.

The two of them reminded Sorcha of a Chihuahua staring down a Pit Bull—and causing the Pit to tremble. "Sure you don't want me to make a point, *dominus*?"

"Please don't, Imp. It's too early in the morning to hide a body. Especially one that size."

Senechal paled as Helly vanished.

Luke pulled his card from his pocket. "If you think of

someone or you hear something, don't hesitate to give us a call."

"I will."

Luke inclined his head. "Thanks for your time."

And with that, he gestured toward the door for Sorcha to lead the way.

She went outside, but her thoughts were whirling. Honestly, she hated bum leads, especially when it involved a young victim. Why couldn't they catch the killer right away like they did on TV?

Find a body and thirty to forty minutes later, arrest the killer and see them in prison for the rest of their lives.

Sadly, real life was nothing like that.

And what really bothered her were the cases like her sister's that went on forever without any conclusion.

Which made her thoughts wander back to what she'd been discussing earlier with Luke. "Is your closure stat really one hundred percent?"

"Yes."

She paused on the sidewalk to look at him. "That's impossible. No one ever closes every single case."

"Not for me, it's not. I have special skills and I cheat." He stepped past her and continued on to the car.

She wasn't sure if that made her feel better or worse. Her own was ninety percent, which was exceptionally high.

One hundred...

She couldn't imagine being that skilled.

Or lucky.

Sorcha rushed to catch up to him. Helly was again lying down on the seat as if she'd never popped into the house to threaten a mountainous man.

Luke gave Sorcha a peeved expression. "The only outstanding case is the matter of the asshole who caused me to be kicked out of Hell. That's ongoing and annoying. So it's more ninety-nine point nine, nine, nine, nine."

She heard the anger in his voice. "Sorry. I know it stings to have something like that hanging over your head."

"I know you do. You're the only one around me who does and I promise you that we will find out what happened to your sister. And I'll personally make sure they regret it."

For some reason, those words touched her a lot more than they should. "Thank you."

He inclined his head. "Send me all the files you have, and I'll see what I can find."

"I will."

As she pulled the UGA ball cap on, she considered everything she'd learned. "So, no witches were involved..."

Luke tied his hair up. "Not if the Malum didn't do it. Witchbreeds wouldn't dare take a soul. They have other malicious things they do."

"Gotcha." Sorcha sighed.

As Luke got into the car, his phone rang. "Teivel, here."

He listened for a few minutes before he nodded. "Thanks. We'll be there shortly."

She arched a brow at his serious tone. "Where to now?"

"Morgue. Conspiracy has something for us."

"He couldn't tell us over the phone?"

Luke started the engine. "Said he wanted us to see it. Apparently, the police looked at it and shrugged. But he thinks it'll interest us."

Sorcha pulled her tablet out and jotted down notes about their encounter with Villan.

Helly leaned over the seat to watch her.

Cringing at the sensation of hot breath on her neck, Sorcha scowled at the imp. "You should be wearing a seatbelt, you know."

"There aren't any."

That stunned her. "What?"

Luke slid her an amused gaze. "1957. They didn't have seatbelts in most cars back then."

She looked down at the one over her lap with a bemused frown.

"Those are aftermarket installs. There's not one for Helly in the backseat."

"What if we get pulled over?" Sorcha asked.

"Luke will handle it like he always does." Helly flashed her fangs at Sorcha. "So what are you writing?"

"Just making notes about what I've learned and what Mr. Villan had to say."

Helly leaned closer so that she could read them. "You always do that?"

"I do. Doesn't Luke take down his own notes?"

They both looked at him.

"I make a few on the board, from time to time, but most of it I keep in my head."

That surprised her. "Aren't you afraid of forgetting something important?"

He snorted. "I wish. Sadly, details stick with me, even when I want to forget them. Like the smell of that cheap ass cologne Villan was wearing."

"Understood." She had a lot of things she'd like to forget, too. Including the stench of Villan's cheap ass cologne.

By the time Sorcha finished making her notes, they were pulling into the Medical Examiner's parking lot.

She looked up and frowned. It was down an inconspicuous street, nestled near a credit union and salon. "This is the morgue?"

"What did you expect? Neon flashing lights that say Dead Bodies Kept Here?"

No, but this was a strange place. The rough gravel road, style of the buildings and broken asphalt reminded her more of Florida than Georgia.

Luke didn't speak as he got out. As usual, Helly climbed over the back and followed him.

With a peculiar feeling in her stomach, she left the car and rushed to catch up to them as they entered the unassuming building.

"Well, hello, Mr. Luke," an enthusiastic female voice called out to them instantly. The receptionist couldn't be any older than her early twenties and the light in her eyes and breathless quality in her voice said that she wanted to wear Luke like a coat. "What can I do to help you today?"

"Looking for Kyle. Is he in his office?"

"Yes, sir." Her smile was wide and flirtatious. Until she saw Sorcha. That smile died instantly.

If looks could kill, Sorcha's head would have exploded and she'd be a pile of ash on the floor. Which made her wonder if Luke could do that to others. Was it one of the powers he refused to talk about?

Personally, she'd love to have that ability. Especially in five o'clock traffic.

Or in the grocery store whenever someone parked their buggy sideways in an aisle.

*No wonder the captain didn't give me a gun.* She totally understood now. With her temper, it was a definite liability.

At any rate, she stepped forward and offered the girl her hand. "I'm Luke's new partner, Detective Sorcha O'Malley."

"Oh." That did away with most of the vicious glare, however ice remained in her demeanor. "Taylor Gaines. I'm the receptionist here. Nice to meet you."

"You, too." Sorcha headed down the hall, after Luke and Helly.

By the time she caught up, they were entering a small office where an adorable man sat, looking very boyish. Probably in his mid-thirties, Kyle had a mop of dark curly hair on top of his head. His dark brown eyes showed immense intelligence as his gaze darted all over the place as if he had a hard time focusing on any one thing.

"Glad you got here so fast." Kyle started pulling papers and files out. "You're not going to believe what I found...it was a canine attack." He froze as he finally saw Sorcha behind the mountain that was Luke. "Who are you?"

"Luke's new partner. Sorcha O'Malley." She held her hand out toward him.

He stared at her hand with a frown. "Did you wash your hands?"

She hesitated as she suddenly felt awkward. "Not since I've been here."

His frown deepened. "Have you any idea how many germs there are? And those are just the regular ones. You could have easily picked up some bio-engineered something. Those are fatal. Horribly fatal." He grabbed a mask and put it on, then handed her a massively large container of hand sanitizer.

"Thank you?" She wasn't sure what to make of this. Especially when he made her do it twice.

By the way he was acting, she half-expected him to raise both hands, form a cross with his forefingers, and hiss at her as if she were a vampire after his blood.

Luke grimaced at her. "Thanks," he grumbled under his breath, letting her know he was rather peeved she'd reminded Kyle they were "unclean, disease-ridden parasites."

After Luke also sanitized his hands twice, Kyle finally removed his mask and let out a relieved breath. "That was close. Y'all could have killed me. You need to be more careful, spreading germs without any thought."

Okay, sure...

As he turned away from them to face his monitor, Sorcha caught Luke's gaze and mouthed the words "wow."

"So... Con... Kyle," Luke cleared his throat as if he just caught himself from calling the man Conspiracy. "You were saying it was a canine attack?"

"Oh yeah. Definitely a canine, but not a dog or wolf. In fact, it's really weird." He pulled a file from under a stack of them. "I'm thinking something bio-engineered." His eyes widened, and then he spoke louder, as if speaking to someone only he could see. "Not that I'm speculating, or anything. Don't want to do that. Just that it's not what we normally see. But..." He lowered his voice to barely above a whisper. "Unofficially thinking they might be doing some kind of super soldier testing at Fort Stewart. I mean, it could be something else. Maybe not. What do you think?"

He spoke so fast that Sorcha could barely follow his words.

Luke handed the file to her. She opened it and had to bite back a gasp as she saw the cleaned-up jagged marks on the student's body. Kyle was right. This was from something much bigger than a dog, wolf, coyote or any canine she'd ever seen. The only canine that size that came to mind was the Dire Wolf they'd investigated in Peachtree City.

Could it be the same person?

Or were there werewolves or other such preternatural creatures roaming the streets of Savannah?

She desperately wanted to ask, but she wasn't sure how much knowledge Kyle had about their agency and the last thing she wanted to do was make him even more paranoid by exposing the poor man to the truth.

*Can you hear my thoughts?* She glanced to Luke who gave her a subtle nod.

*Dire Wolf?*

He shook his head. "So other than military experimentation or Wolverine, what other thoughts do you have about the attack?"

"Oh, I didn't think about Wolverine. I'll add him to my *other* report."

Sorcha scowled. "Other report?"

"The one he doesn't let his superiors see. It holds all the speculations he's not allowed to put in his real work." Luke held the official file up to illustrate what he meant.

Kyle clicked his tongue. "Exactly and it doesn't exist because if it did, it could be subpoenaed and that would be terrible. So I have no other *other* list."

Yeah, she could imagine the horror. If he had to testify in court and someone knew he'd drawn paranoid, or off-kilter speculations, they could use it to discredit him.

Kyle locked gazes with her. "I'm not really a crackpot. I know my theories are out there, but sometimes even the craziest thing becomes reality. You'd be amazed at all the things that sound insane and aren't."

Like her seeing ghosts and Luke's parentage, as well as the Hell imp standing at their side. "I get it. Don't worry. I have some oddball theories myself that I wouldn't want other people to know about. I won't ever judge you."

Kyle smiled. "Thank you." Then he pulled another folder out from his stack. "These are your special notes I made."

Luke took it. "Thanks. Anything else I should know?"

"I sent over some saliva and hair samples to the lab, along with one partial print. I haven't heard back from Jedi, but I'll let you know when I do."

Luke closed the file and nodded. "I'll give him a call and see if he's run them."

"Sounds good. If you need anything else, let me know."

Luke handed her the second folder. "When are you releasing the body?"

"Day after tomorrow."

"Okay. Thanks."

Kyle inclined his head to Luke.

Sorcha didn't say anything as she followed him out of the room, through the building, and back toward the car. "Should I ask about Jedi?"

"Probably not. He's...different."

Different was taking on a whole new meaning with this crew. And here she'd thought she was unusual. The one good thing about all her new colleagues was that they made her feel at home.

"Why Jedi? Does he like *Star Wars*?"

Luke snorted. "His name's Jedidiah Cyprus and he thinks of himself as an alchemist."

"Is he?"

"He's definitely something."

Not quite satisfied with that answer, Sorcha opened the door to the car. "So what do you make of Kyle's findings? If it's not a Dire Wolf, what else could be that size?"

"Hellhound or another shapeshifter."

She looked at Helly. "Pardon?"

"Hellhound," Helly repeated. "Right, boss?"

Luke looked a little green as he got into the car. "Yeah."

Sorcha was confused by how reserved he sounded. "Why does that upset you?"

"Because the only hellhound I know around here is me."

Oh. That would make things a bit sticky. "Maybe one came out to guard you in addition to Helly?"

Luke cleared his throat. "Not possible. I would know if one was anywhere nearby."

"How? Spidey-sense?"

He gave her a sharp stare but said nothing more as he pulled his hair up for the drive.

There was a sudden tension in the air between them that she didn't understand. She'd never felt awkward with him before, but she did now. Kyle's findings really bothered him. She glanced back toward Helly who also appeared a bit shaken.

Luke started the engine at the same time his phone rang. "Teivel." He put the caller on speaker.

"Hey, Luke, it's Jedi. Where are you?"

"Just leaving the ME. I was about to call you. Did you run the evidence for the college student?"

"I did."

"And?"

"We have nothing to match the saliva to or the fur. It's not any known species. Really weird, right?"

Luke winced. "Yeah. What about the print?"

"That's where the train goes off the tracks. I mean, I know it's a partial and all, but there's only one match we can find."

Before he could say anything more, three police cars pulled into the parking lot and surrounded them.

Sorcha froze as she finally understood what Jedi was hinting at.

"The partial's yours, Luke. There's no denying it."

# NINE

The car revved as if it was about to take off. Luke put his hand on the dashboard. "Calm down, Delilah. Don't even think about running through them."

Helly hissed, exposing a set of fangs as those curled horns appeared on her head again.

"Stand down," Luke said as he slowly held his hands up. "Don't do anything, any of you."

"What do you want me to do?" Sorcha asked.

"Call Reyes. Then follow me to jail with Delilah."

"Lucian Teivel," a man said over a speaker. "Get out of the car, slowly. Kneel down on the pavement with your hands locked behind your head and your ankles crossed. Now!"

Stunned, Sorcha watched as he calmly complied. The police swarmed him while he didn't fight them at all.

Another male cop came forward with a gun pointed at her and Helly. "Show me your IDs!"

Did he have to bark that? They weren't fighting or even protesting.

Making sure to keep her hands in plain sight, Sorcha carefully pulled out her Infernal Affairs badge and ID card. "We're law enforcement. Want to tell me why you're arresting my partner?"

The cop scanned her ID. "He's wanted on suspicion of murder."

Was he insane?

Stunned senseless, she scowled at him. "That's ridiculous."

Without commenting, he lowered his gun and looked at Helly. "I need your ID."

Sorcha was surprised when Helly pulled out a Hello Kitty wallet and produced a valid ID for him. "I'm a ride-along."

The cop nodded, then handed her ID back. He spoke into the radio on his shoulder. "They're clear."

Furious over this, Sorcha watched as they put Luke in a patrol car and drove off with him.

This was total bullshit. She wanted to protest, but they were doing their job and interfering with it would only get her and Helly into trouble. Last thing she needed was another mug shot making the rounds.

To this day, she wanted to strangle the officer who'd processed her. *"Prettiest mug shot I've ever seen. You should use this for a modeling photo."*

Asshole. It hadn't been funny. And she could only imagine how humiliating it'd be for Luke. She was still furious about hers, and it'd been almost a year ago.

But to be fair, she had pulled the trigger and earned her arrest.

She was sure Luke was innocent.

Furious on his behalf, she waited for them to clear the scene before she reached into her purse to get her phone.

Reyes answered on the first ring.

"Hi, Captain. It's Sorcha. The local LEOs just arrested Luke."

There was a brief pause as if the captain had to digest the news before she spoke. "For what?" The fury in her voice was tangible.

"Murdering the college student."

Total silence on the other end.

"Hello? You there?" Sorcha asked, afraid the phone had dropped their signal.

"I'm here. Just shocked. What the fuck?"

Yeah, she felt the same way.

Reyes cleared her throat. "Sorry for the profanity. I just can't believe they'd do this and not notify me."

True. Interdepartmental courtesy...they should have notified Reyes before they went after Luke.

"Where do I go to bail him out?"

The captain gave her the address. "I'll meet you there."

"Will do." Sorcha hung up, then hesitated.

She glanced over her shoulder to Helly. "Will the car let me drive her?"

Raising both hands, Helly shrugged. "Delilah?"

The engine revved high then finally settled down. "Get on the driver's side. But you don't touch anything. And I mean *anything*."

Uncertain about this, Sorcha slid over the bench seat to

Luke's side. As soon as she was situated there, the car took off on its own.

This was *so* creepy. Like some *Twilight Zone* episode.

Helly laughed from the backseat. "Don't worry. Delilah won't hurt you. At least I don't think she will."

"Go back to sleep," Delilah said through the radio. "You bore me."

To Sorcha's eternal shock, Helly did.

Sorcha wanted to protest being driven against her will but thought better of it. She wasn't sure how Delilah would react.

And the last thing she wanted was a pissed-off car. So, she put her hands on the wheel to pretend she was driving as the car took her through traffic in record time. That made her wonder if the quick driving that had gotten them to Peachtree City so fast was a result of Luke's powers.

Or Delilah's.

Either way, it was extremely unsettling.

They reached the station where Luke had been taken just as the captain was pulling into the lot.

Elana met her as soon as Sorcha got out of the car. "Luke must be in serious trouble if he let you drive his car."

Sorcha snorted. "The car drove me, but I appreciate the thought."

Elana acknowledged Helly with a nod while she continued speaking to Sorcha. "Did he put up a fight?"

"Surprisingly, no." Sorcha let out a long sigh before she told the captain what had happened.

All in all, Elana took it well. "How could they think Luke would do such a thing?"

"Son of the devil?"

"Yeah, but they don't know that."

True. "I have no idea why they went for him. The forensics say it was a canine attack. All they have is a partial print detected on the body. How they went from that to an actual arrest...anyone's guess."

Elana let out a low curse. "Yeah, and I know for a fact the print isn't Luke's." She pulled Sorcha by the arm. "C'mon, let's go get our boy."

Which was much easier said than done.

Once inside, the desk sergeant refused to let them any farther into the station than the reception area.

Swallowing audibly, he shook his head at Reyes's demands. "I'm sorry, Captain, I really am, but my captain would have my ass if I let y'all back there."

The look on Elana's face said that she was about to have a giant piece of it if he didn't.

Sorcha made a mental note to never anger Elana to that level. It was almost as scary as riding in a driverless antique car.

"This is not a game. One of my finest detectives was arrested for no reason. I want to speak to the watch commander, now. And anyone else who's in charge. I suggest you get them up here immediately."

Again, the sergeant gulped audibly. "Yes, ma'am."

Just as he reached for the phone, the door behind him opened. A captain came through it with Luke trailing. Both were laughing, as was the detective behind them.

Sorcha exchanged a confused glance with Elana.

"Ah! And there she is." Luke gestured toward Helly. "Imp? Tell them where I was night before last."

"Streaming *The Devil's Advocate* with me. Why?"

Luke slapped the captain's arm so hard that the man actually staggered sideways. "Told you."

Rubbing his arm, the captain nodded. "Fine. But I still want to know how your print got on that student."

"That makes two of us." Luke moved to stand next to Elana who continued to look like she was ready to collect badges and kick asses.

"Is my detective cleared?" Elana asked in a tone that let everyone know how displeased she was.

The police captain had the good sense to blush. "Sorry. We just had to talk to him. He's the only lead we had, and this case is under scrutiny."

"Understood, but from what I was told by the ME's office, your suspect should be Cujo not my detective."

Sorcha pressed her lips together to keep from laughing. The police captain wasn't nearly as amused.

Luke cleared his throat. "It's okay, Captain. No harm. No foul. They were actually polite. Just doing their jobs, which I respect."

"Glad you understand." The police captain extended his hand to Luke who shook it.

Then Luke turned to Sorcha and widened his eyes to let her know that he knew something he was dying to impart to her. "Shall we, Captain?" he asked Reyes who looked at him suspiciously.

"Sure." But before she left, she had one last thing to say to the police captain. "I hope the next time you want a chat with one of my people, you'll give me a courtesy call."

"I will."

"Thank you," she said coldly, before following them out of the station.

Luke didn't stop or speak until they were beside Elana's gray Toyota. He glanced to his car, then lowered his voice. "Someone's setting me up."

Sorcha felt her jaw go slack. "What?"

He nodded slowly. "No idea why or who, but this isn't going to stop."

"How do you know that?" Elana asked.

He gave her a dry stare. "Canine shapeshifter? My fingerprint? That didn't happen by accident, and you know why."

Sorcha wanted to believe him, but there was one thing that bugged her. "How could they get your fingerprint if you didn't have contact with the student?"

Luke arched a brow at her question. "Simple. They couldn't get my fingerprint if they wanted to. Period. It's not mine."

There was a peculiar sensation in the air.

One that chilled her to the bone as an extremely preposterous idea went through her head. But it would make sense. "You don't have fingerprints, do you?"

He held his hand up so that she could see the tips of his fingers were completely smooth, without a single ridge. "I do not. In Hell, they burn off."

"Then how did they plant evidence?" Sorcha was so confused.

He gave her a bland stare. "Someone used the fake files we made when I had to be printed for the job."

Imp laughed. "Did they try to take them again in the police station?"

"Thankfully, no. Since I had an alibi...thank you, Imp. They didn't process me. At the moment, I'm cleared."

Elana narrowed her gaze on him. "Really cleared or Luke cleared?"

"Does it matter?" he asked.

"I just need to know if they'll show up at the office later to arrest you again."

"Nah. It should last until we find the killer. At least, I hope."

Sorcha wasn't so quick to be relieved. "Are our personnel files digitized?"

Elana cursed under her breath as she caught on to what Sorcha was thinking. "They're not. I don't want any information about my department online to be hacked and disseminated."

"Then someone was in our offices." A tic started in Luke's jaw.

"Are you sure it wasn't one of our own?" Sorcha asked.

Elana shook her head. "I vet my people too thoroughly. No one would do this to Luke."

"She's right. Everyone at IA knows I'm the son of the devil. They'd be too afraid to screw me over like this and risk my finding out they did it. Especially given the fact that I don't react well to betrayal. It tends to bring out my father in me."

She could only imagine *that* horror.

"Okay," Sorcha said. "So it's an outsider. What else did they take?"

Elana sighed. "I'll let Bernadette know. Right now, I have a meeting at school with my wife about our son peeing on a bush during recess. I don't dare miss another parent-teacher conference or she'll have my head. You two...be careful."

Sorcha sucked her breath in sharply. "Good luck with that."

"Tell me about it. I'm the one who told him a tree was a perfectly good substitution for the bathroom. I'm sure my wife will never let me live this one down."

Laughing at Elana's dire tone, Sorcha watched the captain get in her car and drive off.

Once they were alone, a new thought occurred to her. "You wanted them to arrest you, didn't you? That's why you didn't fight them."

Luke scoffed. "I seldom fight humans. Not worth the busted knuckles...or the headache. But yeah. I was hoping to pick a few details out of the detective while I was here."

"So, did you learn anything?"

"No. I'm stumped. This feels like a total 'Fuck you, Ken' situation."

Sorcha scowled at those unexpected words. "A what?"

Helly let out an evil laugh. "Something we say in Hell when we really want to fuck someone up."

"Yeah. It means you're being royally screwed with for no purpose whatsoever, and the asshole messing with your life has no reason to. They won't profit from it. They're simply enjoying the torment... 'Cause. Fuck. You. Ken." He spat out each word as if it were its own insult.

And given the growl in his voice, she could only imagine what he'd do to whoever was dumb enough to mess with him.

He let out a heavy sigh, then spoke to his car. "Thanks for not harming Sorcha, D."

"You were in a bad enough mood. I wasn't about to make it worse. While you like this car, in one of your moods,

I have no doubt you'd torch me in it. 'Cause fuck you, Delilah."

He actually patted his door affectionately before he got in. "Not today. You bought yourself some good will where I'm concerned."

Sorcha opened her door and let Helly in first. The imp flounced to the backseat. Picking up her ball cap, Sorcha closed the door. "I think I need to get an IA cap for our convertible days."

Before she could put it on, it changed in her hands from the UGA red cap to a black hat bearing the IA shield—a five-pointed white star inside a gold circle that held the words *Infernal Affairs*. The center of the star bore the official Georgia seal.

More powers he'd never explain.

"Thank you."

"You're welcome." He started Delilah and backed out of the parking lot.

As they headed for the office, Sorcha kept running everything through her mind. "What are the odds that there's a Dire running loose in Peachtree City, and another canine shifter in Savannah?"

"Slim. Or not. It really could be a coincidence. I have no idea what the Dire is doing, but at least no one died in Peachtree City."

"And if it's not a coincidence?"

Luke considered it. "I need to get my hands on the hair the ME found." He glanced in the rearview mirror. "Helly?"

"On it, boss." She laid down in the backseat, then vanished.

Sorcha gaped. "Uh...what if she gets caught?"

"She won't."

"But isn't this tampering with evidence?"

"Useless evidence for the humans. They can't identify it and never will. Besides, she'll return it to them as soon as we're done. They'll never know it's gone."

Sorcha didn't know what part of that was the most disturbing. The fact that he thought nothing of breaking their rules or that they could take whatever they wanted without fear of being caught. "Done this a lot, have you?"

"Few times."

*My ulcer just had a baby...*

And that baby was hungry. As they stopped at a light, Sorcha saw a Chick-Fil-A half a block away. "Can we stop for food?"

"Sure. Just tell me where."

She pointed to the restaurant. "Chick-Fil-A."

He started laughing, until he realized she was serious. "Are you shitting me?"

"No. I love their food."

Screwing his face up, he winced. "I'll stop in the lot next to it and you can walk over."

What in the world was wrong with him?

It was the strangest thing to say. "Why?"

He jerked his chin toward the restaurant. "That is true holy ground. I'm not stepping one foot on that property. I can't."

Now she laughed. Until she realized he was equally as serious. "For real?"

"Yes," he said in unison with Delilah as he started forward.

And then he did just what he'd told her he would do. He pulled into the lot next to it.

Bemused, she stared at him. "Okay...are you really telling me you would burst into flames if you ate there?"

"I wish. That would at least warm me up for a bit."

"Explain this. How can you listen to Christian rock and not be able to step foot on Chick-Fil-A property?"

"The music is holy and I can even sing along to it. But there are rules about where I can and can't go, and I'll leave it at that."

Sorcha's breath caught as she realized that she'd just found his Achilles' heel. Something he couldn't do...

She wasn't sure why he wasn't allowed there, but his fear was real. There was no denying it, and she was sure it wasn't something he showed lightly.

Or showed to others as a rule.

"I can eat somewhere else."

That actually lightened the air between them. "You sure?" he asked.

"Absolutely. There has to be a Wendy's or McDonald's nearby."

His relief was tangible.

How absolutely weird. She wasn't quite sure what to make of this.

What a peculiar weakness.

As Luke started to leave, Helly leaned over the seat and shoved her fist in Luke's face.

"Got it, boss!"

"So I see." He put Delilah back in park before he moved her hand out of his face and offered his palm to Helly.

Smiling, she dropped the fur in his hand and sat back. "Did I miss anything while I was gone?"

"We almost stopped at a Chick-Fil-A."

Helly's eyes widened at Sorcha's words, then she hissed like a cat. "Oh, we don't go there. Ever."

So, Luke wasn't the only one with that ban. Just what other weaknesses did they have?

Sorcha scowled as Luke sniffed at the fur Helly had given him. "Where's Timmy, Lassie? I have a Scooby snack if you can find the well."

He slid a murderous glare toward her. Without commenting on her bad humor, he turned in the seat to look at Helly. "Did you smell this?"

She nodded.

Something strange passed between them.

"What is it?" Sorcha asked.

He held it out to her. "Take a whiff."

She screwed her face up in distaste. "Um…no. Rather not."

Scoffing at her reaction, he moved it closer to her nose. "Seriously. It won't bite."

"No, but it might stink." That was her biggest fear. Choking on who knew what.

"Smell it."

Sorcha curled her lip. "You're not going to let this go, are you?"

"I am not." No missing the determination in that gravelly voice.

Irritated, she took his hand and led it closer.

Not sure what to expect, she leaned toward his palm and did as he asked. "I don't smell anything."

"Exactly." He handed the fur back to Helly.

His tone annoyed her. "Okay...what does that mean?"

"It's not a hellhound. If it was, it'd smell like brimstone."

Oh. That was why they were being so strange. "There's a word you don't hear every day. How very archaic of you."

Smirking, he ignored her comment. "Get it back to the lab, Helly. Thanks."

The imp dove out of sight again, then vanished.

Sorcha wasn't sure what to make of the imp's casual teleporting. "Ever wonder if that gives her a complex?"

Luke scowled. "What?"

"Making her dive out of sight in public like a married girlfriend. It can't be pleasant for her."

He snorted. "She's fine. Hiding is what she prefers. It's weird that she's been hanging around you so much. Normally, she avoids humans as much as I do."

"Really?" That made her feel better about all this.

"Yeah. She's not really fond of y'all. She definitely couldn't stand my last partner."

There was no missing that wistful note in his deep voice as he spoke. It made her feel awful for him. "You must get homesick."

"Every minute I'm stuck here. Hate this place."

At first, she was aghast. Until she thought about it more. In a weird way, it made sense. The human plane wasn't exactly the paradise she'd wanted, either. Living was hard, and some days it felt impossible.

Being away from friends and family made it worse. There was only so much Facetime could do to alleviate the loneliness.

Which made her wonder if he could Facetime with the inhabitants of Hell.

That was a truly scary thought. Could demons use it to escape?

Or possess someone?

Before she could ask, both of their phones rang.

*This can't be good.* "Hello," she said at the same time he answered his. "Teivel."

She wasn't sure who called Luke, but her call was from Bernadette.

"We have another body. Is the Sexy Wonder with you?"

Sorcha laughed at Bernadette's term for her partner. "He is."

"Good, then he'll know where to take you. See you there."

She hung up at the same time Luke turned his phone off. "Did you get any details about the new body?" she asked him.

Nodding, he put the car in drive. "Another student. Factors Walk."

"Where's that?"

"Near the river."

She was glad he knew his way around the city. Especially since her relationship with GPS was seldom harmonious. In fact, the damn thing had almost driven her into the river on her arrival in Savannah.

Real evil was modern technology.

She slid her gaze toward Luke, then again, maybe not. Real evil was sitting beside her in the form of a luscious piece of cheese, and yet he didn't seem evil.

*That's exactly what your granddaddy would say.*

She could hear his voice loud and clear in her head. *And no wonder, for Satan himself masquerades as an angel of light. It is not surprising, then, if his servants also masquerade as servants of righteousness. Their end will be what their actions deserve.*

She couldn't remember where that was in the Bible or even why she thought of it now. But her grandfather had quoted it a lot while she was growing up.

Evil was always appealing, and Luke definitely corroborated what her grandfather had preached.

She could only imagine what her granddad would say if he knew about her new partner. No doubt, Granddaddy would be horrified. Maybe she should be, too.

Yet Luke held a kindness and fairness in him that belied his genetics.

Or maybe she was being stupid and seeing only what she wanted to—just like she'd once done with Bert. On paper, he'd looked perfect.

Confirmation bias was a bitch.

*Don't trust Luke.*

*As a dog returneth to his vomit, so a fool returneth to his folly.* Her grandfather's other favorite quote.

It was hard for a leopard to change spots. Or for someone to walk away from their habits.

Luke had spent thousands of years in Hell. Thousands of years collecting souls and damning people.

That evil inclination would still be inside him. All she had was his word that he'd changed.

Just like all those times Bert had told her that he wouldn't hurt her anymore. That he would never lie to her.

How many times had she believed him to her detriment?

Yeah, she had to remember that at the end of the day, Luke was from Hell.

She wasn't.

If Luke returned to his old ways, she was screwed. They all were. That was a sobering thought, and a terrifying one.

Unless the entire world took up residence in a Chick-fil-A, she had no idea how to stop him.

Her thoughts kept spinning, until they reached their destination.

Helly reappeared the instant Luke parked the car.

As they got out, Sorcha saw a small black sign next to a tree that was drowning in Spanish moss. "Emmet Park?"

"Yeah. There are some shops and businesses over there." He jerked his chin to a line of them not far away.

But what held her attention was the large number of other trees being devoured by the Spanish moss hanging from them.

Gorgeous...simply gorgeous.

Her gaze went to the white brick building with red awnings just ahead of them. "Old Harbour Inn..." That place was haunted as shit. Even from this distance, she could feel the spirits that were trapped there. "You do see what I do, right?"

Luke arched a brow. "There are ghosts all over Savannah." He headed toward the hotel where there was an iron bridge with stairs leading down to a cobbled road below where more cars were parked.

Every part of her wanted to run from this place. The last thing she needed was to get closer to the ghosts haunting this area. It was every bit as bad as some of the places she'd gone to in New Orleans.

In fact, this whole area strangely reminded her of that city.

Putting those thoughts and fears out of her mind, she followed Luke down the iron stairs to the alley...or rather road that was paved with mismatched cobblestones that would have turned her ankle had she been wearing her boots or heels. Thank goodness she'd put on her sneakers this morning.

Luke had been right. There were a lot of stores and such around here. This must be one of Savannah's more touristy areas.

Just as there was definitely a spooky feel in the air along with the musk of moss and damp rocks. "How old is this place?"

Luke shrugged. "Over two hundred years."

It felt it.

Even in the hot Georgia sun, she had chills on her arms.

As they neared the end of the cobbled road that dead ended at another hotel, she saw where the police had cordoned off the entire area and blocked traffic from coming up or down a ramp to River Walk. It wasn't until they reached a blue dumpster that she saw the body lying behind it in a strange...

She didn't even know what to call it. It wasn't an alley or really anything. Just an out of place rectangle cinder block area that had two open wrought-iron gates to block it.

At first glance, she'd think it'd been built to protect the dumpster, but the dumpster was outside the small cinder block section, and the gates didn't appear to have a lock.

The body lay in the middle of the rectangle, almost completely obscured by the dumpster. Which was a good thing given the fact that the student was in even worse shape than the last one. Blood coated the cobblestones under the kid and ran down the walkway.

Luke pulled out a pair of latex gloves from his coat pocket.

Bernadette met them while the ME photographed the body.

"Who found the victim?" Luke asked Bernadette.

"Couple of workers about an hour ago. Looks like the same MO. Press is circling like sharks. Serial killers near college campuses make for a bad day for all agencies."

"Yes, they do." He turned toward Sorcha. "You see anything?"

"Only something from the drug-induced nightmares of Tim Burton. Gah, this is awful. That poor…" She couldn't tell if the student was male or female. "Kid."

Bernadette blocked Sorcha from the crime scene. "If you have to barf, run that way." She pointed toward the hotel in the opposite direction. "If we taint evidence, the local LEOs will *never* let us near another crime scene."

"I'm not going to barf." She hoped.

Bernadette gave her a pointed stare. "Cap told me what you did at the cemetery."

Of course, she did. *Damn it, Elana. Why?*

"I'm fine. Cross my heart." She made a small X over her breast.

"What is that?" Luke asked.

At first, she thought he was referring to her gesture. Until she realized he was staring at the cinder block wall.

"Blood splatter," Bernadette said.

"No," he breathed. "I don't think so."

And then Sorcha saw it, too. It was some kind of pattern on the wall. The blood dripped down from what appeared to be a star of some sort.

What was it, indeed...

Moving closer, she scowled at the dried blood. "Is that a snowflake?"

Luke squinted. "Maybe. The blood's run so much that it's hard to see what it was originally."

Bernadette moved to stand between them. "Could just be an optical illusion. What do they call it when people see patterns in abstract drawings?"

"Pareidolia."

Bernadette gaped at Sorcha. "How did you know that?"

"I have no idea how my brain spat that out. I learned it in college and... I don't know. I'm a freak."

Luke didn't comment as he headed toward the ME who wore a pair of light khakis and a short sleeved red shirt as he moved around the body. Skinny and tall, he had dark hair and highly intelligent eyes.

"Hey, Jedi. Did you get a picture of that?" Luke gestured at the wall.

"Yeah. Creepy, right?" Jedi closed the distance between them. "I'm sorry about the arrest. I feel bad that I told them who the print belonged to."

Luke held his hand up. "It's okay. You were just doing your job. I understand."

"Thank you. I knew it couldn't be you. But I had to turn it over. I have no idea how your print got there."

"Me, neither. But strange is what we deal with. Right?"

"Ain't that the truth." Jedi's gaze went past Luke to Sorcha. "You must be the new partner."

"Sorcha O'Malley." She held her gloved hand out toward him.

He shook her hand. "Welcome to the madness."

"I think I was already there. New Orleans broke me in well."

"Bet it did." Bernadette moved closer to the poor student whose final repose was highlighted on the ground with a bright yellow marker. "Were you able to ID the victim?"

Jedi sighed. "Leanne Fields. Nineteen. I'm really tired of photographing kids. Catch this asshole and stop the bloodshed."

"We're trying"

Sorcha turned at the sound of a deep, masculine voice behind her to see a handsome man in his early thirties.

Dressed black on black, he was an intimidating sight. Or he would have been had he stood beside any man other than Luke.

His short black hair had a bit of a spike to it, and he held an air of blunt confidence that was sexy and calm.

He offered her a charming grin. "Detective Rory Corvan, Savannah Homicide." His gaze dipped to her badge and he chuckled. "So you're with the zoo crew. You poor thing."

"Give it a rest, Corvan." Luke stepped past him. "She likes our kind of crazy."

"If you say so." Rory approached the student so that he could examine the scene. "Looks like this one was killed here."

Jedi nodded. "That's the theory I'm going with. Just waiting on Berta to agree when she gets here."

"Berta?" Sorcha asked.

"Blood splatter expert," Rory said.

That was a job she didn't envy.

Nor did she envy theirs at the moment.

Jedi stifled a yawn as he met with Rory. "Aside from the fact that they're both students and torn apart, this is totally different from the last one."

"How so?" Rory asked.

"For one thing, this perp is definitely human and not some kind of animal. Someone very large and very strong." Crouching on the ground, he lifted the student's chin. "These cuts came from a sharp object, probably a knife. Granted, they're similar to the animal attack, but this is definitely made by a weapon and not fangs or claws."

Scowling, Rory knelt on the ground and took the poor kid's hand in his. "What's this?"

Jedi shrugged. "Not sure. I wasn't going to remove it until I was in the lab, but if you want, it's your crime scene."

Rory gently uncurled the bloody fingers to show a small silver pendant. No doubt it was a memento she'd snatched from her attacker.

Arching a brow, Rory turned back toward Luke. "Don't you wear one of these?"

Moving to his side, Luke took it from his hand. "My pendant vanished a few days ago. No idea how. And this is a heptagram. Mine's a hexagram."

Suspicion darkened Rory's eyes as he rose to his feet. "What's the difference?"

"Mine's six-pointed. That has seven. Hence the whole hepta versus hexa. *Big* difference between them."

Rory appeared very skeptical. "If you say so."

Luke gave him a pointed glare. "I do because it is true."

Hands on his hips, he turned toward Sorcha. "'Cause, Fuck You, Ken, right?"

She burst out laughing, then hid it behind a coughing spell. How could he do that to her? Inside jokes didn't belong at a crime scene.

"What the hell does that mean?" Rory asked in an irritated tone.

Luke sneered. "Someone's obviously screwing around with me for some unknown reason."

"That's hard to believe." Rory scoffed. "Who would dare?"

"I have enemies like anyone else. And some of mine hold serious grudges for a really long time." He looked past Rory to Sorcha who saw the fury in those amber eyes.

*What are you thinking?* she asked him with her thoughts.

*That's not a snowflake. It's an effing fairy star painted in blood, and so is the pendant in her hand.*

Sorcha had no idea what he was talking about, but she took her own photo of the blood pattern for later. She was dying to ask him some questions where they could discuss it outside of her head.

Honestly, she knew next to nothing about a fairy star so she Googled it while Luke bickered with Rory.

Those two had some dicey history and it was clear they should never go out drinking together. No doubt, they'd both land in jail for assault.

Even Bernadette moved closer to them, and Sorcha didn't miss the fact that Bernadette rested her hand on her taser as she placed herself between them.

Laughing over that, Sorcha thumbed through her search. The fairy star was a pretty symbol. She'd seen it from time to time while in New Orleans at a lot of the new age, voodoo and occult stores. Even on a few book covers.

Honestly, she'd never paid it much attention.

Now...

Luke knew something and she wanted to pick that gorgeous brain.

"Do I have to separate you two?" Bernadette gently backed Rory up. "Don't make me call your boss, Corvan. We're supposed to be coordinating on this."

Holding his blue-gloved hands up, he stepped away.

Luke took a step toward him. But Bernadette cut him off with a hand to the center of his chest. "Why don't you and Sorcha search the area?"

In other words, they were being banished from Corvan.

Luke's nostrils flared. "Fine." Then, he returned to her side.

"You know something about this. Spill."

Luke glanced to the unis before he nodded. "They need to run the DNA for a fox. That's our canine. Not a wolf of any kind."

She blinked at his words. "Fox? Like a kitsune?"

"I wish." He gave her a bland stare. "This smacks of the sídhe."

"Are you telling me this is from the Unseelie Court?"

"Not that simple. And yes, it could be them or one of the other factions. Off hand, I'm thinking it's a leannán sídhe, given that the victims are art students."

"I'm confused. I thought there were only two sídhe courts. The Seelie and Unseelie."

He screwed up his face. "It's much more complicated than that. In addition to those, they have splinter groups and other factions. The Seelie and Unseelie have better press agents so people know of their existence and tend to want to put all fey into those two groups."

Interesting...

Luke's gaze went past her, toward the small crowd that had gathered to watch them.

At first, she had no idea why he was looking at them. Until something caught her attention. It was an exceptionally tall, handsome man with dark skin and long braids. Given his beauty and demeanor, she assumed he wasn't human. "Friend of yours?"

"Some days." Luke left her side to climb up the ramp to where the "man" was being held back with the other onlookers by the police who were protecting the barrier.

Luke showed his badge to the uni. "This one's with me." He motioned for his "friend" to join them.

Following after him, Sorcha waited for an introduction, but Luke seemed reluctant.

Instead, Luke gave her a pained grimace. "Will you excuse us?"

"Of course." She headed back down the hill wondering why Luke had been so curt with her.

LUKE LED Sorath farther up the road almost to where he'd parked.

Every step they took made him more suspicious. Sorath didn't tread in the human world lightly. He held as much love for this place as Luke—in and out as soon as possible before the stink of humanity clung to him. "What's going on? Did you find out who betrayed me?"

"No."

"Then why are you here?"

Sorath's gaze turned dark and foreboding. "There's something brewing in Hell and I thought you needed to know immediately."

Luke waited for Sorath to continue, but for some reason his friend didn't. "And what do you want me to know?"

"I think the Ancient Orders are on the move. Vying for power."

That wasn't good. For centuries their truce had remained intact. After an eternity of fighting, the Ancient Orders had divided up the world among them with a promise that no one would renew their ambition to subjugate the others. "How do you know?"

"The head of the Phoenix Society just met with your father."

Luke snorted at Sorath's paranoia. "That doesn't mean anything. They could have been reminiscing about old times."

"This is different, Xynzara. Can't you feel it?"

"Don't call me that," Luke growled, hating his name. And he wanted to deny what Sorath was saying, but... "Have you seen or heard anything about The Brotherhood of Shadows?"

"Why?"

"There are art students dying and someone's gathering their souls. I'm thinking leannán sídhe." Not to mention the fact that there was bad blood between him and the little prick who thought he ruled over them.

Freaking sídhe. They were worse than humanity. Worse because they didn't end up in Hell where he could torture them.

Immortal little shits.

"Is that what happened here?" Sorath asked.

"Yeah."

Sorath's eyes flashed red. "Are they blaming us for it?"

"Relax. They think it's a serial killer." The normal LEOs thought of IA as consultants on occult matters. The fact that there were actual preternatural predators out here was more than most of them could handle.

Humans didn't need to know what actually stalked them. Blame the devil while denying Lucifer's existence.

Made all the sense in the world.

Someone whistled. "Hey, sexy! Want to follow me home?"

Luke and Sorath turned to see a young woman hanging out of a car window so that she could catcall to them both.

Sorath lifted his hand in a way that told him his friend was about to strike her with lightning or fire.

Luke grabbed his wrist. "We're in public."

"So? They need a lesson in manners."

"Teach it to them in Hell."

"That's what I was trying to do. Why did you stop me from taking them?"

"We're in public," he repeated. "You know the rules."

With a hiss, Sorath pulled his arm out of Luke's grasp. "You used to be more fun."

"Get me home and I will be again." He raked a glare over Sorath's T-shirt and jeans. "How are you not freezing?"

"I wasn't born in Hell," he reminded Luke.

"You've been there long enough to acclimate."

Sorath scoffed. "I'll never get used to that level of heat."

Luke nodded, knowing what Sorath refused to say out loud. He regretted following Lucifer in his rebellion. As loyal as Sorath was to his father, the angel knew he'd screwed up.

But like Lucifer, he'd never admit it.

Luke had never understood that. But then pride wasn't really his sin.

Lust and wrath were.

Granted the freezing cold here had seriously dampened his lust. The thought of getting naked without being in boiling water didn't appeal to him at all.

At least not until Sorcha had shown up.

Something about her was a lot more tempting than it ought to be, and she might be worth the frostbite.

And speaking of...she was heading for them. The last thing he wanted was for her to be on Sorath's radar. The fallen angel was way too volatile and perceptive.

"Anything else you want to tell me?" he asked Sorath.

He arched a brow at Luke's tone. "You want me to leave?"

"Don't want to have to explain you to humans." He raked Sorath with a smirk. "You tend to stand out."

Sorath passed an interested look toward Sorcha as if he knew Luke specifically didn't want to introduce the fallen angel to her. "As you wish, my lord. But I did learn one thing. Remiel has nothing to do with your banishment." And with that, he turned and headed toward Delilah.

*I hope Helly isn't still there.* She'd never been fond of Sorath. His imp might even scream if she saw him. But Helly could hold her own.

He headed toward Sorcha. "What's up?"

"Sorry to interrupt..." Her voice trailed off as she saw that he was alone. "Your friend left?"

"He had things to do."

"And who was he?"

Luke tsked. "Keep your detective questions on matters related to the students not on my personal business."

She made a sound that let him know he'd just pissed her off. "Okay, then. So... Rory really has a problem with you."

"I'm aware."

"Why? Did you bite him?"

He scoffed at the mere suggestion. "Never. I don't want rabies...or cooties."

"You're the canine," she said as if he didn't know that half of his genetics.

"And Rory's a raven. What's your point?"

"Wait. I'm lost. He's what?"

"Corvus. Corvan... Never mind. I know way too much Latin. Anyway, did you need something more specific?"

"They're about to move the body. I just came to see if you wanted to take another look before they did."

"I think I have what I need."

Sorcha gave him a penetrating stare at his odd behavior and peeved tone. "Did you take issue with something your friend said or are you pissed at me?"

"Neither."

She cocked her head. It didn't sound that way. Luke wasn't his usual happy self. Something in him had changed and she didn't like this version of him. It was...a little scary and lot of off-putting. "Anything I can do to help?"

Luke ground his teeth at her question. Those words tugged at him. He wasn't used to anyone trying to help him.

Seduce. Tempt. Torment. Set up. Punish...those happened all the time.

But never help. He wasn't sure what to do with that.

"Can I get a copy of the photos you took?" he asked.

"Sure. I'll email them when we get in the car."

"Thanks." As Luke started toward Delilah, the hair at the nape of his neck stood up.

Someone was watching him and not just some random lust-filled woman or man.

This was different.

Turning around slowly, he tried to find the source of his discomfort.

Nothing stood out and Sorath was gone.

*Where are you, you bastard. More importantly, who are you?*

"You okay?"

He glanced down at Sorcha. "Sure."

"That's a weak sounding *sure*. Should I be worried?"

Honestly, he didn't know. Something wasn't right. He felt it deep inside.

And if Sorath was right about the truce being broken...

His father was in danger.

*Why do you care?*

Because Lucifer was his father. Rotten soulless bastard that he was and Luke's job was to protect the throne.

Someone had kicked him out of the game, knowing that would leave his father in a position of weakness. Something that could be fatal if the Orders began warring again.

"Luke?"

He ignored Sorcha. "Helly!"

His imp appeared instantly. "You barked, *dominus*?"

"Find my mother and tell her I need to see her. Now."

# TEN

Sorcha had no idea what was wrong with Luke. All the playfulness was gone. He was exquisitely feral. And truthfully, it scared her.

For the first time, she saw the demon in him. It was ruthless and cold.

Distant.

And the last thing she wanted was to be alone with him when he was like this. "I'll go hitch a ride with Bernadette back to the office."

He didn't say a word.

Okay, then. He really wasn't the Luke she'd been getting to know.

This side of him...she didn't like it, and she practically ran back down the cobbled street to where Rory and Bernadette were wrapping up with Jedi.

Bernadette frowned as she saw her. "You okay?"

Not really. She was a lot more shaken than she wanted to admit. "Can I get a ride back to the office with you?"

"I wasn't going straight back. Is Luke—"

"I can take you," Rory said, cutting Bernadette off. "That is, if you don't mind?"

"That'd be great. Thanks."

He inclined his head to her before he slid his phone in his pocket, then went to speak privately with Jedi.

Bernadette continued to eye her. "You sure you're all right? I would say you look like you've seen a ghost, but that doesn't really apply to *you*, does it?"

Sorcha let out a long sight as she realized Bernadette also knew about her powers. "I'm fine." The last thing she wanted to do was complain about Luke on her second day. Especially since she didn't know what was wrong with him.

Maybe this was normal.

Either way, he was allowed to have feelings. She just hated that his were so intense.

Rory returned to her side. "My car's this way." He led her back up the hill and across the road to Houston Street where he'd parked his unmarked black Dodge Charger in front of another hotel. *The Brice.* She loved the crisp, white stucco that stood out from the restaurant next door that was black with yellow awnings. Probably be a nice place to stay.

And it was most likely above her pay grade.

"Where's your partner?" she asked as Rory opened the door for her.

"Out sick today. We're short-handed, so I'm solo."

"Sorry." Sorcha got in as he shut the door behind her.

For some reason, she felt a bit awkward and had no idea why. She'd spent a lot of her career with all kinds of officers and investigators.

Unlike IA, her last precinct had been huge. Sometimes

she'd known the people at a crime scene, but many times she'd walked in blind without knowing anyone other than her partner.

So why was she so nervous now?

She had no idea.

Rory got in and offered her a kind smile. "You all right?"

"I'm fine."

He tsked at her. "Fine never means *fine*. I can tell something upset you. Let me guess...about six and a half feet tall with more baggage than a transatlantic cruise ship?"

She snorted. "Is that your idea of a joke?"

"Yeah, I suck at humor as much as I do at small talk. My sister always said that I should have been a mortician. And maybe I should have. I'd see fewer dead bodies that way."

"Ouch."

"Exactly." He started the car and pulled away from the curb. "Have you been in Savannah long?"

"No."

"Then you probably don't know about Pirate's House, do you?"

She had no idea what he was talking about. In New Orleans pirates had been a big thing, especially Jean Lafitte, and particularly the bar on Bourbon Street that had taken its name from the famous outlaw. "Which pirate?"

He turned left onto Bryan.

Sorcha frowned at the sight of another park. "Are these things all over the city?"

"What things?"

"Small parks."

"You mean the squares, and yes. Savannah loves her

squares." He paused at the next intersection. "And that's the Pirate's House across the street."

She stared at the old gray building that looked like many of the others they'd passed. "Oh, it's a restaurant?"

"Yes, and it's one of the oldest buildings in Savannah. Haunted as all get out, if you like such things. Working for IA, I assume you do."

"Some days. Is it really haunted?"

"Let me take you to dinner there and you can see for yourself."

Sorcha wasn't sure what to say to that. It'd been a long while since anyone had asked her out. Too long, in fact.

Her first instinct was to turn him down. After Bert, she didn't want any part of the dating scene. She no longer trusted herself in that department. Bert had been so good at lying and deceiving that it'd soured her on romantic relationships.

And yet...

It wasn't like she could ever date the son of the devil. And no one else had knocked on her door in a long, long time.

Maybe it wouldn't hurt to try again.

Rory turned to look at her while she silently debated. "I know we just met, but I don't get a lot of free time, and most women have trouble with my job."

"It's okay. I get it. I have the same problem myself, and yes, I'd love to go to dinner with you there."

His mood lifted immediately. "Saturday at six?"

"Sure. I'll text you my address."

Why that made her so nervous, she had no idea.

*You know why.*

It always came back to Bert. He'd all but ruined her on men. *I won't let you take this from me.* Bastard had taken everything else. She wasn't about to let him destroy the rest of her life, too.

She deserved a chance to start over without him ruining it. Especially given the way he'd loved tearing her down and tarnishing any happy moment in her life. It was as if he could only feel pleasure when he caused her pain.

*Why did I ever date such a monster?*

Because of her sister. Her family had been so broken back then. Not that they weren't still. Yet in the aftermath of Siobhan's death, Sorcha had been weak and needy—a shell of who she really was. It'd been hard to make it through a single day.

Bert had come into her life like the mythical knight-in-shining-armor who had pulled her out of her fog. Made her feel something other than grief.

At least in the beginning when she'd thought of him as a gift.

But as she'd gotten back on her feet and returned to her real self, Bert had become resentful. Clingy. Mean and nasty.

An asshole-in-tinfoil who sought to tear her down and make her weak again. Gaslight her until she didn't know who to trust. It turned out that he didn't really care about her. It was all about him, all the time. He'd needed her to worship him. And everything he did, he did to feed his ego and self-importance.

"So...um, do you like to read?"

Sorcha laughed as Rory's question pulled her out of her musings and away from a beast she never wanted to think about again. "You really aren't good with small talk, are you?"

"Not at all. It's why I like being a detective. I ask pertinent questions with no side chatter."

"Then I'll send you my dossier before Saturday."

He smiled. "You joke, but I just might ask you for that."

Laughing, she made a note about it on her tablet. "I'll forward you a copy as soon as I'm back in my office."

Rory fell silent for a few minutes as he drove through town.

Sorcha wasn't sure what had dampened his mood so suddenly. "You okay?"

He let out an elongated breath. "Yeah. I just want you to be careful and I'm not trying to sound like a controling jerk when I say that."

"I don't think you're a jerk, controlling or otherwise, and I'm always careful."

"I'm serious, Sorcha. I know Luke's your partner, but there's something about him...every alarm in my brain rattles whenever he comes near. It's like he's evil or something. And yes, I know how stupid that sounds, but please keep your guard up."

If he only knew how close to the truth he was.

"I'll be careful. Promise."

Rory pulled up to the front of their office. "Okay. See you on Saturday."

"Absolutely." She got out of the car and watched as he drove off.

Another weird day at Infernal Affairs. And it made her wonder how many other women got asked out at a crime scene. Now there was a stat she wasn't about to Google. Either way, the answer would depress her.

Sighing, she headed to the street-level door that opened into the IA garden where her office was located.

She still didn't know what had upset Luke. But then she didn't really know him either.

Maybe the nice Luke had been the fake one. Maybe the defensive asshole she'd just left was his normal state.

Like Bert.

"Get out of my head!" She opened the door to the courtyard to find Christian there with a shocked look on his face.

"You okay?" he asked.

Heat covered her cheeks as she realized he'd heard her angry outburst. *Maybe I do have Tourette's*...which gave her a whole new level of respect for those who dealt with it. Thankfully, she could control hers.

Most of the time.

"Channeling an asshole. Curse of being a medium."

Chris nodded. "Understood. As you saw yesterday, I spontaneously spout idiocy in public. Usually in response to the asshole who stalks me. Respect." He headed for the door she'd just walked through.

Sorcha watched him go. She didn't know why, but she really liked Chris.

Well, all her coworkers so far. They were a good bunch of people...and imp. Helly was in a class by herself.

She had no idea how to classify Luke. Especially today, but maybe he wasn't so much like Bert as he was having a bad day. She had to stop looking at everyone through the Bert lens.

"I won't let you win." She repeated her mantra as she

crossed the yard and went into her office. She would exorcise that demon if it was the last thing she did.

Opening the door, her breath caught as she again saw what Luke had freely given her. Bert had never been so thoughtful. When he gave, it was in order to get something he wanted. Nothing had ever been done "just because."

Not everyone who had a single asshole moment was a permanent asshole like Bert. She was going to force herself to remember that.

Dropping her crossbody bag and tablet in the white chair beside her door, she went to her desk and sat down. Sorcha let out a welcomed sigh at how comfortable her chair was. Perfect lumbar. Just enough cushion that it felt like a cloud. "I forgive you, Luke."

This really had been a thoughtful gesture on his part.

She leaned back and pulled the remote from her desk so that she could turn on her smart board and play with it.

"Hey! Stop that! You're elbowing me!" A loud hiss rang out.

"Brush your teeth if you're going to do that."

"You're stepping on me!"

Each voice belonged to someone different. Some male. Some female. All of them with a guttural growl that sounded otherworldly.

"Just what the hell is this?" Getting up, Sorcha walked toward the wall she shared with Luke's office where the voices seemed to be coming from. "Hello?"

"Who is that?" one of them whispered.

"Shh! Maybe she'll go away."

"You're the one being loud!"

More voices whispering and complaining. And they were definitely coming from inside her wall.

Sorcha opened the closet door only to find that it was completely empty. Not even a coat hanger inside. So who was speaking and where exactly was it coming from?

"Hello?" she tried again. "Who's here?"

"Boo! We're ghosts."

"We're not ghosts, you moron."

"She doesn't know that. Follow my lead. Boo! Boo! Scary ghosts."

"Ghosts don't call themselves ghosts! How stupid are you?"

Another one snorted in anger. "Following your idiotic lead is what got us trapped. I'm not following you anywhere ever again."

"Stop poking me!"

"Watch the horns!"

"Watch my tail!"

Sorcha pulled her phone out of her pocket. Since Elana was at school in a meeting, she dialed Bernadette.

"Hello?"

"Hey, Bernadette. It's Sorcha. I'm in my office and—"

"Who's she talking to?"

"Shh! I think she's on the phone."

"Now you've done it. She's telling on us. We'll all be in trouble."

"I'm not in trouble. I didn't do anything."

"You're talking, too, aren't you? Then you're doing what we are."

"Doom! Despair!

"Rain agony on me!"

Bernadette started laughing in her ear.

Sorcha wasn't amused. At all. "I take it you know what this is?"

"Oh yeah. Coming from your closet, right?"

"Yes. What is it?"

Bernadette kept laughing to the point it was beginning to piss her off. "You know how people keep skeletons in a closet?"

"I'm aware of the phrase, yes."

"Well, your partner keeps demons in his. Real live ones."

Sorcha stood there in complete stupefaction. Of course, Luke kept demons in a closet. Why not? She would laugh at the thought except for the fact that the bickering...demons were still fighting.

"Don't touch me!"

"I didn't touch you."

"Not you, Envee. Stop touching me, Dohlar."

"You wish I was touching you. Stop breathing on me. You stink!"

"Then move away."

"I don't have anywhere to go."

Bernadette laughed even harder.

"Seriously, Bernadette? This isn't funny." Sorcha let out a growl of her own. "Are they always this vocal?"

"I don't know. My office isn't down there. But I know it drove Luke's old partners crazy."

Sorcha's stomach sank at those words. "You put an s on the end of partner. Just how many has he had in the last year?"

"Counting you? Five."

Five...in a year. Five. That number rattled around in her

head as she left the closet and shut the door, then leaned back against it. Five. As in more than four.

In a year...

"You're shitting me."

"Nope. Luke likes to play hard to get along with. And personally, I don't think it's an act."

Lovely. Just lovely.

*And I sold my condo in New Orleans.*

Not that it mattered. It wasn't like she could go back there, anyway. She hadn't just burned that bridge, she'd nuked it and toasted marshmallows over the smoldering remains.

Still, she was regretting the decision to move to Georgia.

*It's a new start. New job. New friends. You'll love it there. Just imagine how great it'll be.* She could kill her father for his optimism.

Someone knocked on the wall in her closet. "Hey, humans? Can one of you let us out? It's not hard. You just have to come over here and twist the knobby thing. Well, unlock it first, then twist. We'd be really grateful."

"We would! You want money? My name may be Dohlar, but I can give you lots."

"I'll give you eternal life!"

"I have to pee!"

Bernadette kept laughing so hard that Sorcha wanted to choke her.

"Why me?" Sorcha asked the ceiling above.

"You shot your partner."

She sucked her breath in sharply at Bernadette's words. "What?"

"Oh, come on. Didn't you learn yesterday that I'm the

company snoop? Nothing gets past me. I knew when I met you what you'd done. I just wanted to see if you'd own up to it."

"Fine, then. I quit."

Bernadette tsked. "No, you don't. Like me, you fit here and you know it. Just don't let those demons out. I'm thinking it'd be really bad if they ran amok."

*You think?*

"No, we won't. We'll behave."

"We're good demons. Just give us a chance."

"I still have to pee!"

Sorcha groaned, worried that one of them might actually need the bathroom. "Thanks for the help, Bernadette. I'll talk to you later."

"Good luck." Bernadette hung up as Sorcha tossed her phone on her desk.

*A closet full of demons...*

She only had one question. "How did all of you get in there?"

"We were tricked."

"We were cursed."

"I followed an idiot."

"We were conjured through a mirror and trapped in here."

"I had to go to the bathroom and opened the wrong door."

There were so many answers, including one who claimed he chased a chicken into the closet. She had no idea what, if anything, they said was true.

No wonder Luke played his music so loud. He was probably trying to drown them out. Which she attempted to do with her own music.

Impossible. They created a lot of noise, especially when they pounded on the walls, demanding freedom.

So she moved to her evidence board where she tried to figure out how to use it. It was actually a lot simpler than she thought. Even better, Luke had already entered in a lot of evidence for her to review and linked their accounts so that they could both access and share information.

That was nice.

Not nice? Two bodies. No souls. One killed and moved. The other killed on site in a place that was fairly public and right across the street from a hotel where they could have been caught at any minute. Obviously, that hadn't been a concern for them.

Who was this brazen perp?

She grimaced at the horrific images she prayed their families never saw. It was what she hated most about trials. The looks on the faces of the people who'd loved the victims. Those who didn't deserve their last memory to be a crime scene photo of their loved one being horribly killed and abandoned.

It wasn't right and she damned the fact that this was the way things worked in the human world.

"I wish we had a better system of justice." Because she lived with the same pain inside her that they did every day. No one should have to share such misery.

And it helped a lot more than it should for her to know for certain there really was a Hell for those who committed such atrocities.

Families and loved ones might not get justice in this lifetime, but there would be justice in the next. And for that, she'd be eternally grateful to Luke and even his awful father.

But her job was to get justice for them while they were here and could see it for themselves. They deserved that.

"Think, Sorcha, think," she whispered to herself as she tried to get inside the head of the monster who'd done this to two innocent students. They had to find the culprit before there was another kid on her board.

The one thing she kept coming back to—why make one look like an animal attack and the other not? Had someone stumbled onto the scene of the second killing before the killer could do whatever they had planned?

Or was this done intentionally to confuse them?

"They were trying to open a portal."

Sorcha screamed as that deep, smooth voice intruded on her thoughts. "Oh my God!"

"Uh, definitely not. Wouldn't even attempt to take on the big guy. Nor do I want any piece of His responsibilities." Luke shut her office door and moved closer to her. "I wanted to tell you that I'm sorry about earlier. I don't normally act like that. Assholes tend to set me off and bring out the worst in me."

"Then I will try not to be an asshole."

Shaking his head, he handed her the pink paper gift bag in his hand.

Sorcha frowned at it. "What's this?"

"An I'm-an-asshole gift to make amends for my stupidity." Those words charmed her a lot more than they should.

She smiled at him. "Thank you, but I'd already forgiven you."

"'Preciate it, but don't thank me yet. You might hate what I got you."

"I doubt that." Sorcha pulled the gold tissue paper off the top to find a bottle of Butterducks Merlot, a red and white striped box that held pralines, turtles and divinity and several small bags of Byrd's cookies. "Should I ask?"

Luke shrugged nonchalantly. "Some of the best of Savannah. I couldn't let you spend another night in town without some Byrd's cookies and treats from Savannah's Candy Kitchen. And Butterducks makes the best wines."

It was incredibly sweet and thoughtful. But then Bert used to do things like this, too.

*I got the cookie for you.* Bert's favorite saying. Fucking bastard would buy things he wanted and pretend like he was an altruist who only thought of others.

He was the real closet demon.

*Get thee behind me, Douchebag!* She was so sick of thinking about him and his cruelty.

Luke cleared his throat. "I don't want anything from you, Sorcha, other than for you to forgive me for popping off when I shouldn't have. While I have a temper, I normally corral it better, and I hate when it gets the best of me. I'm not my father. I don't like snapping at people for no reason."

"It's okay. I have a bit of a nasty temper myself, and a mouth to match it. Means you'll need to share the addresses for Butterducks, Byrd's and Savannah's Candy Kitchen so that I'll know where to go buy gifts for you when I do the same."

He chuckled. "I'm easy as I eat most anything...but ice cream works best for me."

"Really?" Given his aversion to the cold, she'd have thought that was the last thing he'd want to eat.

"Yeah. I freeze my ass off when I eat it, but we don't have it in Hell. Too hot. So I'm trying to get my fill before I go home."

That made sense. Poor thing.

She set the bag down on the floor by her desk and turned her radio down. It was freakishly quiet now. Not a single peep from the closet brigade.

Were they afraid of Luke? Or had something happened to them?

"Made any progress?" Luke asked as he looked over the notes she'd added.

"Not at all. But I did discover one thing."

He turned toward her with an arched brow. "And that is?"

"Want to explain to me about your closet filled with demons?"

# ELEVEN

A slow, playful smile spread across Luke's face before he turned toward her closet and spoke in a loud tone. "Which one of you turds do I kill first?"

Shrieks and chaos ensued from the closet.

"I didn't say anything!"

"Wasn't me, boss."

"Kill Dohlar! He needs to go."

"Shut up, Envee. Take her. She's useless."

Luke pounded on the wall with his fist. "Knock it off, evil spawn."

They went instantly silent.

She was right, they *were* afraid of Luke. "So, how many of them are in there?"

He screwed his face up as he considered it. "Not sure, really. At least a dozen. Maybe two...or more."

"And they live in your office closet?"

"Well, yeah," he said defensively. "They'd drive me insane if I trapped them in my apartment."

"But why are they trapped in the closet…period?"

Luke shrugged. "Why not? You want me to let them out?"

"Depends. Are they dangerous?"

"Depends," he repeated. "They're demons. Low-level, granted, but demons, nonetheless. They tend to run amok when released. There's no telling what they might get into. Ever seen the original *Ghostbusters*? It would probably look a lot like that. Probably worse."

Absolutely terrifying. And it still didn't answer her main question. "Why are they here?"

"We're his pets."

"I love you, master!"

"He adores us. Don't hurt us!"

"I want a cookie!" That sounded like the demon who had to pee earlier.

He gave her a peeved stare. "Humans have cats and dogs. We have demons. Whenever my dad wanted on my good side, he'd send over a new one. And like Helly, they followed me out of Hell because they're fiercely loyal."

"Arf, arf!"

"Meow!"

"Baa, baa."

"That's a sheep, idiot."

"People have sheep."

"No, they don't."

"Yes, they do. They count them to sleep."

"Cu-caw! Cu-caw!"

Like Luke, she ignored the demons. "And what do you feed them?" Other than the cookies they were begging for.

His eyes filled with absolute fear. There was a new

expression she never thought she'd see on Luke's face. "Never, ever feed them. Just keep them corralled in the closet and never release them."

"But we're bored, master!"

"Good. Stay that way." He looked back at Sorcha. "When they're not bored, they're destroying things. Like a pack of puppies set loose in a shoe store. They're worse than piranhas with raw meat."

"I'm your favorite, *dominus*. Can't I come out for a few minutes? I promise to behave."

"And they lie," Luke said.

Sorcha was still confused by all this. "So they just hang out in your closet all the time?"

"Not really. It's a portal. The Feral Bunch can return to Hell, but for some reason they prefer to hang out in there and make me crazy."

Suddenly, the demons began to sing a cappella in unison.

It took a second for her to catch on to the tune. "Is that *Hallelujah*?"

"Their favorite song. You will come to loathe it. I think they do it mostly to piss off Delilah. For that reason alone, I don't banish them."

She had to admit that they made a beautiful choir.

Luke knocked on the wall again. "Okay, sycophants. Knock it off."

There was one last voice that sang a final *hallelujah*.

Luke rolled his eyes. "That's Envee. She always pushes her luck and she's Helly's best friend. Never, *ever* let the two of them loose in this world together. It would be a catastrophe."

"Good to know. Any other surprises I need to be aware of?"

"I hope not, but with the way this day's been going... Might as well place a bet."

"Can I have a cookie, too?" one of the demons begged.

"Snickerdoodle!"

"Choco chip is the best!"

"Can we eat babies?"

Luke gave her wall a dry stare before he spoke. "*It rubs the lotion on its skin, or else it gets the hose again.*"

Stunned beyond belief, Sorcha couldn't move for a minute. "Did you just quote *Silence of the Lambs*?"

"They love horror movies. And they need to be quiet now so that I can work."

"Jingle bells—" the words ended in a short umph, followed by a tussle.

"Don't make him mad or we won't get TV time. Shh!"

Luke let out a long, exasperated breath. "It's like herding caffeinated toddlers after an ice cream and cake bender."

Maybe, but she was dying to know what they looked like. All kinds of images were going through her mind.

"Do you have a picture of them?"

"Why would I want a picture of those hyenas?"

"They're your pets. People usually love to share pet photos."

"Hmm. Never thought of that. But if you're curious..." He opened the door to her closet, snapped his finger and the wall turned clear.

The two demons closest to the wall shrieked, then covered themselves with their hands.

"I'm naked!" The female demon really wasn't. She wore

a tight red sweater and matching skirt. She was actually beautiful with her curly blonde hair that matched her short horns.

"That's Envee," Luke said with a sigh.

Three more pushed her aside so that they could press themselves against the wall like children or zombies on a window. A cute male with red eyes and horns even placed his mouth on the wall and blew his cheeks out.

"Hey, boss! Can you share those cookies?" That was an adorable teenage girl with black hair and a pair of red horns and eyes.

"Xesbeth," Luke said to Sorcha. "They look so cute, don't they?"

"They do."

He snapped his fingers and they turned into shadow beasts.

Sorcha gasped. "Is that what they really look like?"

"Yes. And they smell."

"No, we don't!"

"You smell." It sounded like one demon shoved another.

"You smell worse!"

Now, there was definitely a scuffle in the closet that caused the ones she could see to turn around and start yelling at the combatants.

"Enough!" Luke hit the wall twice with his fist and the wall turned opaque again. "Go bother Sorath."

"Okay."

Then there was silence.

Sorcha let out a long, relieved breath. "They are a handful."

"I know. Makes me wish my father kept count and that

my pets came with an expiration date, like normal creatures."

"Meaning?"

"They never die. Believe me, I have tried."

Her eyebrows shot north at something she didn't expect to hear. She wasn't sure what part of that disturbed her most. The fact that the demons were immortal or that Luke had tried to kill them. "I thought you said everything, except God, could die?"

"I did. Doesn't mean it's easy to accomplish. Demons can be killed. I just haven't found the means for the ones in my closet. Yet."

Unsure of what to say to that, she nodded slowly. "I'm just going to do my work now."

"Sounds good." Luke pulled his coat tighter around him before he sat down in what she thought was going to be thin air.

But right as he sat, his black throne-like office chair appeared beneath him.

"Nice. Wish I could do that. It would have saved my dignity a few times."

He wrinkled his nose playfully. "I won't let you fall, Sorcha. I'll always make sure there's a chair to catch you."

Those words meant more to her than they should, and she quickly turned her mind away from how incredibly sexy he looked, and to their case. "The fairy star on the wall... what are you thinking?"

"My first thought was a leannán sídhe."

"Bless you."

Sighing at her joke, he rubbed at his eyebrow, then

explained. "They're fey in origin, similar to a Greek muse. They find an artist and inspire them."

Made sense given that both students were art students. "Do they normally tear someone apart?"

"Yeah, they do. It's kind of their thing. They suck what they need out of their target and kill them violently. They're also shapeshifters."

"Let me guess. They like taking the form of a fox?"

He nodded. "Sometimes."

"Do they take souls?"

"They can." But there was a note in his voice that said he wasn't buying it.

"And?"

"New information makes me think it might be a message from the Brotherhood of Shadows...an elite group of the sídhe aristocracy."

"Why would they want to kill college students?" she asked.

"Normally, they wouldn't care. But something about this bothers me."

She snorted. "There's a lot about this that bothers me."

Using his hand instead of the remote she needed, he swiped through the files on her screen. When he got to the one of the bloodstain, he made it larger so that she could see it better.

Her jaw went slack as she saw writing in the center of it. Impossible to see unless it was blown up. "What is that?"

"Xynzara."

"What's that mean?"

"It's my birth name."

# TWELVE

Sorcha took a step back and ran into the edge of her desk. Which was good as she needed that extra stability. "Why is your name written inside the blood splatter of our victim?"

"Wish I knew."

Her mind reeled. "How did the student know your name?"

"There's no way she could. That's not for public consumption. Only a tiny number of creatures know my real name. And I'm thinking whoever did that wanted to get my explicit attention."

"Why?"

"No idea." He stood up and moved closer to the screen. "It's in English and with your alphabet. Whoever did it wanted humans to be able to read it, too."

"*Your* alphabet?"

He nodded. "We have a different script in Hell that we use. Same for witches and other groups."

"So it's not like Greek or Cuneiform?"

"Why would we use those?"

"To be aggravating?"

He pressed his fingers to the bridge of his nose as if he had a headache. "While there is some truth to that, we just created our own way back when." Using his finger, he drew an odd assortment of symbols on the screen. The first looked like an eye. The next appeared as an unfinished star followed by a misshaped E, a weird W then an actual star. Something she couldn't make out and a final five-pointed star...those must be the As in his name.

"That's pretty."

"It's how a human might write my name if they knew our letters." He then combined them into a peculiar shape. "This is how my name would be written by someone from Hell who actually uses our script."

Yeah, that was very different. These weren't runes or alchemy symbols. It was unlike anything she'd ever seen before. "So it isn't a message to you."

"I still think it is. Whoever or whatever is doing this is trying to set me up. Makes me wonder if it's the same shit who had me tossed out of Hell."

"Why would they do that?"

"That's the question, detective. Why *would* they?"

By the ferocity of his expression, she would imagine what he intended to do to whoever had done this. Gone was any of the playful Luke she'd seen.

This was the demonic partner who wanted blood.

"Can I ask you something if you promise not to get angry?"

He frowned before he answered. "Sure."

"What does Xynzara mean?"

"Blade of Rebellion. My mother gave it to me because she intended for me to be my father's heir."

That was a disturbing thought. "As in take over Hell?"

"As I said, everything can be killed. But I have never coveted my father's throne. Which is why he agreed to name me his heir once I was grown. He knew I'd never lead an attack against him." He gestured toward the closet. "I can barely ride herd on my tiny troop of demons. Last thing I want is the headache my father deals with constantly. He can keep that forever, and I've always made sure to watch his back because I don't want to inherit any part of that drama."

"So why ban you from Hell?"

He gave her a peeved stare. "Yeah. See the problem?"

Yes, she did. "So you think someone is trying to over-throw Lucifer?"

"I don't know. I have a lot of enemies and siblings who would do this to me just for shits and giggles. Again, the old, *Fuck you, Ken.* My fear is that you're right and someone is coming for his throne. But why frame me here where I really pose no threat?"

She wished she had an answer.

Luke's phone rang out with *Hell's Bells.* Without commenting on his ringtone, he answered it and put it on speaker. "Teivel."

"Why did you kill me?"

The color faded from his face as Sorcha's breath caught in her throat. What?

Luke's eyes darkened dangerously. "Who is this?"

"You know who I am. Why did you kill me?"

"I haven't killed anyone and I don't appreciate your bullshit."

The voice began sobbing. "I did what you wanted. Why did you laugh while you hurt me?"

"Fuck you!" He hung up, then turned to face Sorcha. His eyes were no longer amber. They were a fiery red unlike anything she'd ever seen before. These didn't glow. They swirled.

"Helly!" he growled in a guttural tone.

She appeared instantly and drew up short as she caught sight of his state. "Yes, *dominus*?"

"Find out where the last call on my phone came from."

Nodding, she turned into a dark mist and covered his phone.

That was one way to do a trace. Personally, she preferred the more conventional means.

"Shouldn't we tell the captain or Bernadette about this?"

"Tell them what? I'm being harassed?"

"Stalked and set up. They need to know."

"What can they do?"

He was right. This wasn't human. What could a mere mortal do to help with someone far beyond the normal realm?

"I do have one question and please don't take this the wrong way. I'm just trying to fact find. Have you killed anyone recently?"

The look he gave her was blistering. "No."

"Okay. Don't get angry. I'm only curious why they're saying you did."

"I really don't know." The sincerity in his tone and on his face told her that he was innocent.

"Just breathe, Luke. We'll get through this. We'll find out who's after you and stop it."

Luke adored the conviction he saw in her eyes and heard in her voice. But she was human.

What could she do?

Bleed?

His anger rose high and it took everything he had to keep it under control. Nothing would please him more than to explode everything around him. To throw a fit the size of a tsunami. But it would solve nothing.

Worse? It would terrify Sorcha.

She reached out and placed her hand on his.

And for the first time in his life, he calmed down.

SHADDIX PASSED a droll stare at her imp, a gift from her father on the day she'd been born. "Careful, Enos. Else I'll yank out the stubs where your wings used to be."

Enos mumbled something incomprehensible.

"What was that?"

Her imp shook its head. "Nothing, *domina*. Just my stomach rumbling."

Right... Shaddix narrowed her gaze on the beast. "Control your body."

"Yes, *domina*."

Sneering at it, she craved real company. Pets held no interest for her right now. Not when she was now her father's favorite. Her newfound power was addictive.

How could Luke have ever complained about it?

He'd never deserved his position. Never appreciated it.

*But I do...*

She left her room and headed for the fiery pit where her father oversaw his dominion.

At a full seven feet in height, Samael was a creature of extreme and utter beauty. His once solid gold wings were now tipped with black, and he had them folded against his lean, well-muscled body. Long blond hair framed a face that had been chiseled to perfection. Ironically, he was an exact copy of Luke, except for his hair color and much paler skin.

And icy blue eyes.

But the shape of their lips, eyes, chin and nose were identical in every way. Even the way they carried themselves.

Shaddix had always hated that arrogance. It'd bothered her when her father did it. When Luke had come along...

He was such an undeserving bastard.

Literally.

She was a pure-blooded angel. Why her father had ever favored such a mutant creature, she'd never understand.

Samael stood beside a pale, sinister man. She would say human, but he wasn't completely human. He reeked of blood and bile.

Vampire. She'd know that unique stench anywhere.

Her father looked over to her and smiled. "Ah, my daughter. Shaddix, come here and meet Antoine Dufresne."

Moving closer, she inclined her head to the stranger. Until she knew if he was an equal or higher, she had no intention of speaking to him.

The vampire scowled at her father. "I thought your son was your second?"

Samael's eyes turned to a furious red as his wings fanned out.

Dufresne realized too late that he'd stepped on the wrong topic. "Forgive me, my lord. I must have been misinformed."

Samael's wings tucked down against his back again, but his eyes remained vibrant red. "Shaddix will be dealing with the subject at hand."

"And that is?" she asked.

"The Order of Blackthorn is looking for a daughter of theirs who has escaped the fold."

Shaddix frowned at her father. "Why would that concern us?"

Dufresne returned her frown. "As your main ally, we were hoping to borrow a hellhound to track her down."

"Why not use one of your werewolves or other shapeshifters?" Surely, they'd be just as good, and a lot easier to stomach. Hellhounds came with a nasty arrogance that made it hard for her to tolerate them.

Her father looked less than pleased with her question. "Obviously, they don't want the woman to know they're coming after her. She'll be looking for their kind. She won't think to be wary of a hellhound."

Shaddix always hated when her father took that tone that implied she was stupid. She despised it twice as much when he did it in front of others.

Never once had he ever embarrassed Luke. That little prick got a pass on everything.

Her anger was such that she was surprised steam wasn't coming out of her nostrils. But she knew better than to let it show. That would only incur more wrath from her father.

Lucifer couldn't handle anyone challenging him.

Well, it was more like he wouldn't tolerate it and the last thing she wanted was for him to start in on her.

"I shall take care of Mr. Dufresne, Father. You can rely on me."

"Then I'll leave you to it." He vanished instantly.

Dufresne arched a brow at her. "What happened to Luke?"

"What do you know of my brother?"

"It's rare for your father to grant an audience. So I've always done business with Luke."

Because her father had no respect for vampires or much of anyone. "Luke no longer holds his confidence." Thanks to her father's paranoia. She still couldn't believe he'd kicked Luke out of Hell.

"What does that mean?"

"Sadly, my brother isn't welcome here anymore."

The disbelief in the vampire's eyes would have been comical had the subject not been so serious. "I take it you're replacing him."

Shaddix nodded. "I am."

He inclined his head to her. "My condolences on the loss of your brother."

"Thank you. I do miss him." Not really, but no one else needed to know that.

"Have you any idea where he's gone?"

That made the hair on the back of her neck rise. "Why do you ask?"

"Curiosity."

"That tends to get people into trouble. Especially vampires...and cats."

A strange glint appeared in his eyes. "I'll take care."

"You should and don't worry. I have no idea where my brother has gone. Once he was cast out, he vanished."

Dufresne wasn't sure what game the fallen angel in front of him was playing. She was hiding something. He just didn't know what.

Not that it mattered. He had much more pressing issues at present. "Could you please summon a hellhound for me?"

"Of course." She snapped her fingers.

A tall, beautiful dark-skinned woman with amber eyes appeared in the room, beside the angel.

Her eyes flared with anger as she saw Shaddix. "What's the meaning of this?" she growled.

"My father wishes for us to help the vampire. Given that it's a direct order, I thought you'd be the one best suited to carry it out."

The hellhound's nostrils flared. How the angel could appear so nonchalant against that level of fury, he had no idea. Even at his distance, he was scared. "You don't command me."

Antoine had never met the hound before this, but she was terrifying. The angel was either incredibly brave or more likely stupid.

Shaddix shrugged. "Help or don't. I really couldn't care less. But if you choose not to, I will make sure my father knows you refused his orders." Then, she vanished as quickly as Lucifer had done.

Alone with the hellhound, Antoine wasn't sure what to do. The last thing he wanted was to incur her wrath.

She turned toward him with a menacing glower that almost succeeded in loosening his bowels.

"Hi," he said, trying to befriend her.

Sadly, that didn't appease her at all. "Who are you, vampire?"

"Antoine Dufresne."

That took a degree of anger from her amber eyes. "I've heard of you. You're a friend of my son's."

"Your son?"

"Luke."

Antoine wasn't sure how to take that. In all the centuries he'd known Luke, they'd never spoken of mothers. For some reason, he'd assumed Luke's was either dead or another angel.

But a hellhound...

Interesting.

"Luke's why I came here. I was hoping to speak with him."

"Why?" She wasn't very chatty, which only added to the sinister quality of the beast.

"I have a missing daughter. I would like to say she was kidnapped, but more likely I think she's fallen in love with a human, and I need to get her back before anyone finds out."

That seemed to confuse the hellhound. "Why would you not want her happy?" Such a simple question. If only it were that easy.

"Vampires and humans don't mix. I mean, it's fine to feed on them, but not to live with one. She's broken one of our most sacred rules."

The hellhound nodded. "Understood. It's fine to feed on humans, but never to keep one."

There was a lot more to it than that. It wasn't just that Amandine had broken their rules. Being with any human put all of them at risk. As a rule, the human race was never to know they existed.

Ever.

And it wasn't bad enough that she'd flaunted a rule that had kept them safe for centuries. Oh no. His daughter had taken up with the son of the Phoenix Society leader—the very group they had made their truce with.

For hundreds of years, their groups had been at war. It'd been bloody and costly on both sides.

Until the vampires had made a truce with the Phoenix leader that strictly forbade vampires from breeding with humans and letting the mundane humans know they existed.

In return, the Phoenixes kept humans from hunting vampires, including their own members. More than that, they helped conceal his species and should a group of humans find them, the Phoenixes took care of it so that the vampires could live in peace.

For over two hundred years, his people had known a tranquility they'd never dreamed of. Even after that bastard Stoker had shined a light on them, they had still managed to stay hidden. Granted the truce kept them from breeding their own children, but it'd been worth it for the peace of mind that came with living without being hunted by roving mobs of imbeciles.

Of having their homes burned during the daylight when they were most vulnerable.

And idiots staking them because they stupidly believed it would kill them.

No vampire wanted this truce to end.

If any member of his Order learned of this, they'd

demand he kill his own daughter for her violation. The same daughter he'd become a vampire eight hundred years ago to save.

She was his life. He refused to be her death.

"Please help me find my daughter."

The hellhound inclined her head to him. "I understand the need to protect a child. I'll make sure you find her."

"Thank you."

"Do you have any idea where to start?"

He nodded. "They're both students at Savannah College of Art and Design."

# THIRTEEN

"We have the students' photos."

Luke glanced toward Sorcha who stood in the door of his office. "Did you upload them?"

"In the folder."

"Thank you." Luke opened the file, then gasped as he saw the unravaged faces of the girls who'd been slaughtered.

Sighing, Sorcha closed the door to his office and moved to stand next to him. She did her best not to breathe in his intoxicating scent. Leather and a sweet smokiness that she couldn't define. That alone made her ache to take a bite of him.

She forced her thoughts away from that. "I know. It's so sad. They look enough alike, they could be sisters."

Luke got up and moved closer to the screen. "That's not what has my attention."

"What, then?"

He lifted his hand and waved it in front of the screen.

Using his powers, he posted a third photo in the middle of the two student IDs. Like the murdered women, this one also had long dark hair and eyes. She was dressed in a pair of jeans with a green sweater and brown jacket. They were so similar in looks that they could easily be related.

This was looking more and more like a serial killer.

Sorcha gasped audibly. "Is that another open case?"

He shook his head slowly. "She's Amandine Dufresne. Daughter of the head of one of the most powerful hidden Orders."

"What do you mean?"

"I told you about them earlier. The secret organizations that basically run the entire world."

"I think I saw this episode of *Ancient Aliens.*"

He rolled his eyes at her sarcasm. "That show's a lot more right than you think."

Sorcha felt the blood drain from her face. She wanted to call bullshit on what he said, but how could she? He was the son of the devil. If anyone knew about secret societies, Luke was the...demon. "Who exactly are these organizations?"

"I'm sure you've heard of the Illuminati."

"Of course."

"They're real and it's a large group of humans. Then there's Brotherhood of Shadows. That is made up of elves and sídhe."

Sorcha's head swam at what he was telling her. "Awesome. Any other ulcer inducing groups I should know about?"

"Probably."

"And does Santa have his own?"

He smirked at her. "Don't be a smart ass."

"Sorry. I believe you. It's just a little hard to wrap my head around this."

"I know. It's why they're secret societies who go out of their way to make sure humans have no idea they exist."

No kidding. As chaotic as the world was, she could only imagine how much worse it'd be if anyone knew the fey and others had power and pulled strings. "Makes sense. Please go on."

"Centuries ago, the Free Masons founded the Phoenix Society, and they're usually crossed up with the Dragon Society."

"Shapeshifters?"

"No. Triads."

That shocked her. "As in the Chinese mafia?"

"Yes, but this particular sect has some special skills and friends that make them IA eligible."

Which meant they were packed with psychic abilities, shapeshifters, cambions or who knew what. "Great! I'm so glad I work here and am learning about all these fun entities."

"I know, and you're going to love this next group even more."

What could be worse?

Oh wait, a Celtic paranormal group. "Lucky Charms Society?"

"No. The Star Overlords."

Sorcha burst out laughing. Until she saw that Luke wasn't amused so this had to be a real thing. "You're kidding, right?"

He shook his head slowly. "Ancient alien astronaut theorists would have a field day with them. They're made up of a number of representatives from various worlds who want to stake a claim here on Earth. Why do you think they created the UN Office for Outer Space Affairs?"

Her head reeling, she moved to take a seat in the black suede chair in front of his desk. "But the group goes by the name Star Overlords?"

"No one ever said they were creative."

"No, but they are a bit conceited."

"Again, not of this earth. They view humanity as a parasite they want to corral and put in a cage. It's been hard to keep them back, but so far, diplomacy and treaties have worked."

That made her feel all warm and fluffy. "You think if we buy E.T. a phone they'd go home and leave Earth alone?"

"Tried and failed."

Her jaw went slack. Of course they'd tried. This felt more and more surreal. "And the rest of the Orders?" she asked, afraid of the answer.

"La Quinta Columna."

"Spanish?"

"Close. Aztec and Mayan. In English they're known as the Fifth Column."

"Beautimous. Next?"

"Sisters of the Cauldron who are sometimes known as Magespawn."

"Why Magespawn?"

"Some of the males and others of their Order get a little miffed at being called sisters. They wanted a more gender-neutral moniker."

"But those in the Brotherhood of Shadows are okay with that?"

Luke shrugged. "I'm not the one who created the groups or who participates in them. Take it up with their ancestors and members."

"Fine. How many are left?"

"Just a few more such as the Infernal Order—"

"Your father?"

"You would think, but no. That group was founded by the Templars and is run by their descendants."

Knights Templar. She should have known they'd have a hand in world affairs. "Do any of them know the secret of Oak Island?" She couldn't resist asking.

"Probably and we need to have a serious conversation about your streaming addiction soon."

Sorcha would argue that, but he was right. She spent way too much time watching everything Hulu and Netflix had to offer. *And don't get me started on Amazon Prime.* "Fine. Does your father have his own group?"

"Of course, he does. Circle of Fyre."

That made sense. "Isn't that a bit on the nose?"

"Not as much as Infernal Order would have been."

"Point taken. Is there any group we're missing I need to know about?"

"Just the Order of Blackthorn." He pointed to the pictures on his screen. "That's why I don't think this is being done by a serial killer."

"Why? The victims all look alike. It's an easy MO that makes sense."

"Yes, and killing the heir to the Order of Blackthorn makes a lot more sense."

It might, but she wasn't quite ready to go there. She really wanted this to be human in nature and not a turf war between preternatural superpowers. "Walk me through your thinking."

"I ran across Amandine a few weeks ago. Didn't think anything about it as she was with a friend in a coffee shop, studying late at night. I mean, don't get me wrong, it was weird. An immortal being attending classes at a local university? Granted eternity can get boring. Not as boring as class, if you ask me. But who am I to judge kink? Anyway, I put it out of my thoughts until now. Now I'm thinking what if our perp is trying to get Amandine and the others were a mistake? It would explain the condition of the bodies."

"How so?"

"Order of Blackthorn is made up of the more usual paranormal creatures. Vampires, werewolves, boogeymen, etcetera."

"And Amandine is..."

"Vampire. They're hard to kill. But if you bleed them out and ravage their body, they can't regenerate."

He was right. That would explain the overkill. "But wouldn't staking their heart be quicker and easier?" Not to mention a lot less messy.

Creating a bottle of water out of thin air, Luke opened it and took a drink. "Stop watching movies and bad TV. Nothing is *that* easy to kill...well, maybe a Daimon. But not all their marks are in the center of their chests either, and you better have the strength of a Dark-Hunter when you stake that mark or all you'll do is piss the Daimon off."

Sorcha's eyes widened as she made a note on her tablet about that. "Daimons...must pierce their mark. Don't stake vampires unless I'm wearing tennis shoes."

Luke moved to stand beside her. "Exactly. They tend to take those stakes and return the favor."

She cringed at the image that went through her head. "Ouch. Duly noted. But I still don't see how these all tie together."

Luke gestured at the photos with the water bottle in his hand. "Look at them. They could easily be mistaken for each other."

"True. And?"

"If you were given a picture of Amandine so that you could find her..."

"It would be easy to mistake them." She finally saw what he did. "But why kill them and frame you for it?"

"I was my father's heir. If you wanted to start a war between the secret factions..."

"Murder the heir of one organization and blame it on the heir of another."

Setting the water aside, Luke nodded slowly. "I'm thinking the killer thought each one was Amandine and framed me for the kill so that her father would demand my head for it."

"But you're no longer the heir. Why bother?"

"I'm sure my father hasn't told anyone that I'm gone. He's paranoid and doesn't like for anyone to know his business. The only ones who would know about my absence would be those who witnessed it. And I'm sure half, if not most of them, are probably dead or locked up."

Wincing, Sorcha closed her tablet and held it up against her chest. "That's shitty."

"Yes, it is. But it makes a lot of sense. If Antoine Dufresne saw any of the evidence, he'd believe that it led to me and he'd want my cute, adorable ass on a chopping block."

She ignored his comment because he did have a cute, adorable ass. "Have you ever met Dufresne?"

"Many times. My father seldom deals with those he thinks less of. In the past, he sent me in to interface with the other organizations."

"So you're like an ambassador?"

"Exactly." There was a foreign light in those amber eyes that told her he was still mulling all this as he paced back and forth like a feral predator.

"What else are you thinking?"

He crossed his arms over his chest and sighed. "Originally, that the first murder was someone fucking with me."

"Yeah...the whole 'Fuck You, Ken' scenario. Now you're thinking your banishment is unrelated?"

"No... Not... Maybe... I don't know. I can't shake this feeling that everything's related. But I'm not sure how. If someone is trying to break the treaties, what better way than to target the heirs?"

She set her tablet aside. "But why wait a year between your banishment and these deaths?"

"Exactly. But what if it's not a year? Like I said, my father wouldn't have sent out postcards to let anyone know I'm gone. Same with the other factions. What if other heirs are dead or missing and we just haven't heard anything? Maybe it's been going on, and no one has caught on to the pattern. Could have started even before my banishment. How would we know?"

That sent a chill down her spine. She wanted to deny it, but Luke was right. It made a lot of sense.

Except for one thing... "What's the motive?"

"Oldest one out there...rule the world."

Sorcha screwed her face up at his simple answer. "That's a bit trite, don't you think?"

"Occam's razor. Sometimes trite is the only answer. Besides, you're not dealing with people. We're talking about creatures who view people as food. They'd love nothing more than to have the ability to stick humanity into incubators like meat in a freezer or on farms where humans are treated as cattle." He let out a bitter laugh. "Hell, my father would love nothing better than to take over every last bit of this planet and burn it to the ground for no other reason than to lay waste to everything the good Lord created."

She didn't like the sound of that at all. "Is that his ultimate plan?"

Putting his hands in his pockets, Luke sighed. "That was the plan when he got here. But he was stopped before he could do it. If he could reactivate his quest, he wouldn't hesitate to do so. Again, I'm not here to sugarcoat the devil and say he's just misunderstood. He's not. He's everything you've heard and worse. No one wants to dance with him unless they're ready to be damned to a place much worse than anything a horror writer has ever conceived."

Her head was starting to hurt. There were so many more predators out there than she'd ever known. Real ones that terrified her.

*Think about work.*

For some reason, murder was a safer topic. "Any chance I can nab a water from air?"

He snorted. "'Course." He opened his palm and a bottle of water appeared before he offered it to her.

Nice. She'd love to have that ability. Taking the bottle, she took a sip before she returned to their topic at hand. "Okay. Assuming you're right," and she had no doubt that he was, "we need to speak with this girl...Amandine."

"Already on it." He showed her his phone where he'd used the IA database to pull up Amandine's address.

She gave him an amused smirk and used his words. "Wouldn't it be easier to call her?"

He shook his head. "The bolt factor is high with this one."

"Thanks, Yoda." And he dared to comment on her addiction to streaming networks. He quoted as many, if not more, movies as she did. "Shall we saddle up?"

With a laugh, he gestured toward his door so that she could lead them to the garage.

They got into Delilah and headed toward the modest home Amandine was renting not far from Forsyth Park.

"This is rather underwhelming for someone who is the heiress of a vampire dynasty. Don't you think?"

Luke shrugged. "You never know. I live in an apartment above a garage that gives my mother hives whenever she visits. Some of us don't need all the bells and whistles."

He had a point. "Why do you live in a small apartment?" She would think he'd be more at home in a grand palace or mansion.

"It's convenient and I don't want to draw attention to myself."

She couldn't stop the mad laughter that exploded from her.

Luke turned his head to give her an annoyed glare. "What was that?"

"Do you own a mirror? You're nine feet tall, exceptionally handsome and wear a black leather coat in the dead heat of summer. Dude! You do nothing *but* stick out."

"Dude?" he repeated.

"It's one of my favorites. I know it annoys many people so I try to limit its use around strangers."

He gave her a lopsided grin. "Doesn't bother me. And...I can't help my looks."

"Aren't you a shapeshifter?"

"Human appearance or hellhound. I only have two forms. Well, unless you count the wings I keep hidden. I guess that could be considered a third form."

For some reason, that surprised her. "You have wings?"

"I do."

Interesting. "So you could fly if you had to?"

"Yes, but rather not. With human paranoia being what it is, I might get shot down. And while it wouldn't kill me, it'd definitely hurt and piss me off to no uncertain end. With my luck, some old woman somewhere would find me and put me in her cage and force me to say, 'I think I saw a puddy cat' for eternity."

Sorcha tried hard not to laugh at his dry humor, but...

He arched a brow. "Don't you dare laugh. I'm still waiting for those nude photos of me to show up someplace. It's why I don't dare run for office."

Now she was laughing so hard, she was grateful she was sitting in the car. Otherwise, she might have fallen.

Luke appeared a bit peeved as he took his hair down.

She didn't know why, but his movements made him seem even hotter than normal. His presence was so disturbing. They just didn't make men like this in the flesh, and it was hard to pretend he was normal when he exuded an unholy sex appeal.

Getting out of the car, she needed to put some distance between them.

Luke joined her on the curb and led her toward the nondescript white house that had been converted into apartments. He led her up the stairs to the second floor, then stopped in front of the first door on the left and knocked.

A man in his early twenties opened it. With dark blond hair, he barely reached Luke's shoulder. His blue eyes widened as he saw Luke dominating the hallway.

Luke scowled at him. "Eli...what are you doing here?"

"Same to you."

The confusion on both their faces might be comical if it wasn't undercut by a ferocity Sorcha didn't understand.

"I'm here on business," Luke said simply.

"Satan's?"

Luke tsked. "He doesn't like being called that." Then, he paused a second. "Like I care. Screw it. Satan it is. And no, I'm not here on his business. But it's official and important." He showed his badge. "Where's Amandine?"

"Eli? Is something wrong?"

He started to close the door in Luke's face, but Luke caught the door and held it open. "It's me, Amandine. I need a word with you."

"Lucian?" She gently nudged Eli aside so that she could open the door wider. "Why are you here?"

"Can I come inside?"

"No!" Eli's tone was emphatic.

"Of course." Amandine opened the door wider. Tall and

slender, there was a fey-like quality to the vampiress. She had long dark hair and was dressed in a flowing black skirt and top.

The girl gave Sorcha a once over that wasn't exactly complimentary.

Eli's face was so red, she was surprised he wasn't screaming at them.

Until Amandine cupped his cheek in her hand and smiled up at him. "Breathe, love. I'm not going to run off with Luke. He's not my type."

Luke scoffed. "I'm everyone's type." He flashed a charming grin at Eli who finally calmed down.

"Why are you here?" Eli asked.

Amandine tsked. "Be more hospitable. Luke wouldn't come without a good reason. Right, Luke?"

"Right." He stepped back. "Want to take this one, Sorcha?"

All attention turned to her, which suddenly was very disconcerting. Shaking it off, she stepped forward. "Sure. Have you heard about the students who were murdered lately?"

Amandine winced. "It's awful. I know they were drained of blood, but you can't possibly think *I* had anything to do with it. Vampires don't kill like that."

"I know. But Luke noticed something the cops didn't." She turned her notebook on and showed Amandine the actual photos of the women they'd found.

Both Amandine and Eli gasped.

"They look like me?"

Sorcha nodded. "Luke thinks the killer is after you and

that killing them was a mistake." Not her finest moment of letting someone know they had a killer out to get them, but she had yet to find a more delicate way to convey that message.

Amandine turned even paler as she stepped back and sat down on her afghan-covered sofa. She held Sorcha's notebook in both hands as she stared at their victims. "Who would want me dead?" She glanced to Luke, then to Eli. "Your father?"

"No. He might not be happy about our relationship, but he wouldn't dare go after you. It'd be all kinds of suicide. The other Orders would have a fit if someone did that. Right?" he asked Luke.

Luke glanced to Sorcha. "I want to say yes, but..."

"My father didn't do this!" Eli insisted.

"That I believe. However..." Luke trailed off with the thought.

"What?" Sorcha asked.

"I have a long history with the Hellfire Club. I could see one of them wanting to come after me."

That confused her. "I thought Eli was part of the Phoenix Society?"

"Their modern name. Two hundred years ago, they were the Hellfire Club...a dig at my father. We have definite history between us. Most of which isn't suitable for younger audiences."

That explained Eli's rude greeting. It could also explain why they were setting up Luke for the killings.

It was beginning to make sense.

And before she could say anything, a loud explosion

sounded beside her. It took a moment to realize that someone had thrown a bottle through their window. One filled with something flammable. Before she realized what it was, it set fire to the closed curtains and spread across the room.

# FOURTEEN

Screaming, Amandine started for the next room.

Luke grabbed her before she could do something stupid. "We have to get out of here."

Amandine's eyes widened. "I can't go outside. It's daylight."

"You can't survive a fire, either," Luke reminded her before he told Eli and Sorcha to leave. He shrugged his leather coat off. Covering Amandine from head to foot, he picked her up and ran with her, out the door and toward the stairs.

Other occupants were filling the hallway. "What was that?"

"Fire!" Luke shouted. "Get out of the building!" He rushed down the stairs to find Eli and Sorcha waiting for him by his car. "Delilah! Start your engine and raise the top." He turned to Sorcha. "Get in. We have to get Amandine to the office as fast as we can."

Luke gently put Amandine in the back as the convertible

top raised to shield them. As soon as Eli was in and Sorcha belted, they raced to their offices.

Once they were in the garage, Luke called out. "Helly!"

She appeared instantly, then gasped as she saw Eli and Amandine.

"Close the garage door and take care of Delilah, please." He carried Amandine out the back, to his office, while they ran behind him to catch up.

By the time Sorcha was inside Luke's office, he'd already closed the blinds, pulled his coat off a bedraggled Amandine and shrugged it back on.

"You okay?" Sorcha asked Luke.

He nodded as he turned toward Amandine. "What about you, princess?"

Amandine was running her hands over her body, looking for damage. "I think I'm okay. Thank you for getting me out of there so fast."

That confused Sorcha. "You weren't kidding about vampires and daylight?"

Eli knelt down by Amandine's side. "Sunlight won't kill them, but it weakens them enough that they can be killed."

"And it blisters terribly. The pain is unbearable." Amandine looked to Luke. "Thank you for saving me."

Inclining his head to her, Luke passed a furious glare toward Sorcha. "And fire definitely kills them." He pulled his phone out.

Before she could ask him who he was calling, he started speaking. "Hey, boss. Sorcha and I just fled an apartment house near Forsyth. Someone tossed a Molotov through the windows. I had to rush a college kid out and I don't want the local LEOs to think we had anything to do with it." He paused a few minutes. "Yeah, we're in my office. We'll stay here and wait. Thanks." He hung up.

"Reyes?" she asked.

He nodded. "I think this confirms our theory about the real target." He jerked his chin toward their guest.

Amandine stood up. "I won't be intimidated or threatened!"

"Better intimidated than dead."

She glared at Luke for his comment. "What am I supposed to do? Give up my life because someone takes issue with my father?"

Luke swept his gaze from Amandine to Eli. "If the Orders find out about the two of you, you'll have a lot more than just your father to contend with."

Eli gnashed his teeth. "They're locked in the Middle Ages. There's nothing wrong with our relationship. It doesn't threaten anything other than their overly rigid sensibilities."

Luke made a snort so dismissive that it sounded equine in nature. "Historically speaking, that's not true. When two Orders unite, they have the ability to do some serious damage to the others *and* to the world. But there might be a compromise."

They looked at Luke hopefully.

"What?" Eli asked.

"Abdicate. One or both of you. Give up your inheritance and the other Orders can't complain. If there's no conflict, there's no conflict."

Sorcha was impressed at his King Solomonesque approach. It made complete sense.

Amandine's face lit up. "It's perfect! We should have thought of that ourselves!"

Eli wasn't so quick to agree. "Wait… What?"

Rising to her feet, Amandine took his hand. "Think about it. If we're not the heirs, our union won't make the others nervous. Let's do this!"

He shook his head. "I can't do that."

Grimacing at Eli's reaction, Sorcha bit her lip to keep from speaking. This wasn't right. If he really loved her, how could he refuse such a simple request?

And it ruffled Amandine. "What do you mean, you can't do that?" The anger in those last four words was savage.

Eli went pale. "My brother is an idiot. If he takes over… you've met him. He's worthless."

The fury in Amandine's eyes said that Eli needed to stop talking. Fast. "He'll be fine."

Unfortunately, he wasn't smart enough to shut up. "Would you be okay with your brother ruling in your stead?"

"I was until you took *that* tone. It doesn't sound like you care about your brother so much as you don't want to give up the power and money."

"And there is *that*," Eli said in an equally irritated tone. "We're talking a fortune. Can you honestly look at me and say that you'd be good with having to work three jobs to pay for tuition?"

Rage descended on her face. "My father was right. You *never* loved me. You just wanted vampiric sex. Get out!"

Sorcha actually took an involuntary step toward the door. That deep, demonic command that was hard to resist.

"Mandy," Eli pleaded.

"Don't you even, you bastard. Out!"

When he failed to listen, Amandine threw her hands up and an invisible shove pushed Eli to the door, plastering him up against it.

"Mandy, stop!" That shrieking tone was impressive. So was the fact that he was shoved aside while the door opened itself and then he was forced outside.

The door slammed shut with a resounding finality.

"Feckless bastard!" Amandine turned toward Luke who held his hands up and took a step back.

"Might be a bastard, but I'm not a feckless one."

That succeeded in breaking through Amandine's tears. "Are all men worthless?"

He glanced toward Sorcha. "Yes seems to be the right answer since I'm outnumbered."

Baring fangs at Luke, she turned toward Sorcha. "Did I do the right thing?"

"You're asking the wrong person. I have a bad history with men. If there's a loser, I always gravitate straight to him." Sorcha hesitated a second, as this was really off topic. "Can I ask you something?"

Crossing her arms over her chest, Amandine lifted a brow. "Sure."

"What's vampiric sex?"

Luke gave her a grin. "Ever heard of tantric sex? It's *that* on steroids."

Sorcha both could and couldn't believe that. Was it like Schrodinger's sex? She had no idea. "Is he right?" she asked Amandine.

Before Amandine could answer, a large black dog appeared in front of the closed door. While not quite as big as a German Shepherd, it was still an intimidating beast. Sleek and hairless, it had large shoulders and glowing red eyes.

Never had Sorcha seen anything like this.

But if she had to guess, hellhound came to mind.

She looked at Luke for confirmation. "Mom?"

He nodded. "And she's on a hunt."

In response to those words, the hellhound transformed into a tall, elegant woman whose eyes were a perfect match for Luke's. Other than that, Sorcha saw no family resemblance whatsoever.

Unless someone counted that devastating presence that commanded attention. Was that an inherited trait or something Luke picked up from living with his mother?

"You found the heiress?" Her voice was smooth and deep. A female version of Luke's.

Luke tsked at his mother. "She wasn't lost."

"According to her father, she was."

Luke ignored that comment. "Sorcha? Meet my mother, Senka. Mom, this is my new partner, and I take it that you're familiar with Amandine."

She inclined her head to Sorcha before she glanced about the room. "Where's your imp?"

"I sent her to Delilah."

"Good." She turned toward Amandine. "Come, child. Your father awaits."

Amandine jutted out her chin in childish defiance. "I'm not going."

Senka arched an irritated brow. "Pardon?"

Luke cleared his throat to get Amandine's attention.

"You don't want to tell her no. It's not a word she hears often, and it doesn't ever bode well for the one saying it."

"I am Amandine Dufresne, daughter of Antoine, leader of the Order of Blackthorn. No one tells me what to do."

The way Senka's eyes flared, Sorcha felt the disaster that was brewing. Even the air felt electric. Rife with conflict and anger.

This was about to be an epic showdown between two creatures who profaned the word *no*. And she was sure that Senka's bite would be much more vicious than her bark.

Luke moved to stand between them. "No destroying my office, Mum. Seriously." He turned toward Amandine. "She's a hellhound. Last thing you want is for her to drag you out of here. Grabbing those who are reluctant to leave is what she specializes in. Don't run or fight. She will hunt you down, and it won't end well for you."

"My father—"

"Is the one who sent her after you. Means he knows how my mother's breed functions and that was what he wanted for you. Go peacefully. Please. For your own sake."

Sorcha saw the rebellion that glowed in the younger woman's eyes. It was obvious that she wanted to run. Craved it.

And Sorcha couldn't blame her. She didn't like being ordered around, either. But it wasn't in Sorcha's nature to back down or run. She'd fight to the bitter end.

Thankfully, Amandine saw the truth in Luke's eyes and sighed. "Fine. I'll go home."

Senka moved toward Luke and pulled his head down so that their foreheads touched. "Thank you." She kissed his cheek. "And just so you know, I like this one much better than your old partner. She smells better, too." And with that she lifted her arm and summoned a purple cloud to engulf the two of them. Then, she vanished along with Amandine.

Stunned, Sorcha stood there. "I smell better?"

He laughed. "Don't ask."

Okie dokie.

Suddenly, someone started knocking furiously on Luke's door.

"Amandine! Talk to me!"

Sorcha cringed at the pain-filled tone. She would say poor kid, but he'd been a bastard to Amandine. If what he'd shown them was his true nature, better Amandine learn it now than years down the road.

Luke opened the door but refused to let Eli enter his office. "You're too late. She's on her way home."

Eli's jaw went slack as he lost all color in his cheeks. "What? How?"

"Her father sent a hellhound to collect her."

Eli growled deep in his throat. "I've lost my woman. My apartment...this isn't right!"

"Them's the breaks." Luke shut the door in Eli's face.

Sorcha bit back her laughter. "That was rude."

"Not really. Rude would have been to slap him first. And I was tempted. I'd like a little credit for my restraint. Which is a lot harder for me than most."

Sorcha would have commented on that except she realized something. "Wait...did we just solve our case?"

"Part of it."

"Part? No, I disagree. I think we solved it. Amandine was the target. It's not a serial killer on the loose. Right?"

"True, but we still don't know who killed the students or

set me up. All we know is who their target is. Until we find the merciless moron who's been doing this, Amandine isn't safe."

He had a point and she hated that she'd jumped ahead. She'd just been so glad to know the reason behind the killings. Nothing else had mattered.

Dang it!

Why couldn't Luke use his powers and just have it solved?

If only life worked that way...

Crossing her arms over her chest, she looked at Luke. "You're not safe, either. Whoever it is wants you to pay for something."

He shrugged. "I'm not afraid. I just want the throat of whatever asshole thinks they can frame me and live happily-ever-after. But at least Amandine's home now, and hopefully it'll stop the killer from targeting anyone else."

"What if it doesn't?"

"That's why we're still looking and the case isn't closed."

Another knock sounded on the door.

Luke growled. "Eli! How many times do I have to tell you —" His words broke off as he opened the door to find a wide-eyed Rory standing on the other side.

Screwing up his face, Luke slammed the door and gave Sorcha a fierce scowl. "What is this? Annual Asshole Day?"

"What?" she asked with a laugh.

Rory knocked again. "Open the door, Teivel. I'm here to take statements."

With obvious reluctance, Luke pulled the door open so

he could glare at Rory. "My statement? I stand by the fact that you're an asshole."

"Real mature." Holding a steel clipboard, Rory walked into the room without an invitation. "Where's the girl?"

Luke gestured toward Sorcha.

Rory growled at him. "Not her. The one you were seen running away with from the fire."

"She left."

Rory's jaw dropped. "And you let her go without a statement?"

"Didn't know I was supposed to knee cap her. Last time I checked, keeping someone against their will is false imprisonment." *Remind me sometime to tell you how I learned that lesson when I first got here.*

Sorcha inwardly groaned as Luke passed that thought to her. She could only imagine what the lunatic had done before he'd learned they had rules in this dimension.

Poor victim...

Opening his clipboard and pulling out a sheet of paper, Rory made the sound of a low, frustrated growl. "Why are all conversations with you impossible and migraine inducing?"

"Because we don't converse. I find conversation with you to be utterly trivial and boring."

Sorcha really wanted to laugh at the expression on Luke's face. But the last thing she wanted was to contribute to their mutual disdain. So, she decided to distract them. "Would you like my statement, Rory?"

"Please." He passed an angry grimace toward Luke before he crossed the room to where she stood. Only then did he glance about with a fierce grimace of distaste. "Fire your decorator. This is darker than most caves. How can anyone work in this environment? It looks like a teen-aged Goth threw up."

Completely unrepentant, Luke moved to his desk chair and sat down as if he were...well, the prince of Hell. "If you don't like my cave, door's in the wall." He put his booted feet up on his desk, then turned his smart board on and somehow began watching a baseball game.

Rory curled his lips. "What are you doing?"

"Watching the Savannah Bananas. Why aren't you?"

Clipping a piece of paper to his pad, Rory shook his head. "How do you work with him?" he asked Sorcha.

"I think he's funny." But not nearly as funny as the weird ball game he was watching. "What *is* that?"

"It's Banana Ball. You should try it after you finish giving your statement to the monkey who inspired me to watch it."

What was it about the two of them that they couldn't even pretend to get along?

"Is there somewhere else we could go to do this? *Any*where else?" Rory asked.

Luke glared at him. "Right here is fine."

"I need to take statements from both of you. I'd rather do it individually."

"Why?" Luke asked like a petulant toddler. "We're both professionals and I don't feel comfortable leaving my partner alone with you. She might get rabies or something."

Rory rolled his eyes. "Fine. I'll take your statements here." He glanced to Sorcha. "Normally, I'd force him to the station for this, but I know he'll make friends with my boss and probably get me fired. Or written up...again."

The shit-eating grin that spread across Luke's face said that he might do it anyway. "I challenge you to take me in."

"Behave!" she said to Luke.

"Why? Misbehaving is so much more fun."

Ignoring Luke, Rory cleared his throat. "Can you walk me through what happened at the apartment?"

"Sure." While Luke watched his Banana Ball, Sorcha relayed everything from the moment they arrived until they returned here with Amandine and Eli. She omitted mentioning Luke's mom and how Amandine actually left.

Instead, she shrugged. "The girl became angry at her boyfriend and stormed out of here. No idea where she's gone."

"Thank you." He looked over to Luke. "You?"

"That's about the size of it," he said in an affected Southern drawl. "No need in doing two reports unless you love paperwork. I've nothing to add to what Detective O'Malley said."

"All right." He tucked the paper he'd filled out into the metal clipboard case. "If there's nothing else..." He headed to the door and stopped to look back at Sorcha. "Did we say seven or eight?"

"Thought we said six, but seven works."

He smiled kindly. "I'll see you, then."

The moment he was gone, Luke turned off the board with his thoughts. "What's this? You're meeting up with the Snozzle?"

"Snozzle? What?"

"If I use the term I normally use for him, you'll be highly offended. Snozzle is the wholesome alternative."

She took a long breath as she moved to sit in front of his desk. "I really don't understand the animosity between you two. What did he do? Steal your bone?"

Luke ignored her dig at his heritage. "He's a pompous dickweed. How can you stand being around him?"

She gave him a dry, pointed stare.

"Fine. I'm a dickweed, too. I acknowledge my whole dickweedery." He gestured at the door Rory had just walked through. "He's a cambion and he's too stupid to know it."

That made her stomach drop. "What?"

"Oh yeah. Before you go on a date with him, be careful. Prince—bleeped for your delicate sensibilities—is not fully human."

"How do you know that?"

The look he gave her was bone-chilling. "I can smell it on him. It's an unmistakable *odeur*."

That was interesting, but she still didn't know why he was so angry over it. "I would think that would make you get along all the more."

"Not when he's something fetid to me."

"And that is?"

"Nephilim." Luke spat the word as if it choked him to even pronounce those syllables.

Oh. That made sense. Sort of...

"How do you know that?"

"He oozes that desperate *like me, like me 'cause I'm good* pheromone. It chokes me every time I'm near the beast."

There was so much to unpack from those words that she wasn't sure where to begin. But she kept coming back to one thing. "You're friends with an angel. Why does Rory irritate you so?"

"Remi is Remi. He never judges, as it's not his place. Rory judges the shit out of me, so I return the favor. With interest. No pencil-neck shit-stain is going to look down his way-too-long nose at me like I'm the runt of my litter or something that just pissed on his leg."

He said that, but there was more to it than just what he told her.

Much more.

"Oh my God! You're jealous!"

Luke scoffed. "I'm not jealous," he said petulantly. He even poked his lip out.

"Then you're childish."

After considering that for a few seconds, Luke nodded. "That, I'll cop to. Especially if you want to spank me for misbehaving." He flashed that grin at her.

This time, it didn't work. She was too pissed at him. "Ugh. We so need an HR department."

"Wouldn't do any good. I'd only make Helly take the boring class." He sat up. "So...Detective. What fun shall we get into now?"

Something in his tone made the hair on the back of her neck rise as she imagined the evil he could do. "Guess we need to find something to do before you get arrested again."

"Well, so long as it's for something I actually did, I don't mind. It did piss me off to be arrested for someone else's bullshit. Makes the beast in me want to hunt down the bastard responsible and rip out his throat. Which I just might do before everything is said and done."

"How do you know it's a man?"

"Women want me for other things...so do some men. But I haven't met a woman yet who wanted to frame me for a crime...that smacks of male assholery."

"You say that, but women can be exceptionally petty. It would make sense to me that it's a female culprit."

"Fine. I'll keep my options open."

His reversal confused her. Especially given the lightning quickness of it. "Just like that?"

He shrugged nonchalantly. "Why not?"

Now she fully understood Rory's complaint about Luke. He was hard to have a conversation with when he got into this mood.

And speaking of Rory...

"Can I clarify this for my sanity so that I fully understand it?"

Luke put his hands behind his head as he leaned back in his office chair. "Sure."

"You're a...hellhound not a demon."

"Yeah."

"Helly is an imp. Your mother is a full-blooded hellhound."

"And Jesus is Lord, what's your point?"

Narrowing her gaze, she smirked at his blasphemous question. "When we met, you said that I wasn't fully human, either."

"Correct."

"And you know for a fact that Rory is a cambion? Nephilim?"

"You're on a roll."

She ignored his sarcasm. "Is this like a TV show where every other person in Savannah isn't human?"

He made a deep, guttural sound of irritation before he answered. "No. Cambions are rare. Well, not so much rare as they don't normally survive childhood."

"Why?"

"We're abominations. Part of the world, but not really.

Most things that go bump in the night would rather mixed breeds not exist, so they tend to hunt us down and eat us before we learn to protect ourselves. The fact that the Snozzle is still alive means that his non-human parent is protecting him vigorously or he has powers he's not letting us know about. Either way, it pisses me off because he's either lying to everyone about his origins, or his head parent is outside my ability to detect them. And I don't like things hanging about that I can't sense."

Understood. That whole prospect was unsettling. And Rory's words about not fitting in took on a whole new meaning.

Did Rory know he wasn't completely human?

And more disturbing... "How do you know who is what? Is there a way for someone who isn't you to know if someone has paranormal origins?"

"That's the fun part. Most people have no way of knowing until it's too late. Then the land mine explodes and they're left bleeding...or dead. That's why Reyes hired me. I'm the only one on staff who can sniff out *anything* paranormal. Not just some things. Even someone like you who is cloaked by something. I know you're one of us. Just can't detect the specifics...yet. But I know when someone is touched by preternatural things or is one."

Sorcha ran her hands over her face as she struggled with this. "Why did I take this job again?"

"So you could spend your days admiring my cute, adorable ass."

She laughed in spite of herself. "It's not *that* cute."

"We both know otherwise. But don't worry. You're safe from my charms."

"Meaning what?"

"It's too fucking cold here for sex. I bathe in boiling water, wearing a wetsuit. Just the thought of being naked in the human world…" He visibly shivered. "No idea how y'all do it. Literally and figuratively. While I love being licked like a popsicle at home, I don't want to be a popsicle here."

She didn't want to be amused by that, and yet she found him hysterical.

More the pity that the temperature here kept him from sex. Not that she would ever breach that etiquette to sleep with a coworker. But it was a shame for someone she could tell wasn't used to celibacy to be forced into it.

"A little restraint is good for you."

Lowering his arms, he scoffed. "I've had enough. Let's find out who's after Amandine and see if it's the same little turd I need to kill for my banishment. Ice cream aside, I'm ready to go home."

Sorcha understood that. She missed New Orleans.

No, she missed *home*. In her case, that meant being a kid with her sister, safely tucked away in their parents' house. She missed the part of her that she'd lost the day her sister had been taken.

The part of herself that she'd never see again.

Siobhan.

They were supposed to be together forever. According to her mother, they'd come into this world holding hands. The doctor and nurses had been shocked during the C-section when they'd found the two of them with their hands entwined…which was why they'd done the C-section to begin with. After viewing the sonogram, the doctor had been afraid their hands were fused together.

Neither of them cried until the doctor gently separated their hands and parted them. Then they'd been inconsolable until one of the nurses had thought to lay them side by side so that they could touch.

They'd quieted instantly.

And they had slept that way until they'd gone off to separate colleges.

That first night at school had been the absolute hardest one of her life.

Until her sister's murder.

The emptiness in her heart was so severe that some days she had trouble breathing. Every day without Siobhan was the real Hell. She'd gladly give up her soul and burn for eternity if she could have her sister back for one single day.

One conversation.

Suddenly, Luke was beside her. Gently, he tilted her chin up until she was staring into those amber eyes. "Don't make offers like that, Sorcha. Even in your head. Someone might answer. If I could, I'd let you have that day without any bargain because no one should be left adrift. But this is where we are."

She understood and she knew he was right. Still, it was hard. "Do you have any siblings?"

"Many and I miss none of them."

She couldn't imagine an existence where she wasn't close to her sister. How awful for him. "I'm sorry."

"Don't be. They're bottom feeders, not worth missing. But I feel bad for you that you don't have yours." He meant that. She could sense his sincerity.

"Can I ask something personal?"

Suspicion darkened his gaze. "Sure."

"What do you miss about Hell? Really?"

One corner of his mouth lifted into an incredible lopsided grin. "The weather. My bed. Being able to sleep naked. The music...we have so many great musicians. You wouldn't believe it. It's nonstop concerts. And the tiger nut cake...worth it."

"Tiger nut cake?"

He nodded. "It's an old Egyptian recipe and delicious beyond belief."

She'd take his word for it, and she noticed something that was missing from his list. "You didn't mention any person there that you miss."

"Helly came with me."

That made her feel horrible for him. "Just Helly?"

"We don't attach, Sorcha. Not like humans. That emotion you have for your sister is not something we feel."

"Then why go home?"

# FIFTEEN

*hy go home...*

Luke sat alone at his desk, hating the fact that Sorcha's words had really impacted him.

*It's home. Why wouldn't I want to go back?*

But then he'd never realized how empty that single word was. *Home.*

A place where someone belonged.

The only people he had feelings for were his mother and Helly.

To a lesser degree, his father. But he wasn't protective of Old Scratch in the same way he was for his mother or Helly. As his father used to say, if you can't protect yourself, don't expect anyone else to do so.

And while he'd had fun with Sorath, he could see the fallen angel anytime he wanted. He actually saw him more here than he'd seen him in Hell.

Same for his mother.

So why was he so hell-bent on returning?

"Don't be stupid. You don't belong here," he sneered at his melancholy.

What was he supposed to do? Get a house in the burbs? Have some little demons of his own?

The very thought made him want to vomit. He wasn't a father any more than Lucifer had been.

He could barely corral Helly, and the Closet Demons were impossible. He couldn't imagine trying to actually parent something.

As if she sensed his dark mood, Helly appeared in front of him. "What'cha doing, boss?"

"Moping."

"Can I help?"

He snorted at her question. "You want to mope, too?"

"If it'll make you feel better." She flopped down in the chair in front of his desk. Then, she pouted like a toddler who had broken a favorite toy. "So, what are we moping about?"

He started not to tell her, but he was interested in her opinion. "Do you miss Hell?"

"Not at all. Why?"

That was what he figured. Still... "Did you have friends or family there?"

Her eyebrow shot north. "What?" The way she asked that was comical.

"I'm serious. Did you leave friends or family behind?"

She seemed baffled by his question. "After all these centuries, you're asking me about this now?"

"It dawned on me that I never asked you about it before. Bad oversight."

She cocked her head to stare at him. "Who are you and where's my *dominus*?"

"It's me, Imp. I was just curious."

She got up and propped her head against his desk so that she could stare up at him like a small child, seeking something. "You're my only family, *dominus*. Didn't you know that? It's why I left with you."

He would have considered himself more a burden for her than family...

Then again, family could be a burden, couldn't it?

"Surely you have other friends and real family."

She shook her head. "You *are* my real family. Ever since you were born and your mother grabbed me by the neck and told me to guard you or die. I've had no one but you."

"That hardly forms a bond."

"It does if you don't want to die."

He pursed his lips. "You know what I mean."

"I do and I admit that you were a little hard to love when all you did was cry, pee, shit and vomit. But after a while, you learned to wipe your chin, use the bathroom and talk. Eventually, you became fun."

"Eventually?" he asked incredulously.

She nodded. "And if it matters to you, I did learn to love you before you became fun."

He gave her a piercing stare at something she'd never said to him before. Something that was incomprehensible. "You love me?"

"I do." She offered him a bright smile. "I have for a long time now. You're my baby, *dominus*. Why wouldn't I love you?"

He scoffed. "I'm your assignment."

"You're my best friend. My only friend, actually. And I've cherished the centuries we've spent together."

That made him feel terrible. "I haven't been kind to you."

"Better than anyone else."

That made it all the worse. And in that moment, he hated himself for every cross word he'd ever given her. Every order he'd barked or growled. She deserved much better than that and he would try to remember in the future that she was his family, too. "I'm such an asshole."

"You're my asshole, and I find no fault with you."

She was like his mother. Actually, she was better. His mother found fault with him all the time.

Helly had never done such.

With a frown, Helly closed the distance between them. "What's wrong? Really?"

"I never realized until today that I'm alone."

She pulled her head back and frowned. "You're not alone, *dominus*. I'm here. Always." She moved to pull him into her arms.

Normally, Luke would have rebuffed her for that gesture. But tonight...

He folded the tiny imp into his arms and held her tight against him. Closing his eyes, he savored the hug. "This is a first."

She nodded against his shoulder. "Weird, isn't it?"

Laughing, he released her. "Maybe. A little."

"We never have to speak of this again."

That actually made him smile and he was grateful for it. "Thank you, Imp."

"I'm here to serve. In most ways. Remember, you're like

a son to me so there are limits to the serving. I hope. Please don't ever ask me to serve like *that*. It would be all kinds of gross."

Shaking his head, he gently pushed her away. She was right, they were family. And he should have seen it sooner.

In all his life, she'd been his only real constant. The one who'd been with him through the worst moments. Even now, he could see her popping in when he'd been banished. Determined to stay with him no matter where he went.

He ruffled her hair playfully. "Do you want to go back to Hell, Imp?"

"I will follow you to Hell itself." She flashed a fanged grin at him. "Wherever you go, *dominus*, I go."

He appreciated that thought, but it didn't answer his question. "I'm not asking if you *will*. I'm asking what you want. Do you miss home?"

"Oh. I do not miss anything about it."

For some reason that surprised him. "Nothing?"

She gave him a gimlet stare. "It was an entirely different experience for those of us who weren't the prince of Hell."

That made sense. And he felt guilty about it. Especially where she was concerned. "I never noticed."

"Why should you? You had everything you wanted."

Maybe. But he'd realized something after being around Sorcha...

He wasn't the most important creature in the room at any given time. Others mattered, too.

Such a simple concept and yet it'd taken him far too long to realize it.

"Come, *dominus*...let's leave your office and have some fun."

"Only if you call me Luke."

Helly choked. "P-pardon?"

"It's time you called me something other than lord. I'm no one's lord here and as you said, we're family."

"Okay, I'll try. But I make no promises."

Saturday night... Sorcha still couldn't believe that she was out on a date. It'd been so long that she could barely remember one.

Her mother would die of shock if she told her.

Which was why the only one who knew was Luke. And he wasn't happy about this at all. He'd been spitting and cursing all day.

But while he continued to complain, he couldn't say anything bad about Rory.

*The man's part angel. How bad can he be?*

She kept coming back to that fact. Her only real question was if Rory knew it.

Sorcha glanced about the unique pirate decor from her seat in a wooden booth. "They really bought into the whole pirate motif, huh?"

"Yes, they have. This was originally a pirate's den in 1753. You can read the history on the back of the menu."

Hmm... She flipped it over. Sure enough, it was all there. Interesting.

She turned the menu back over so that she could read it. "What's good here?"

"Fried chicken is my favorite. But I promise it's all good. I've never had anything that wasn't delicious."

Sorcha tried to focus on the paper in her hand, but the ghost to her right was making it really hard to do so. It didn't help that the ghost weirdly reminded her of Jack Sparrow. A little more clean-shaven, but Johnny Depp had some serious competition here.

Worse, he kept trying to tell her something. He wasn't speaking. Just gesturing toward the gated cellar stairway. The brick there looked about three hundred years old, as did the old wooden stairs and the green shutters that rested above a creepy red light.

Still, the ghost kept gesturing at it with purpose. It was so annoying that she finally gave up trying to read. "What is that area over there?"

Rory glanced at the stairway where the ghost stood. "It goes to a cellar, and rumors say there used to be tunnels where they'd drag passed out men from here to ships so that they could shanghai sailors."

Made sense. No wonder the ghost was looking so distressed. He was probably trying to warn patrons not to drink too much and fall victim to being kidnapped.

How she hated her powers.

Which made her wonder something. "Do you have any peculiar habits or abilities?"

Rory glanced up with a frown. "Like what? A third nipple?"

"Or a parent who's not quite human?"

He laughed out loud. "My mom can be a bear if you wake her up too early. Other than that, no. Why?"

She shrugged. "Just wondering. Personally, I can pick up things with my toes."

"Okay."

Awkward silence fell as he looked over the menu, and she continued to wonder if Luke could be wrong about the detective. He seemed so "normal."

Which took her thoughts back to her partner.

It wasn't until this moment that Sorcha realized how much she enjoyed Luke's company. If he were here, he'd be telling her what the poor departed soul wanted. As well as the history of this place.

She wouldn't be surprised if he'd sat at a table here and hustled souls for his father. Indeed, she could easily picture him dressed as a pirate, drinking from a tankard while he chatted up the desperate sailors.

A part of her wanted to pick up her phone and call him to ask about it. But even she knew how rude that would be while on a date with another man. Not that Rory was bad or boring. He was just so...

Normal.

While she'd craved normal during the years she'd dated the horrible hairy monster known as Bert, Luke had taught her that there was something to be said for those who were offbeat.

*But you're not on a date with Luke...*

She needed to put him out of her thoughts, for at least tonight, and remember that she was on a date with someone else.

Just as she opened her mouth to speak to Rory, her phone rang.

Of course, it did.

Expecting it to be Luke, she glanced down and arched a brow in surprise. It was her mom. "Ah crap." If she didn't take this, her mother would worry herself sick.

Last thing she wanted was to see her mother hysterical, thinking something had happened to her. Having seen the nightmare over her sister, she wasn't about to put her mother through that.

"Something wrong?" Rory asked.

"No, I just need to be rude for a second. Hang on." She answered the phone. "Hi, Mom."

"Baby! How are you doing?"

"I'm fine and actually on a date. Mind if I call you back?"

"Goodness no! Tell him I said hi." Her mom hung up immediately.

She set her phone aside. "My mom says hi."

"Okay."

"I know and I'm sorry. It's just she worries about me, so I try to never roll her calls. If I do, her mind goes to dark places. Same if I text. If she doesn't hear my voice, she thinks someone has taken me and is using the phone to toy with her." Her mom had been bad before Siobhan's death. Since then...

Sorcha always picked up.

"Totally understood. I do the same with my mom. Being a cop, she always thinks I'm dead in a ditch somewhere." His eyes widened as he realized what he'd said to her. "I mean... I—"

"It's okay, Rory. I know you weren't being insensitive." It was easy for people who'd never experienced her nightmare to make comments like that. And while it sometimes hurt, she didn't want others to have to dance around eggshells because tragedy had decided to assault her and her family. She didn't want anyone to go through their nightmare.

Before he could comment, his phone rang. He glanced at

it, then frowned. "Not my mom...worse." He answered it. "Corvan."

As the waitress neared their table, Sorcha waved the girl away, since she wasn't sure how personal that call was. In the event it was work, she was sure Rory wouldn't want the stranger to overhear.

"I'm on my way."

Definitely not personal. "Crime call?"

He let out a long sigh. "And this is why I don't date. Most wouldn't be happy that I had to leave before we even got to order."

Rory was right. She understood, as she'd been in his shoes before. There was nothing worse than that disappointed look on someone's face when she had to get up and leave at a moment's notice. One of her dates had even once said, "They're dead. Can't they wait?"

Needless to say, there had never been another date with that jerk.

But Rory understood and so did she.

"Can I ride along?" she asked him.

"Sure. Especially since this might be one of yours more than mine."

Oh fun. "What is it?"

"Another student."

Her stomach shrank at those words. *Please don't be our unknown shredder...* She didn't want to see another mangled kid. "Like the others?"

"Yeah."

Why would the perp keep going after Amandine when she was no longer here? Had he missed the memo?

She wanted to call Luke, but given the animosity

between him and Rory, she thought better of it. No need to get them fighting at the scene again.

Rory dropped a handful of bills on the table to cover their drinks before they left the restaurant.

By the time they arrived at the Wormsloe historic site, it was almost dark. Even so, the huge stone archway they drove under was impossible to miss. "What is this place?"

"An old colonial site."

The Spanish moss-draped trees made an eerie curtain as they drove down the paved road. It was like something from a horror movie.

Under other circumstances, the drive might be lovely. But in the fading light, it was quite spooky.

Now... In spite of the heat, She shivered in heartfelt pain over another family being torn apart.

They left the car and headed for what appeared to be another cemetery on the premises.

Police lights guided them to where the ME and other officers were already working on site. She took her badge out and clipped it to her belt before she put on a pair of latex gloves.

Rory was right. It looked just like their other crime scenes. Including the mutilated body that had been dumped next to a grave that had a small gate around it.

"Inigo Jones?"

Rory gave her a blank stare. "So it appears."

"Inigo?" she repeated, thinking he'd recognize the reference.

He didn't. "Yeah?"

Obviously, Rory had never seen or read *The Princess Bride.*

Maybe Luke was right and she did have a streaming addiction.

She trailed along behind him as he approached one of the officers.

"Hey, Brian. What's going on here?"

"A student who was geocaching."

"Geo what?" she asked.

The officer scratched at his ear. "I didn't know either until the ME explained it. Geocaching. It's like a huge global treasure hunt where people log into an app and use it to locate items that have notes or other things in them. Then they photograph themselves with the item and log it in for others to enjoy. I don't get it, but apparently, it's a thing."

It sounded really interesting to her. So she pulled out her phone in order to explore the trend.

"Any other details?" Rory asked.

"When the student didn't return from her search, the roommate came out here to find her. Since they were using their phone to track the item, it was easy for the roommate to locate the body. She says she didn't touch anything before she called us." He jerked his chin toward the ambulance. "She's over there if you want to interview her."

Feeling for the roommate's pain, Sorcha made her way over to the girl who was wrapped in a weighted blanket, for comfort.

The young woman was pale and shaking. "Please don't ask me any more questions. I can't keep reliving this."

"I know and I'm sorry. I just wanted to offer you a hug."

The girl threw herself against Sorcha and started crying even harder.

Sorcha just held her as she was taken back to that

moment when the police had shown up at her house on that cold winter night.

Because of Mono, she'd been home, instead of at school, in her dorm.

For reasons she still didn't understand, she'd gone to bed fully clothed that night. It was as if some part of her had known that she'd need to be dressed to deal with what was coming for her family.

Just before dawn, her mother had been getting ready for work. Sorcha had awakened to the sound of someone knocking on her bedroom window.

"Sorcha?"

It'd sounded just like her sister's voice. Thinking Siobhan had snuck home to see her, she had gone to the window and pulled back the curtains.

At that exact moment, the police car had rolled into their driveway.

Her mother had gone outside to meet them, and Sorcha had watched curiously as everything unfolded in slow motion. "What happened? Did my daughter have a car wreck?"

Such a simple question.

"No, ma'am. We're here to inform you..."

Sorcha wouldn't allow those words to finish even now. If she lived a thousand years, she'd never forget them. Or the sight of her mother screaming and falling to the ground. Of the police having to carry her petite mother into the house where Sorcha waited in stunned silence.

Her mother's hysterical screams had awakened her father.

Sorcha had staggered back to her bed and just sat there, trying to fathom the horror.

Tears gathered in her eyes as she held the girl and tried not to remember the one memory she'd give anything to forget.

After several minutes, the student pulled away and wiped at her tears with the back of her hand. "You do know, don't you?"

Too choked up to speak, she nodded.

"Miss Norton—"

Sorcha held her hand up to cut off Rory's words. "She made a statement to the police already. I think she needs to be taken home."

Rory nodded. "I'll get an officer to do it."

As he walked off, Sorcha had a peculiar chill go down her spine. That crinkly feeling that came from being watched.

Turning around slowly, all she saw were the officers and support staff...police cars, an ambulance, flashing lights. The moss-covered trees.

Nothing was out...

Her thought trailed off as she caught sight of a black dog in the shrubbery. At first glance, it looked like Luke's mom. But there was something different, too.

Without thinking, she started for the dog.

Baring its teeth, it growled at her before it vanished into a cloud of gray smoke.

"What did I miss?"

Sorcha actually screamed at the deep, resonant bass in her ear. "Jesus!"

"Not even close." Luke flashed a grin at her. "You okay?"

"I don't know." She gestured toward the bushes where the dog had been. "I think I just saw a hellhound."

Luke scowled at her. "Where?"

"Over there."

Without another word, he headed for it.

After a couple of minutes, he returned to her side. "Not a hellhound."

"What then?"

"Definitely a shifter. Just not one of ours."

She was getting irritated by his short answers. "Why do you say that?"

"The scent of chocolate is all over the place. Can't miss it. Precludes a real canine as they'd be lying in a bush somewhere, dead or sick. Plus, I can't find a trail so whoever it was teleported out of here."

The fact he knew that without her telling him was terrifying.

He was a vital asset to their group. Reyes had been wise to hire him.

Even if he was the devil's own.

Strange how that wasn't as scary to her anymore.

And before he could say anything else, Rory approached them with a determined stride. The fury in his dark eyes was tangible. He held his hand right under Luke's nose. "This the right number of star points?"

Pulling Rory's hand back, Luke glanced down at the pendant Rory held. "Still not mine."

"That's convenient."

"The truth often is."

Rory narrowed his gaze on Luke. "There's something not right about you."

"It's the fleas. They make me itchy."

Rolling his eyes, Rory clenched the pendant in his fist. "I still think you're involved."

"We're even. I still think you're a dickweed."

Rory was so angry, she was surprised smoke wasn't coming out of his nostrils. "I can't believe this is how our date ends."

*I've had worse.* Sorcha barely bit those words back. "Not the first time a murder has intruded on my personal life."

Rory calmed down. "It appears the same MO. But it's more similar to the first body. Killed elsewhere and dumped here."

"In a cemetery," she said under her breath.

While they talked, Luke wandered over to the body.

"What are we missing?" Rory asked her.

"Besides sleep? A viable perp." Sorcha felt sick to her stomach. "I want this bastard before he hurts anyone else."

"So do I."

"Corvan!" One of the officers called him away.

As he headed off, Sorcha wandered over to where Luke stood by the body.

He held that adorable smirk as he looked at the name on the grave. "My name is Inigo Jones... You killed my father..."

She laughed at his perfect imitation. Except for the name. "I knew you'd get it."

"I have as much of a life as you do. And apparently a subscription bill the size of the GNP of some countries."

While she really liked Rory, there was something infectious about Luke. Something that made her want to take a bite out of him.

But that would be extremely unprofessional.

"Who are we looking for?"

Luke shrugged. "I have to be honest. I don't know of a single shapeshifter who swallows souls. We've been down the list. And I can't believe there's a creature we don't know."

No sooner had he spoken than a foreign light sparked in those amber depths. "Ankou."

"Bless you."

He scowled at her. "We normally say 'damn you' when we sneeze."

"Seriously?"

"What do you think?"

Made sense, but dang...vicious.

"So what aneurysm did you just have?"

"Ankou," Luke repeated. "Celtic in nature. They're nasty little critters. And they shift."

"Why would one want to frame you?"

Luke didn't answer. Instead, he stepped away from the gathering crowd, off toward the woods.

Curious, she followed after him. "What are we doing?"

"Looking for a fairy mound."

"Excuse me?"

"They're here. Trust me. Little bastards are never far away. And this time of night, they like to frolic. Twilight is their special, happy time."

Why not? Made as much sense as anything else they dealt with. But as they went deeper into the woods, her heart began to pound. "Aren't there gators in Savannah?" She remembered her father warning her to be careful of them. And having lived and worked in New Orleans, she knew they could turn up in the most unexpected places.

Like any crime scene around water. They'd even found a gator in a swimming pool during one investigation.

She did *not* want to repeat that experience.

Luke paused to give her a salacious smile. When he spoke, his voice held a deep Cajun drawl. "You afraid of a little ole gator, *cher*? I promise you, he's not the scariest thing out in these woods."

"Given who you are, I'd agree. But I don't want a death roll or missing body part."

He tsked. "I won't let nothing vicious take you, darlin'. Don't worry."

She appreciated that, but it didn't stop her from worrying. Every shadow seemed to be moving. More than that, the rhythmic chattering of cicadas added to the spookiness. "If I get swallowed by something, I swear I'll haunt you forever."

"You won't be the first."

Interesting as she'd never seen any spirit near him.

Just as she was about to ask Luke to lead her back, he stopped mid step. Off to the side was a small mound of moss-covered rocks. It was actually quite pretty.

Sorcha took out her phone and turned on the light so that she could get a better look at it.

Luke used his powers to take her phone from her hand and turn off the light. "Don't scare them away."

"Who?"

He didn't answer her as he knelt on the ground and uncovered more of the rock formation. Then he began making a strange chittering noise. Similar to the cicadas, yet very different. She had no idea how to describe the pleasant sound.

Suddenly, a light appeared from the mound. The size of it was similar to a firefly. Only this was an eerie green.

The light danced on an erratic path around the grass until Luke captured it in his fist.

Hissing, Sorcha covered her ears as a horrendous screech sounded.

"Stop it," Luke growled at his fist. "Or I'll pull your wings off."

The sound stopped instantly.

"Better. Now show yourself." Luke opened his fist.

That light made a circular glowing pattern in the darkness. It grew bigger until it formed the body of a handsome man in his early twenties. With short black curly hair, he only came to the middle of Luke's chest. His wings were so clear, they looked as if they'd been made of gossamer. They also appeared so soft that she wanted to reach out and touch them.

And it made her curious as to what Luke's wings would look like. Definitely not so fragile.

No. His would probably be more akin to a bat. Leathery and battle ready.

The much shorter fey sneered at her partner. "What do you want, Prince of Perdition?"

Luke tsked. "That's a tough one. Thinking of pulling off a pair of wings to add to my collection. Yours are just so pretty..."

The fey started to leave only to cry out in frustration. "What have you done to me?"

"Fey trap. I find them as helpful as a lure. Poor you that your parents didn't teach you how to avoid them."

The fey began to laugh. "You're right. They didn't. But my brothers taught me something more important."

No sooner had he spoken than a dozen more lights shot out from the rocks. Like the fey had done, they spiraled and became much larger.

Sorcha reached for her weapon, only to remember that Reyes still hadn't issued her one. Crap!

While her blood was rushing through her veins, Luke didn't appear shaken at all.

In fact, he laughed at them. "You might want to rethink what you're doing, boys."

"You might want to release our brother." That one was almost as tall as Luke. Not quite as muscular, but by his tone, she surmised that he thought he was equal to Luke in height, weight and martial abilities.

With a deep sigh, Luke shook his head. "Let's not get in a pissing contest. I promise mine is bigger and shoots farther."

Ew! She didn't even want to think about that.

A blond fey tripled his size so that he towered over Luke.

With a laugh, Luke stepped back from the first fey so that he could punch the huge one. That blow sent the fey flying into the darkness. Luke turned toward the others. "Next victim. Step forward."

They attacked at once.

Sorcha started to help, then realized why Reyes had told her not to worry about being armed around Luke.

Using his powers, he flipped one fey into the air and as he went for a second one, a harsh light flashed, blinding her.

She closed her eyes to shield them, but she could hear fierce growling.

By the time her eyes adjusted, all the fey lay on the ground, scattered around Luke. Each one had a huge black dog on top of his chest. Except for the one who'd first gone for Luke. He had a furious Helly holding him down by his throat.

Sorcha wasn't sure what to make of the sight. "Hell-hounds?" she asked Luke.

"They tend to come out whenever I'm attacked. You can count on it."

"So does Helly." The imp flashed a grin at Sorcha.

"And a scary Helly you are."

Holding her fists up, she made a fierce grimace, then growled like an ogre.

Luke plucked the first fey he'd captured up by his shirt and held the poor thing in front of him. "Let's try this again. I'm evil and you're stupid for thinking you could attack me and go along on your merry way. Do you understand the idiocy of what you just did?"

The fey nodded.

"Good. Now give us your name."

"Oliver."

Scowling, she mouthed the name to Luke. It was such an odd name for a fey creature. She'd been expecting Oberon or Aeron or some such.

But Oliver? That just didn't seem right.

Luke took the name in stride. "Thank you, Oliver. Now be a good fairy and tell me about a stray Ankou who may or may not be following orders from your council."

"All the Ankou are stray. I don't understand the question."

That made two of them. Sorcha had no idea what an Ankou was.

Luke let out a long, disappointed breath. "Okay, Ollie. Listen and follow. You know Ankou, yes?"

"Of course."

"You like this little fairy portal I just plucked you from, yes?"

"Yes."

Luke grimaced before he continued. "There's an Ankou who recently went through it. Yes?"

"I don't know."

Luke's eyes turned vibrant red. "Do you know what I used to do for my father?"

Oliver paled. "I do."

"Have you any idea how much I loved doing what I did and how much I miss it?"

He shook his head. "No."

Luke let out a laugh so evil that it actually scared her. "Imagine the greatest orgasm you've ever had. Put that on steroids and magnify it by one hundred and you might be in the ballpark of how much I loved my former job."

His eyes widening, Oliver gulped audibly.

Luke patted him on the cheek. "Now you can answer my questions with your skin on or with it laying in a nasty pile at your feet. Your choice."

Could he really do that? That disturbed her on numerous levels.

Oliver gulped. "I want to keep my skin on my body."

"Good choice." Luke glanced around at the other fey that

were still pinned down by hounds. "Now... Answer me this or I'll let one of the hounds have at one of your friends. Understood?"

"Understood."

"What Ankou recently accessed your little doorway?"

"I really don't know, I swear. But Matilda does."

Luke gave him a cold smile. "Get her."

"Matilda!"

Sorcha blinked as an adorable Tinker Bell showed up. There was really no other way to describe her. She was even dressed in a flimsy, layered green dress and corset. Though to be fair, she had dark hair instead of blonde, and it was long and crowned with a circlet of flowers.

Exquisite was the only way to describe her.

As soon as she saw Luke and the others, she drew up short and tucked her green wings down by her side. "What is going on here?"

"Matilda?" Luke asked.

"Yes."

"I'm looking for an Ankou who accessed your portal a short while ago. Ollie here said you would know who it is."

She glanced about at the fey group that was pinned by hellhounds. "May I ask why? I hope you don't intend to tie him down and beat him. Or feed him to one of your dogs."

"Can't make any promises. Since I don't know what he'll say, I like to keep my options open."

"Don't do it, Tilly!" Oliver said. "You know you can't trust the devil's own."

"Can't trust an Ankou either." Tilly finally saw Sorcha. A frown creased her delicate brow. "A human, not human."

She turned back toward Luke. "You keep interesting company."

"So I've been told."

Tilly screwed her face up. "Elizar was the last Ankou to come through the portal. Maybe two hours ago."

That was the kind of name Sorcha would expect, and the time would align to the poor kid's murder.

"Where can I find this Elizar?" Luke asked.

Matilda looked past Luke to the fey he held. It was obvious she didn't want to say, but she knew better than to lie or remain silent while Oliver was being held. "He sits at the right hand of our queen."

Sorcha wasn't sure what that meant. Nor did she have any idea of what an Ankou was. But her self-preservation wasn't about to stop this conversation.

The look on Luke's face, however, said it wasn't a good thing for them. He obviously understood it all.

Luke's nostrils flared. "Which one of you little parasites has royal blood?"

No one made a sound.

"All right, Helly. Pick one to kill. If it's the royal one, oops. But if we start taking heads, either the right one will speak up, a friend will out him or we have a collection of heads for your bedroom. Win-win, all the way around."

Stunned, Sorcha tried to say something. No words would come out.

Surely, he wouldn't be so cold.

Yet Helly closed her eyes and pointed randomly. "That one!"

Luke handed Oliver over to Helly as he headed for the one she'd chosen. "Lucky you."

The fey actually wet himself. "He's the prince!" He pointed to a handsome dark-haired fey not far from Sorcha.

"Thank you. You get to live." Luke let him go and went to the one on the ground. "You and I are going to chat now."

"My mother will demand your life for this. No one hurts me!"

Luke nudged the hellhound aside and plucked him up from the ground with a terrifying ease. "Color me not afraid. Now, how do you want this to go? I beat the shit out of you? You hand over information of your own accord with no damage done? I rip out your throat...dealer's choice and the clock is ticking."

The fey gulped audibly before he spoke. "I can take you to Elizar."

"Good choice. Wasn't one of the options, but you know what? I'm feeling a little merciful this evening. You're in luck." He glanced toward Tilly. "Open the portal for all of us."

"Just do it," the prince said. "Let my mother deal with him."

Without another word, Tilly did as her prince asked and opened the shimmery portal. It was beautiful. Like rippling waves that hovered in front of them.

Luke snapped his fingers and the hellhounds let their captives up, then escorted them to the portal. One by one, they walked through.

When she started to enter the portal, Luke placed a gentle hand on her shoulder. "Let me go in first. In case there's a trap, I want to disarm it before you get there."

"Given that I'm unarmed and I lack your bodyguards and talents, have at it, big guy."

He winked at her before he stepped through it.

Sorcha started to go in, but the moment she took a step, it closed completely.

Gasping she turned toward Helly who was equally as stunned.

"*Dominus!*" Helly cried.

But it was no use. Luke was completely gone and there was nothing they could do.

CHAPTER
# SIXTEEN

Luke arched a brow as the portal closed behind him, cutting off Sorcha, Helly and the hellhounds.

"Get him!" the tiny prince shrieked.

The fey guard rushed him.

Luke set fire to the entire group, then turned toward their prince. "Anyone else you want to be extra crispy?"

"Variance, stop!"

Luke knew the sound of that sharp tone. Tanith. Queen of all fey, regardless of court. They might name others king or queen, but she was the one who ruled them all with an iron fist to compete against his father's.

Prince Variance stepped aside at her approach and actually bowed before her. "Sorry, Mother. I was trying—"

"Doesn't matter." She offered Luke a warm smile that chilled him more than a cold Savannah night. With dark skin and black eyes that contrasted sharply with her white hair, she would be beautiful if he didn't know her personally. She might appear to be beauty incarnate, but inside...

There were demons in Hell he'd much rather cuddle. In fact, he had a closet full of them.

And if she was waiting for him to bow to her, his father would be herding icebergs first.

Steeling his features, he cleared his throat. "Queen Tanith."

She tsked at him. "No need in such formalities, Luke. Welcome to my kingdom. I believe this is your first visit to it, isn't it?"

"It is."

He assumed she gestured with her arm to indicate the cold white walls around them, but what it really emphasized was the glittering gems in her gauzy white gown that hugged a perfect body.

"What do you think of Mag Mell?"

"Nice place to visit, but I wouldn't want to build a summer home here."

She tsked playfully as she stepped forward and took his arm. "It grows on you."

"That's what they say about Spanish moss, but I don't intend to stay long enough for that to happen."

Clearing her throat, she gave him a sympathetic pout. "I heard about your father. Wouldn't you prefer a place where you really fit in? I offer you shelter here."

That set off every alarm in his body. "Pardon?"

"Mag Mell is a beautiful realm. You should rest here awhile and see what you think."

"No, thank you. I'm just stopping by to collect an Ankou who murdered three humans. Would you be so kind as to direct me to Elizar?"

She tsked at him. "You don't want that, love."

Those words...they infuriated him. This was a game his father had invented, and it was one that triggered him in the worst way. "Don't gaslight me, Tanith. Not a fan."

"Sorry, love. But I'm so glad you're here."

What did that mean? There was a peculiar note in her voice. One he didn't quite understand and as she led him toward a door, he realized that his head held total silence. He had no idea what anyone here was thinking.

How was that possible?

That silence was deafening.

Tanith smiled up at him. "So very glad."

Those whispered words went through his head like a hypnotic dream. The next thing he knew, the room was spinning.

Then everything went black.

"Sorcha!"

Helly bared her fangs at the sound of Rory's call. "Can I bite him?"

"Please don't. Keep working on the portal while I get rid of him." That sounded a lot worse than she meant for it to.

Trying not to appear worried, she headed back toward Rory. "I'm right here."

"Why are you in the woods?"

"Luke thought he saw something."

"Did he?"

She shook her head. "Why don't you go back to the grave and body, and we'll be with you shortly."

That did the opposite of what she wanted. Instead of

reassuring him, it made him instantly paranoid. "What's going on?"

Damn detectives and their inquisitiveness. And yes, she included herself with that. No wonder her parents lost patience with her so often.

"It's all right. Really." Even though it wasn't.

Trying not to show impatience, she went with him until they were with the group. She excused herself to go to Jedi who was processing the poor victim.

He looked up at her and smiled. "Hi, Detective. What can I do for you?"

"Can you monopolize Rory for a few minutes?"

"May I ask why?"

"So that I'll owe you a favor."

He laughed. "Okay. I'll respect your privacy. Send him over and I'll do my best."

"Thank you!" After patting him on the shoulder, she went back to Rory. "Hey, I was just speaking with Jedi, and he needs you for a second. I think he has something to show you."

Rory nodded. "I'll be there as soon as I finish here."

That was just what she wanted.

Keeping her gaze locked on him until he was out of sight, she slowly returned to where Helly waited in the woods.

The imp let out a frustrated breath at her approach. "I've tried everything to get inside. I don't know how to open it."

"What about his mom? Could she get in?"

"Maybe. But I'm scared to let her know. She might get mad at me for not protecting him."

"Aren't you more scared not to and to risk him needing

help and not having it? Wouldn't she be more upset if he is in danger and we left him to it?"

Helly made a face at her. "You're mean!" Then she sobered. "But correct. I'll be right back. Keep my space warm."

Unsure what to make of that, Sorcha waited next to the portal. Alone.

This wasn't the best plan she'd ever made. And as the sound of cicadas grew louder, she felt more and more unsure about it. What had she been thinking?

What would his mom do?

*I don't like this.*

Every shadow appeared worse than the one before. Her heart pounded furiously, especially as she remembered that she was out here, alone, without a single weapon.

Crap...

Reyes really needed to issue her a weapon. While she might not need it around Luke, she definitely needed it when she wasn't with him.

Like now.

Now would be good.

Something grumbled in the woods. Not in the direction of the police, but deeper in. Was it hungry or angry?

Hangry would probably be the worst of all.

Just as she was ready to run back to Rory, a flash temporarily blinded her. She put her hand up to protect her eyes and only lowered it once the light was gone.

Senka stood in her human form with half a dozen silent hellhounds standing at her side. That was a terrifying sight. "Where's my son?"

Wishing she was invisible, Sorcha pointed to the small

mound where Luke had captured Oliver. "They opened a portal and I think they took him there."

Senka glared at it with a fierce snarl. "Mag Mell? That bitch has some nerve."

Sorcha would ask who that was, but this didn't seem like the best moment to say anything. His mother's anger was too tangible for that.

With a flick of her hand, Senka opened the portal and stepped through.

Helly appeared at Sorcha's side, then ran forward, pulling her. "Let's not get left behind again."

Tightening her grip, she ran with Helly until they were safely on the other side.

But as soon as she stepped through the portal, Sorcha let go. Stunned by the beauty, she couldn't believe this came from a group of mushrooms.

Unless someone ate the mushrooms.

*I've become Alice.* That was how it felt. Everything felt larger around her, even though it wasn't. Harsh white was everywhere. The ceiling, the marble floor, the walls. It was almost as if someone was afraid of color.

She would have thought the fey lived in a green, forest-like settings. This was a contemporary and harsh environment. One that seemed at odds with the...

Cartoons she'd seen?

Yeah, okay. She'd never known anything about the fey other than what she'd seen in anime and Disney movies. And this proved to her just how little she knew.

"Have you been here before?" she asked Helly.

"No. But it looks like what I'd expect from Queen

Tanith." Helly gestured toward the queen who was the tall, slender fey, wearing a crown. One whose hair matched the walls and her shimmery dress.

The same queen who was currently cornered by Senka while her fellow hellhounds were being held at bay by a group of fey guards.

"Where's my son?"

Tanith lifted her chin defiantly after she finished sweeping a disdainful sneer over his mother. "You don't question me, beast. Ever."

"And you don't want to ruin your dress...with blood. Show me my child. Now!"

Still, Tanith refused. "I'm the queen here. You don't command me!"

Senka's eyes flared. "And I stand at the side of the leader of the most powerful Order to ever exist. Would you like me to summon *my* lord?"

The threat made the queen smirk at Senka. "From what I hear, Luke no longer holds any favor with his father. In fact, I've been told that the High One wants nothing to do with our boy. So why would you interfere with a brand-new existence where he'll be treated like the prince he is?"

"If he's to be a prince here as you say, let me see him and he'll tell me what he prefers."

"I'm afraid I can't do that. He's rather tied up at the moment."

The fury in Senka's amber eyes was terrifying. She took a step toward the queen, only to have the fey guards cut off her access with the tips of their spears.

Before anyone could move, Senka let out a howl that

belied her graceful form. One so piercing that Sorcha had to plug her ears, as did Tanith.

It caused the guards to drop their spears while the other hellhounds ran down the hallway to the left.

Falling to the floor, Tanith cringed, still pressing her fingers deep into her ears. Not the most dignifying pose for a queen.

Helly cupped her hands over Sorcha's. "Now you'll be fine." She reluctantly let the imp pull her hands away. Even though she could still hear the howl, it was no longer piercing or debilitating.

Beyond grateful for the relief, she gave Helly a hug. "Let's find Luke."

They went down the hallway, after the hellhounds. On their way to find him, they passed a number of fey who were on the ground, also holding their ears.

"What is the noise his mother's making?" she asked Helly.

"The Bale-cry. It's how hellhounds locate each other when they're hurt."

Made sense.

And it left a nasty after-ring.

They followed the rest of the hounds to a huge bedroom that was every bit as stark and white as the room they'd first entered and the hallway they'd run down.

The hounds circled a body on the floor, whining as if they were in physical pain.

It took Sorcha a full minute to recognize Luke. Wearing only a pair of black shorts, he was on the ground in a fetal ball, shaking.

Her heart broke at the sight of him in such pain. "He's freezing. Grab a blanket, please," she said to Helly.

Without thinking, she pulled him against her, trying to warm him up.

"It's okay, Luke. We're here."

His teeth chattered so hard that she was surprised they hadn't shattered.

Helly returned with a comforter and blankets.

Sorcha wrapped them around him and still he shook from the cold. Even his lips were turning blue. "We have to get him warm." She looked around for anything else.

There was nothing.

Sorcha could only thing of one more thing. "Find his clothes."

Helly rushed off to look.

Gently, Sorcha rubbed at his stubbled cheeks in an attempt to get blood flowing so that his lips wouldn't be so blue. When that didn't work, she pressed her cheek against his, hoping the warmth of her body would help.

Luke buried his hand in her hair.

Pulling back slightly, she saw that his eyes had changed from gold to red.

That fiery gaze held hers enthralled. Her breath caught in her throat at the sight of his agony and hope. It was electric.

Then he pressed his lips against hers.

Sorcha felt a surge of heat at the contact. It was unlike anything she'd ever experienced in her life. Her entire body on fire, she deepened the kiss until she wrung a feral growl from Luke.

This was so unprofessional and yet she couldn't stop

herself. He tasted sweet and intoxicating. Never had anyone kissed her like this.

Like she was the air he needed.

Luke's head swam as welcomed warmth flowed through him. He had no idea what it was about her kiss, but it drove out every last bit of the cold that had seized him so fiercely, he'd been unable to stand.

"Um ... do you still need his coat?"

Luke broke away from the kiss with a laugh at Helly's question. "Yes!" He grabbed it from her hands and quickly shrugged it on with Sorcha's help.

"You all right?" Sorcha asked breathlessly.

"Couldn't be better at the moment." He was finally warm enough that he could summon his powers to clothe himself.

Which made him even angrier.

Who had told Tanith that cold made him vulnerable? While he could tolerate a fair amount of it, there came a point when he was too cold to access his powers. That wasn't something many creatures knew about.

Had Sorcha not shown up when she had...

He wasn't sure what Tanith had planned for him, but he would have been helpless against her.

Now, he was helpless against Sorcha. She'd not only restored his body temperature, she'd fired something inside him that had stayed dormant since he'd been banished.

And awakened something he didn't recognize. Something he'd never felt before.

That terrified him.

He felt reborn. Stronger than ever.

More lethal.

"Xynzara? Are you all right?" his mother asked as she joined them.

He nodded. "Thanks for the howl and the help." He looked past her shoulder for anything fey. In the mood he was in, he wanted to start collecting heads. "Where's the queen?"

"In the portal room. Would you like the honor of tearing out her throat?"

His mother knew him so well.

"Only after I get a few answers."

Sorcha stepped in front of him. "You're not really going to kill her, are you?"

Before he could stop himself, he gave her another quick kiss on the lips.

Yeah, there was no mistaking that sensation. Another wave of fire exploded through his veins, warming him to the core of his blackened heart. And he hoped they could explore this a little more in-depth...

After he dealt with Tanith.

Not wanting to stress Sorcha, he winked at her. "As much as I would love to shred her, I won't. It'd cause too big a schism between factions, and we don't need that kind of power vacuum. But I have no intention of letting this go without a strong understanding between us."

And with that, he left them and headed back to where the queen still cowered on the floor, surrounded by more hellhounds.

*Go, Mum.*

The moment Tanith saw him, she turned as pale as her hair.

She tried to use her powers, but his mother had her

trapped. There was nothing the queen could do. She was as helpless as she'd made him.

For that alone, Luke could kiss his mother.

"Not so much fun, is it?" he asked bitterly.

Tanith pressed herself back against the wall. "What are you going to do with me?"

"I would love to add your wings to my collection." But that would no doubt upset Sorcha and right now, that was the last thing he wanted to do.

Tanith tucked her wings around her body as if that would stop him from taking them if he really wanted to. "I made a fair offer to you!"

Luke was aghast. "Being your concubine isn't an offer at all."

Senka's eyes flared. "You wanted to turn my son into a pet?"

"No! Just a concubine."

"Which is a fancy word for pet." Senka approached the queen, then reached for her throat.

Luke caught his mother's wrist. "Only I get the privilege."

His mother held up her hands. "Have at it, then. Make her feel my wrath."

Luke straightened his coat with a tug. "Let's talk about Elizar…"

Tanith glanced to his mother before she answered. "He's my servant."

"Who's been killing women who bear a striking resemblance to Amandine Dufresne."

"No. He's only supposed to capture her and bring her to me. Not kill anyone. He sometimes gets confused."

Sorcha gasped.

Luke was befuddled by those words. Had she really just said that?

He squatted on the floor beside the queen. "So let me get this straight, if I cut your throat instead of letting you go, your heir won't say anything because I was confused by my orders?"

"That would be entirely different."

Not really.

"May I kill her now?" his mother asked.

"I'm tempted." *'Cause what difference would it make according to fairy logic?* Killing and letting go were apparently the same thing.

Luke let out a disgusted sigh. "Why are you trying to capture Amandine and, more to the point, why were you framing me for the crimes?"

Genuine shock went across her face. There was no mistaking that. She had no idea he'd been framed for the murders.

Interesting.

He leaned forward on his haunches. "I see we have a problem here. How 'bout you send for ole Elizar and let me have a little chat with him."

Tanith nodded slowly before Luke offered his hand to her so that he could pull her up from the floor.

It was strange how quickly she recovered her regal bearing to stare up her nose at him. Especially given the fact that she'd been on the verge of making him her bedroom pet. He was still pissed off about that.

Even in Hell, he'd had more decency than that. He'd never forced anyone into his bed. But then, it'd been Hell. All he had to do was ask if the objects of his attraction wanted to go someplace where they weren't being tortured and they quickly acquiesced.

A large number of them had even offered themselves before he had a chance to ask.

Still, they'd all had a choice. He'd never kept anyone against their will, and he would die before he forced himself on anyone else. As demonic as he was, there were some atrocities and violations he would never commit.

"What are you going to do to me?" Tanith asked.

"I haven't decided yet. Depends on what your Ankou has to say." He should probably alleviate her fears, but the part of him that belonged to his father wanted to prolong her fears. Especially given what she'd done to him.

It was bad enough he hated the cold. But she'd tried to take away his autonomy. To control him, and that was where his hellhound genes took over.

He was no one's bitch. No one would ever have sovereignty over him.

Not even his father.

Tanith quickened her steps as they neared a room at the end of the hallway. She opened a door on the left, then started to leave.

Luke caught her arm and smiled coldly at her. "I thought you wanted my company, Majesty. Why are you trying to leave so quickly?"

"I've business to attend."

"But our business is so much more pressing. Please"— he indicated the room with his hand—"introduce me."

She glanced over his shoulder to where Sorcha and Helly stood before she entered the room with all the regal grace she could muster. Luke was impressed at how quickly she'd regained her composure.

No doubt she didn't want her Ankou to see her begging and weak. That would never go over well.

Clearing her throat, she moved to her throne and took a seat as if she didn't have a care in the world.

"I summon you, Elizar."

Almost immediately, the hooded figure appeared and bowed to his queen. It was said that Ankou were created whenever a fey creature became disfigured or was born with any malady. To keep them from being run off by others of their kind, they were given the ability for glamour, and to shapeshift into a non-repellent form.

Yet that wasn't enough. According to legend, their jealousy was such that it blackened their hearts. Made them so angry at the "regular" fey that over time it caused them to become even more malformed and twisted.

Once that happened, the Ankou spirit took over, and they were only good for collecting the souls of the fallen fey and escorting them to the Eternal Summerlands.

Unlike Hell, it was supposed to be a wonderful eternity. The fey didn't have a place of punishment. Turning into an Ankou was their only version of Hell.

To be honest, he'd much prefer theirs to his.

Although now that he was looking at the twisted, hideous creature that appeared to be in extreme pain...

Maybe Hell wasn't so bad.

"My queen," Elizar breathed. "What may I do for you?"

She gestured toward Luke.

The moment he turned and saw Luke behind him, he

held up his arm to shield himself, screamed and shrank toward the gilded throne.

Appropriate response given Luke's mood.

"Save me, Majesty."

Luke rolled his eyes at the whiny tone. "Stop shitting your britches, bruh. I just have a few things to ask you."

Elizar lowered his arm and peeked around the throne. In any other mood that would be comical. "You're not here to kill me?"

Luke exchanged a bemused stare with Sorcha. "Really wish you wouldn't hold that against me."

Sorcha screwed up her face. "Let's hear what he has to say first. I might change my mind."

With a lopsided grin, he turned back to the Ankou. "Then I'd start speaking, old man. My first question, who told you to go after Amandine Dufresne?"

Elizar looked to his queen.

"Don't you dare lay something at my feet that I didn't do." She turned her cold gaze to Luke. "Had I done so, I would have told you. Good or bad, I own my actions."

"I know you do. So the question is, who else has control of your assassin?"

"No one else is supposed to." Tanith came off her throne with such force that it made her gown sound like small bells tinkling. "Answer him! Who dared to command you in my stead?"

"Prince Elwin."

Luke thought *he* was angry, but the fury on her face far surpassed his.

"Absolute Guard!"

Senka inclined her head to Luke to let him know that she

was allowing her hounds to release the queen's elite guardians.

They appeared instantly around the throne and took a knee before their queen. Dressed in blue and green armor, they made an auspicious sight.

"Find Elwin and bring him to me. Now!"

They vanished instantly.

Senka approached the throne. "Why did you seek to take my son?"

Tanith gave her an impudent stare. She gestured at him with her whole hand. "Look at the beast you birthed. Just because you're his mother doesn't mean you don't know what an exceptional piece of masculinity he is. Congratulations on that, by the way. I couldn't believe my luck when he stepped through my portal after all these centuries of my salivating over him. Why kidnap a human male to father a child when I could combine my DNA with *that*?"

Sorcha bit back a laugh at the queen's tone. The fey had a point. "You kidnap humans?"

"All the time. But don't worry. Once I get what I need, they're returned no worse for the wear."

Gaping, Sorcha didn't know how to take that as Luke stepped behind her. "What are you doing?" she asked him.

"I'm feeling the need for some protection. She's actually scaring me."

Sorcha laughed. "I'm surprised you're not agreeing to stay."

"No, thank you," he said quickly. "It would have been nice to have been asked, though." He directed his next comments to the queen. "Maybe you should try that in the future instead of drugging someone and chaining them to your bed."

"How did you get free?" Tanith asked.

"My howl would have caused him to automatically shift into his hellhound form."

"Which caused the chains to fall off." He glared at Tanith. "Better be glad I didn't come to on my own and find them on me. The outcome would have been far different for you, Majesty." The growl in that deep voice sent a shiver over Sorcha.

Though to be honest, she wasn't sure he could have done much given the condition she'd found him in. But the queen didn't need to know that.

Luke gently took her hand and gave a light squeeze before he stepped away.

Puzzled by that, she wanted to ask him why he'd squeezed her hand. But this was far too public for that inquiry.

After a few moments, the fey guard returned with an exceptionally angry fey prince.

He glared at all of them. "What is the meaning of this?"

Luke threw out his hand and a visible fey trap appeared under the prince's feet. This time it wasn't just an unseen forcefield, rather this trap had symbols she couldn't understand. Two of those strange shapes rose up from the floor to wrap themselves around the prince's legs. They crawled over his body until they encircled his arms and even his neck.

"Sucks, doesn't it?" Luke approached the prince. "Not being able to move. Being held against your will."

He towered over the much smaller prince. "So answer

this, why did you frame me? Speak carefully. I know a lie when I hear one and I won't take it in stride."

With a panicked expression, he looked over at Tanith. "Mother?"

She was merciless with her response. "You knocked on the devil's door, Elwin. What have I told you about keeping bad company? Answer his questions and afterward, I have my own for you."

That made the prince turn even paler. With a furious shriek, he tried to break free.

Luke tsked at him. "Not going to happen, pup. Who told you to go after Amandine and frame me?"

Elwin drew a ragged breath. "No one. At least not a person."

Luke used his powers to bring the prince so close to him that their noses almost touched. "Explain."

"A falcon brought a letter to me. It said that if I didn't send out the Ankou to kill Amandine and frame you for it, they would come and tear down my mother's kingdom and spread our ashes to the winds."

The expression on Luke's face said that he wasn't quite willing to believe the prince's story. "Where's this order now?"

"It disintegrated as soon as I read it."

Luke smirked. "How convenient."

"It's the truth! I swear."

Luke wanted to deny it, but he saw in the prince's eyes that Elwin was telling the truth. A part of him was dying to snap the prince's neck just on principle and make a gift of his head to the queen.

If he were in Hell...

But this was a different time and place.

Stepping back, he glanced to Sorcha who watched him with an unsettling intensity. She feared what he was going to do next.

A part of him did, too. But the last thing he wanted was to see disappointment in those beautiful blue eyes.

Right now, she looked at him with respect and comradery. *I won't sacrifice that.* Not for this worthless piece of fey excrement.

Reluctantly, he released the prince and shoved him toward Tanith. "No more killing. And no more framing me. One more body or evidence planting and I promise my wrath will make that threat look like a VIP trip to Disneyland."

He turned his attention to the Ankou.

Elizar shrank back to hide behind the throne again.

"You understand, Elizar?"

"Yes, master."

"Elwin?"

The fey prince nodded. "But what do we do if they come for us?"

Luke glanced to his mother.

Tanith folded her arms over her chest. "The treaty between the Orders will protect us. If we're attacked, the other Orders will come to our defense. Hence the point of our treaty. Had you come to me instead of taking matters into your own hands, I would have told you that." She met Luke's gaze. "Now I know why you were so angry when you arrived. But don't worry. This ends. I will make sure that my people leave you alone."

"Thank you."

Senka wasn't so easily sated. "Should I leave a few of my people behind to assure compliance?"

Tanith arched a brow. "Depends. Are any as handsome as your son?"

Luke growled in his throat. "We're done, *Mata*. Please don't leave anyone here. I think it would be a mistake."

Senka inclined her head to him. "But if I return...it will be at the head of my army. And no treaty will protect you."

Even though rebellion shined in Tanith's eyes, she was wise enough to not taunt the hellhound Alpha. "Noted."

With that, Luke turned toward the three most important women in his life. His imp, his mother and his partner.

Better known as his family. For the first time, he understood that word. Looking at them, it actually meant something, and it caused another wave of warmth to flood through him.

"Shall we?" He gestured toward the door that led back to the fey portal chambers.

His mother smiled grimly. "After you, my son."

That tone...

She had something planned and he didn't want to be a witness to it. More to the point, he didn't want to implicate either Sorcha or Helly. So he quickly led them to the portal and back to Sorcha's world.

In the dark forest, Sorcha gave him a curious stare. "How do we write up this report? I mean, we solved the crimes, but..."

"Rory can add them to his unsolved list. A black mark on his record. I like it."

She shook her head at him. "He will continue to suspect you of the killings."

Luke shrugged. "Yeah, but he already hates me." Something pricked and itched at his neck.

Grimacing, he rubbed at it, then froze as he saw what it was. Completely stunned, he pulled his hand away and stared in awe at his fingertips.

"What's wrong?" Sorcha asked.

Unable to believe it, Luke wiped at his forehead. It wasn't a dream. There was more moisture there.

"I'm sweating."

Sorcha laughed at him. "People do that when they're hot."

"Yeah, but..." He trailed off his words as he realized she was right.

He *was* hot.

For the first time since he'd been kicked to earth, he felt the heat here. Georgia *was* hot in the summer. Shrugging his coat off, he handed it to a very confused Helly.

"*Dominus?*"

"Luke," he reminded her. Amazed that he wasn't freezing, he rubbed his ringed hand down his bare forearm.

Sorcha scowled at him. "You're really not cold?"

"Not even a little." It was the most incredible thing on earth. He wanted to shout as joy swept over him. Yeah, it was a little thing.

And at the same time, this was major.

"Sorcha?"

Luke cursed at the sound of Rory's voice through the woods. "He's always going to be a thorn in my ass, isn't he?"

"Probably. Let's go tell him we're okay."

"I promise, I'm not the one he's worried about." Luke hung back with Helly as Sorcha headed for Rory.

"It's her, isn't it?"

He grimaced at Helly's question. "What?"

"I think she's restoring your soul."

He scoffed at the very idea. "That's not possible."

She covered her mouth in a way that was almost comical. "You're not the same, *dom*...Luke. You've changed. And now you are warm. I saw the way you kissed her."

"It was nothing."

She arched her brow.

Because he was actually lying and they both knew it.

"That, too, is a new one for you, *dominus*. What is it you always say about liars?"

She was right. And deep inside, in a place where he never wanted to look, he knew the truth.

He was afraid. All these centuries, he'd known exactly who and what he was. No goals. No ambition. Just hedonistic pleasure.

It'd been a good life. He'd treasured every heartbeat of it.

Until he'd been tossed out.

The anger and rage of it still simmered inside. But in the few days since he'd met Sorcha, that rage had quieted. Not completely gone, but it no longer controlled him.

And he enjoyed that quiet.

He enjoyed spending time with her.

*What is wrong with me? I'm a prince of Hell.*

And she was...

He still didn't know. Any more than he knew who had done this to him.

His mother emerged from the portal.

"What took you so long?" he asked.

"Loose ends."

He winced at her tone. "Is the queen dead?"

"No. She even retains all her body parts. But she will never trespass on you again. I made sure of it."

For that, he was truly grateful. "Thank you."

She closed the distance between them and buried her hand in his hair. With a gentle ferocity, she pulled his head until their foreheads touched. "You are mine, Xynzara. No one will harm you without my wrath."

*Even my father?* He bit back that question because at the end of the day, he wasn't sure if she'd choose him or not. And he didn't want to test her.

"It's ever my honor to call your mother."

She smiled, then placed a tender kiss on his forehead. "I will bring you home. Faith, child."

"I have never doubted you."

She glanced to Helly. "Guard him, Imp."

"Always, *domina*."

Then she was gone.

Luke stood in the darkness, listening to the whisper of people speaking and the serenade of cicadas. A light breeze brushed against his arms and instead of the freezing kiss he was used to, it warmed him.

*I am changing.*

And a part of him actually liked it.

"Luke?"

He drew a ragged sigh at the sound of Sorcha's call. All his life, he'd prided himself on never answering to anyone's command. Not even his mother's.

Especially not his father's.

Yet he headed for Sorcha and into a most uncertain future with a partner who baffled him.

With a light chuckle, he glanced up to the sky and whispered. "You must really be bored. But wherever You lead, I am following."

His father would die to know he spoke to his grandfather. In Hell, it was forbidden.

And while Luke knew he'd never meet the Great Creator, he was grateful tonight for having been created. Grateful for this uncertain journey that would lead him along paths unknown.

# EPILOGUE

Outside of Luke's apartment, Sorcha frowned at the blaring sound of...

*K-Pop Demon Hunters?*

*Soda Pop?* It took her a moment to come to terms with what was playing. This was definitely not the norm for her raucous partner. Way too mellow for his normal playlist.

And happy.

Had he been kidnapped again?

She had no idea until his door opened of its own accord. Suddenly, Luke was there, dressed in a pair of black shorts and matching T-shirt. With an adorable smile, he pulled her inside where he, Helly and the Feral Closet Demons appeared to be having a party.

There was even a disco ball on the ceiling of the room, sending glittering prisms dancing all over his black walls.

Sorcha was still trying to absorb the sounds and sights as Luke took her hand so that she could dance with him and Helly whose horns and wings were on full display.

Unlike Luke, Helly sang off-key.

As did the demons who were still locked in the closet. Only the walls were clear so that she could see them all. The closet looked like a tight, silent disco. Yet the demons were into the song which they must be singing off-key on purpose. Some were even twerking.

Shivering at the sight, she danced until the song ended… without any twerking on her part. "What are y'all doing?" she asked with a laugh.

That infectious grin answered her. "It's Friday. We always celebrate."

"Why?"

"Why not? We're all fed and no one's dead. Best of all, I'm not freezing."

She swept a hungry gaze over that luscious body. "So, I see." Then she glanced to the closet. "I thought the demons were banned from your room."

"Don't remind him!" Dohlar shouted.

"What happened to the music?" another added.

"I want to dance!"

"Gimme more *Soda Pop*!"

"Gimme Abby!"

"Who ate the last piece of pizza?"

"Stop stepping on my tail, you animal."

"I still have to pee!"

Luke leaned his head back and groaned. "Go watch your movie, hyenas." The wall solidified.

"Please, master. One more pizza!"

"Shut up!" Envee shouted. "He might take our movie from us."

"Help! I need *Chuck E Cheese Hell*!"

Sorcha opened her mouth and made a face at that last comment. "Should I ask about *Chuck E Cheese Hell*?"

Luke laughed. "It's a song I should never have allowed any of them to hear. Stupid me, I thought it'd be torture for *them*. Turns out, they really loved it and now they make demands for it so much that I'm the one who's being punished. *'Cause, Fuck You, Ken.*"

"Is that really going to be a thing?"

"Yes, it is. Because it fits in so well with so much random bullshit that happens."

He had a point.

Luke went to get a towel from the kitchen counter to wipe the sweat from his brow. "So what brings you to my door? Another body?"

"Just a quick thank you." She pulled a small wrapped box out from her purse and handed it to him.

He stared at it with a stern frown. "What's this?"

"A gift. I saw it in a store by the river. I don't know why, but it reminded me of you. So I wanted you to have it as a way of saying *thank you* for welcoming me into IA."

Luke didn't know what to say. He wasn't used to anyone showing him appreciation. Especially being sincere about it.

Huh...taking the package, he opened it to find a silver necklace. Four interlocking Celtic hearts were surrounded by a circle where sun rays fanned out and twisted together. It was quite lovely.

With a smile, Sorcha took it from his hand and placed it around his neck. Chills ran all over him as her delicate fingers brushed against his skin.

His body out of control, all he could do was hold his

breath at the sensation of her touch. The one thing he truly craved. "Thank you."

"My pleasure." As she started away, he gently cupped her cheek.

Never in eternity had he met her equal. Her blonde hair begged him to bury his face in it and there was nothing he wanted more than to see it fanned out across his pillows.

Especially when she looked up at him as she did now. Not with fear or judgement. With tenderness.

That was a look he'd never really had from anyone.

It made him feel...

He would say human, but that was impossible. He shared nothing with mankind. And yet...

Maybe Helly was right.

Was this what having a soul felt like?

And when he saw sadness darken her gaze, it caused an actual ache in his heart. "What's wrong?"

"Nothing."

He brushed his thumb against her cheek. "Not nothing, Sorcha. What are you thinking?"

"Don't you know?"

"I could. But I'd rather give you your privacy. I know how much it bothers you for me to go snooping in your thoughts."

Sorcha smiled. Over the last two months, that was what she'd come to appreciate most about him. He didn't give in to his evil ways as much.

He was respectful and kind.

"I was just thinking that when you go home and long after I'm gone, it'll be a token for you to remember me."

He winced as if that thought pained him. "I will never forget you."

As she started to step away, he leaned down toward her lips.

Common sense told her to step away.

No, *run* away.

How could she? He'd come to mean so much to her that she couldn't even explain it.

Savoring his scent, she lifted herself on her tiptoes so that she could kiss him.

Luke drank in her warmth. For whatever reason, she was the key to his being able to tolerate the human realm. Something he'd learned when she went home to visit her parents.

Longest week of his life.

Not only had he missed her, but by day five, he'd had to start bundling himself up again. On the seventh day, he'd been afraid frostbite would set in.

Then she'd returned.

Her smile alone had warmed him.

And her kiss had set him on fire. And so long as she stayed by his side, he didn't get cold at all. It was a miracle he didn't understand.

But definitely one he could taste.

Suddenly, Helly cleared her throat to remind them of her presence. "Should I leave, boss?"

Laughing, Sorcha pulled away. "You need to make more noise."

"I thought I was. If you want, I can go watch *The Conjuring* with the FCD. I love the sounds they make whenever the exorcism part starts."

Sorcha widened her eyes. "Does it really affect the Feral Closet Demons?"

Luke shook his head. "They just play act like they're being banished. But they are entertaining when they do it."

That was interesting. "Can they be banished?"

"Everyone can be banished. Sometimes it only takes a glance or unkind word."

She caught the note in his voice. He wasn't just talking about exorcism. And it made her heart go out to him. "I'm sorry."

"For what?"

"Everything you've lost."

Luke was caught off guard by her sincerity. Before she'd come here, he'd felt that pain.

Now...

He'd gained so much more. Being banished from home no longer had the sting it used to. He was actually beginning to like it here. "*Vade retro me satana.*"

She frowned at him. "What does that mean?"

"Get thee behind me, Satan. It'll work on a number of Hell-beings."

"Including you?"

"Only if it comes from you." The thought of her banishing him...

He didn't even want his mind to go there.

She was starting to mean too much to him. And just as he reached for her again, both their phones went off.

Luke cursed at the sound. He pulled his phone out of his pocket as she grabbed hers from her purse.

"Teivel."

"O'Malley."

"Hey gorgeous," Bernadette said with a smile in her voice. "There's a body we need you to look at. Pretty sure it's IA, but boss lady wants me to run it past you anyway."

"On my way." He hung up at the same time Sorcha did.

"Should I ask?"

He frowned at her. "What do you mean?"

"I don't know. I have a weird feeling about this."

"Yeah, Bernadette was a little vague." Conjuring black jeans, he grabbed his wallet and keys, then opened the door for Sorcha. "After you, O'Malley."

SORCHA WASN'T sure what to expect as they pulled up to a small, tidy light blue house on Tybee Island. Whoever owned it had decorated it like a cute beach getaway. There were even a pair of pink flamingos on the porch. "I like the flamingos."

"They're different." Luke pulled his hair down as they got out and approached the crime scene.

Rory met them on the porch.

"What's going on?" Sorcha asked.

"Body in the garage. Dead as a doornail."

Sorcha had no idea what he meant or why Rory thought that was funny until they entered the garage and she saw a body that was actually pinned to the garage door by a giant spike through the victim's chest. "You're not funny."

Rory grinned. "Sure, I am. You just can't appreciate it, yet." He glanced to Luke, then met Sorcha's gaze. "You still owe me another *stab* at dinner."

She groaned at his bad pun over the poor victim. "You're vexing me, Corvan."

"That's what all the women say."

Corvan's boss approached and gave them all a stink eye. "I need y'all to be serious right now. We got reporters showing up all over the place. Last thing I need or want is for any of them to start saying that Savannah's finest is treating this matter with anything less than all due respect. You hear me?"

Rory cleared his throat. "Yes, sir."

He glared at Sorcha and Luke. "That goes double for you two. We got enough problems with your unit. I don't want to become a laughingstock, too."

Luke inclined his head.

"Yes, sir," Sorcha repeated.

"Good. Now get your gear on and don't be contaminating my crime scene or compromising my evidence log."

Sorcha pulled a pair of latex gloves out of the roll she kept inside her purse.

Covering her blonde hair and face, she quickly set about examining the garage while Jedi and others did their jobs.

Rory stepped carefully around the broken glass on the ground so as not to slice through his shoe coverings.

"Who called this in?" Sorcha asked.

"Wife. A uni is taking her statement inside." Rory glanced at her. "Apparently, she came home from work and found him like this."

Luke frowned. "Alone?"

"That's what she said."

Sorcha averted her gaze as they struggled to remove the

spike so that they could get the body down. "You believe her?"

Rory shrugged as he glanced up at the heavy-set man hanging from what appeared to be a piece of the garage door track that had somehow broken off and pierced him straight through his heart. "I don't think a four foot ten, ninety-pound woman could do *that* to him. She couldn't even reach that high, standing on a chair."

That made sense. Unless she was Helly...

Sorcha went over to pick up a piece of crumpled paper from underneath the red SUV that was parked in the other bay. Straightening it out, she glanced over it.

Luke came over. "What'd you find?"

"Credit card statement. Looks like he's been spending a lot of time at the Emerald Princess Casino." It was the only casino in Georgia. A riverboat that sailed out of Brunswick about an hour and a half south of Savannah.

"Yeah." Luke leaned over her shoulder. "Look at the amount."

Sorcha saw Rory's boss heading toward the door. "What's he doing?" she asked Rory.

He shrugged. "There's no need in keeping everyone on scene. It's an easy open-and-shut accident. The cap's going to make a statement to the press."

As they began pulling the man down from the door, she and Luke went inside to find the man's widow sitting on the couch.

Visibly shaken, the tiny woman sat with swollen eyes as she blew her nose into a Kleenex. "I just can't believe this happened while I was away. Oh my goodness, what a terrible, awful day!"

"Mrs. Gary? Were you aware of your husband's gambling?" Sorcha wasn't sure why she felt the need to ask.

She nodded. "Tony couldn't help himself. In fact, it was in a casino in New Orleans where he first met me." She looked up with a wistful smile. "He really liked to play the odds."

The doorbell rang.

"If you'll excuse me now, I must go. I'm sure that's my sister come to comfort me in my time of woe." She got up and walked off.

The moment she left, Luke let out a peculiar snort.

"What's wrong?"

He glanced toward the door, then reached down for something that was partially buried in the woman's pocketbook and pulled it out. "Met in New Orleans, right?"

"That's what she said. Why?"

Luke showed her a poppet that was dressed identically to the victim. A poppet with a large spike through its chest that held a note that read—*I-O-U*. "Apparently, the casino wasn't the only one Tony Gary owed a debt to."

She sucked her breath in sharply between her teeth as she realized the woman must be one of the Witchbreeds Luke had talked about. "What are the odds Rory would believe us?"

"About as likely as winning the lottery." He tucked the doll back into her purse. "It's IA, but as you always say, how do we write this one up?"

Bernadette joined them. "Did y'all find something?"

"An inexplicable truth."

She winced at Luke's words. "Well, we'll just let Savannah's finest handle it, then."

"Yes, ma'am."

Sorcha didn't say anything. It wasn't her place.

Removing her gloves, she followed Luke back to Delilah. "That was interesting."

"Yeah, and for some reason, I'm craving a corn dog."

She groaned out loud. "You are absolutely awful."

He wrinkled his nose at her. "Yes, I am."

Just as she opened the door, Helly appeared in the back seat. Panicked and breathless, she sat up and grabbed Luke's arm. "We have a problem. Please don't kill me."

The storm in his eyes made Sorcha catch her breath. "What did you do, Helly?"

"Nothing. I swear. It wasn't me."

"What wasn't you?"

Biting her lip, Helly glanced to Sorcha, then back to Luke. "The demons are out of the closet."

Xolotl knelt on the ground and allowed her white Dire Wolf companion to lick her cheek as she faced her most worthless accomplice. "Your plan failed. Luke's still on the human plane."

"I know. No matter what we try, he always lands on his feet. I swear he's more feline than hound."

Perhaps, but it didn't change the fact that they'd lost for the moment. "Time is running out for us to disband the Orders."

Shimmering in the darkness, the shadow put more space between them. "The fey won't be intimidated so easily in the future. Not after Senka's chat with their queen."

Xolotl wasn't that concerned with the fey. "They're only one Order. We have others we can use."

The shadow nodded. "This isn't over. I won't stop until he's in chains and we have taken our rightful place in the universe."

"Good." Because Luke Teivel was the only one who could stop them. Damn him for it. "Find a way to kill him."

"Working on it. You'll have his head as soon as I can find his weakness."

Xolotl nodded. "Torture or slay whoever you have to."

"That an order?" the shadow asked.

"Call it a request. And in the meantime…" Xolotl sent her wolf off to cause havoc and fear in the human world. "We'll keep him off kilter."

"I won't fail." The shadow disintegrated into the darkness.

Xolotl didn't move until it was completely gone.

Alone now, she walked over to the fiery calendar that counted down to the time when just the right configuration would be in place. On that day, the jail that held the lawless ones would weaken.

She couldn't wait.

Once they were freed, there would be no one to stop her.

As it was in the beginning, it would be in the end.

For too long, they'd been relegated to myths and darkness. Mankind had made a mockery of this world. They didn't deserve it.

Xolotl and her kind did.

And death would take the Prince and King of Perdition.

A new world order was coming, and Xolotl would rule it.

# ALSO BY SHERRILYN KENYON
## (LISTED IN CORRECT READING ORDER)

### INFERNAL AFFAIRS

Hell to Pay

Hell's Half Acre

### MYTHS & OUTLAWS

House of Fire and Magic

House of Ice & Shadows

### NICK CHRONICLES

*Infinity*

*Invincible*

*Infamous*

*Inferno*

*Illusion*

*Instinct*

*Invision*

*Intensity*

### SHADOWS OF FIRE

*Sabotage*

*Last Christmas*

*Savage*

*Simi*

**THE LEAGUE**

*Born of Night*

*Born of Fire*

*Born of Ice*

*Fire & Ice*

*Born of Shadows*

*Born of Silence*

*Cloak & Silence*

*Born of Fury*

*Born of Defiance*

*Born of Betrayal*

*Born of Legend*

*Born of Vengeance*

*Born of Blood*

*Born of Trouble*

*Born of Darkness*

**THE LEAGUE: EVE OF DESTRUCTION**

Eve of Destruction

Born of Blood

Eve of Ruin

**DARK HUNTER**

*Night Pleasures*

*Night Embrace*

*Dance with the Devil*

*Kiss of the Night*

*Night Play*

*Sword of Darkness*

*Knight of Darkness*

*Seize the Night*

*Sins of the Night*

*Unleash the Night*

*Dark Side of the Moon*

*The Dream-Hunter*

*Devil May Cry*

*Upon the Midnight Clear*

*Dream Chaser*

*Acheron*

*One Silent Night*

*Dream Warrior*

*Bad Moon Rising*

*No Mercy*

*Retribution*

*The Guardian*

*The Dark-Hunter Companion*

*Time Untime*

*Styxx*

*Dark Bites*

*Son of No One*

*Dragonbane*

*Dragonmark*

*Dragonsworn*

*Stygian*

**Deadman's Cross**

*Deadmen Walking*

*Death Doesn't Bargain*

*At Death's Door*

**Lords of Avalon**

*(written as Kinley MacGregor)*

Sword of Darkness

Knight of Darkness

**Standalones & Collections**

Dark Places

# ABOUT THE AUTHOR

Defying all odds is what #1 New York Times and international bestselling author Sherrilyn Kenyon does best. Rising from extreme poverty as a child that culminated in being a homeless mother with an infant, she has become one of the most popular and influential authors in the world (in both adult and young adult fiction), with dedicated legions of fans known as  Paladins–thousands of whom proudly sport tattoos from her numerous genre-defying series.

Since her first book debuted in 1993 while she was still in college, she has placed more than 80 novels on the New York Times list in all formats and genres, including manga and graphic novels, and has more than 70 million books in print worldwide. Her current series include: Dark-Hunters®, Chronicles of Nick®, Deadman's Cross™, Black Hat Society™, Nevermore™, Silent Swans™, Lords of Avalon® and, The League®.

Over the years, her Lords of Avalon® novels have been

adapted by Marvel, and her Dark-Hunters® and Chronicles of Nick® are New York Times bestselling manga and comics and are #1 bestselling adult coloring books.

Join her and her Paladins online at QueenofAllShadows.com and www.facebook.com/mysherrilyn.

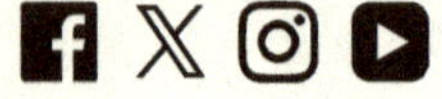

A small press bound by the belief that every voice matters.

Sign up for our newsletter to learn about new releases and more.
https://oliver-heberbooks.com/subscribe/

Follow us on social media:

facebook.com/oliverheberbooks
instagram.com/oliverheberbooks
amazon.com/oliverheberbooks
youtube.com/@OliverHeberBooksPublisher